THE
SEVENTH
REALITY

Syderra Jaks

For Azaan,
my partner in SpaceTime

The Sanskrit name for God is Sat-Chit-Ananda:
Existence, Consciousness, and Bliss.
Brahman is God the formless;
The Universal Spirit;
The Ultimate Reality;
Pure Consciousness;
The One Existence;
The Absolute.

When people asked the Buddha,
"Are you a god?"
The Buddha replied, "No."
"An angel?"
"No."
"A saint?"
"No."
"Then what are you?"
The Buddha answered, "I am awake."

(www.age-of-the-sage.org)

Listen Israel, YHVH is our God, YHVH is One.

(Deuteronomy, 6:4)

*That you will know that God is the Supreme Being
and there is none besides Him.*

(Deuteronomy, 4:35)

In the beginning God created the heaven and the earth.
And the earth was without form, and void;
and darkness was upon the face of the deep.
And the Spirit of God moved upon the face of the waters.

King James Bible (John 1:1-5)

Say: He is Allah, the One and Only;
Allah, the Eternal, Absolute;
He begetteth not, nor is He begotten;
And there is none like unto Him.

Sura Ikhlas 112:1-4 Quran
(Abdullah Yusuf Ali Translation)

PROLOGUE

The Tractate
$\{\Sigma\infty\}$

Know ye:

There is no other universe but one.
The Whole is the Singularity
And the Singularity is the Sum of all Infinity.

There is no beginning.
There is no end.

There are six coetaneous Realities in the universe,
Each spawned of the Seventh Reality is a manifestation of It.

Deeds performed by thee awaken thy Consciousness,
Lifting the veils that obscure Enlightenment.

Deeds with positive mana draw thy noumenon
towards the Singularity,
Unto an evolution of pure energy and knowledge.

Deeds with negative mana create disharmony and obstruct
transcendence to the Seventh Reality.

Which deeds to perform is always thine to choose.

(*Extract from* The Tractate on Enlightened Consciousness,
an encyclical of no known source, origin or chronology)

15

CHAPTER I

SYNCHRONICITY

Zenad Reality
India

He was saturated with ecstasy, an exhilaration that he had never experienced before. He wanted the feeling to last forever. Never, ever end.

But even as he wallowed in joyous exultation, a blinding light turned his euphoria into an agonized scream as he felt his entire body tear apart. Something was ripped out of his body. He couldn't breathe. Suddenly weightless, he hurtled down a long tunnel, spinning like an electron, a subparticle ejected into spacetime.

Then all was dark. All was silent.

δ

Only a few hours ago Izem was standing captivated by the splendor of the *Dargah Sharif* in Ajmer. It was the occasion of *Urs* of the much revered Sufi Saint Khwaja Moinuddin Chisti. His death anniversary was celebrated with the pomp and splendor of a wedding, because centuries ago the Saint had attained the much sought after union with God. Izem was ecstatic, for his long cherished dream of participating in a group *zikr* at the *Dargah Sharif* was about to come true.

Izem wore the white cotton pajamas and flowing, long-sleeved shirt favored by most locals to beat the dry heat of Ajmer, but his features set him apart as an obvious foreigner. His generous lips, aquiline nose, dusky skin and piercing gray eyes hinted at ancient ancestors from the nomadic Berbers of the African Sahara.

His full name was Ameqran Izem, a name given by his parents because he was the eldest son. In school, he preferred to use only Izem, not because it meant lion, lord of the jungle, but because it was easy for his friends and teachers to pronounce and remember.

A brilliant scientist and an expert in acoustics theory, Izem's sojourn into the realms of particle physics had drawn him deep into the mysteries of the divine, instilling in him the urge to discover for himself the Ultimate Truth. His search for answers to the meaning of life, led him to conclude that meditation was the best method, and *zikr* the best approach to meditate. The Sufi meditation technique, when practiced correctly, freed the mind from earthly desires, allowing it to experience a deep spiritual awareness that was said to bring one closer to the Divine Presence, the Supreme Oneness, the Singularity.

Izem knew full well that the process had to be achieved in

stages, for *zikr* was the proclaimed source of power for all journeys and the foundation of all successes. It was the reviver from the slumber of heedlessness. It was the eye opener that revealed the material world as nothing but a mirage that seduced humans to forget the One. *Zikr* was the bridge to the Ultimate Truth, the way to remembrance, to reverting to the true path. Because of its potency, performing the act of *zikr* was a challenge, but like all challenges in his life, Izem was determined to meet it headlong.

Today, because of the *Urs,* the courtyard surrounding the shrine was even more crowded than usual, for it was believed that all who came to the Sufi Saint for help were never turned away empty handed. So there were people of all colors and castes – Hindus, Muslims, Christians, Sikhs, men, women, children, beggars, the maimed, the blind and the one-eyed. All were there.

The shrine itself was ablaze with light. Intricate gold and jewel-toned patterns carved on the doors gleamed, chandeliers glittered, and fairy lights outlining the structure of the domes and pillars, shimmered in the twilight. A group of *quwwals* sat to one side, singing in accompaniment to the harmonium and a rhythmic clapping of hands. Their *ghazals* praised the saint's wisdom and propagated his teachings.

The songs became louder and more high pitched when the *quwwals* noticed the *kalanders* from Mehrauli entering the *Dargah.* The *kalanders* were devotees of the Saint, and each year they walked some four hundred kilometers from their home town to the holy city of Ajmer, to attend the *Urs.* Between them they carried a richly embroidered *chador* spread open for all to see and admire. This covering, symbolizing the reverence that the *kalanders* held for the Saint, would remain draped over his tomb until replaced at the next *Urs*, again by the *kalanders*.

Izem had arrived at the shrine the day before, and had persuaded one of the minor Sufi guides, sometimes called a *pir*, to accept him as a *murid*, a student of the pir. For only by becoming a *murid* could one learn the *tariqa*, the path to *zikr*. Learning the *tariqa* was a lengthy process, but Izem had only a week's leave from work, so he had coaxed and cajoled the religious guide until he had agreed to allow Izem to join a group of *murids* about to commence a *zikr* session.

The Sufi guide had been extremely reluctant to allow a novice to participate. Several steps had to be completed before a *murid* was considered competent enough to launch into a full-fledged *zikr* for it could prove dangerous for the uninitiated. But eventually, Izem's sincerity, dedication and commitment to seeking divine knowledge, as well as a generous fee, helped to overcome the guide's resistance, who reasoned that being an inexperienced foreigner, Izem wouldn't be able to reach the heights of meditation that could get him into any serious trouble. In his opinion, Izem, at best, would be able to rise to only the initial, shallow levels of transcendence, and should therefore remain quite safe.

Having crossed that hurdle, Izem now waited patiently to join the circle of *murids* who sat repeatedly murmuring the Quranic phrase, "There is no god but God," in preparation of initiating the *zikr*. The guide beckoned with a wave of his hand and Izem quickly eased himself into a gap in the tight circle where, sitting shoulder to shoulder with the *murids*, he too took up the chant. The murmurings ebbed as the guide began to recite from the Quran, heralding the formal commencement of the meditation process. The recitation came to an end, and closing their eyes and swaying their bodies to the rhythm of the chant, the *murids* emptied their minds of everything but the simple truth "there is no god but God."

Their voices rose in a crescendo and as the murmurings grew louder and louder, icy fingers trailed down Izem's spine chilling him to the bone. The hair on his nape bristled up in goosebumps. His breath now came in short spurts as his heartbeat rose alarmingly, and he began to drown in a tidal wave of fear and dread. An immense desire to escape before he got lost in the unknown, washed over him. He was about to move away and disrupt the crucial continuity of the circle, when he sensed a reduction in his mental and physical stress. He once again began to breathe normally as the chanting subsided, first into whispers and then into silence.

There was a moment of utter stillness and then the murmurings began anew.

The cycle of crescendo to diminuendo and back to crescendo continued until each *murid* was swaying to an inner rhythm, oblivious of his surroundings, aware only of the resonance of the chant. Each kept to the path of the *tariqa*, transcending to a level of consciousness that his individual ability allowed him to reach. Some amongst them were unable to empty their minds so that the material world kept enticing them back. These had to return to the first steps of the *tariqa*, restarting their journeys over and over again. Others, who had more practice, transcended to a level of consciousness that would eventually prise open the door, and if they were lucky, perhaps offer them a glimpse of the divine Oneness.

Izem too, swayed to the mesmerizing chant. Initially his

mind wandered to the mathematical model he was developing with his two colleagues and wondered if there were still errors lurking in the matrices. He wondered if the Veil Lifter Project was ready for launching, and how successful it would be in harnessing energy from dark matter. Then his mind flitted off in another direction and he began to compare meditation techniques, wondering if *zikr* was the best meditation technique that could free his mind to seek the elusive meaning of life.

Following the guide's instructions, Izem let his thoughts flow through him, not blocking them, nor trying to divert their erratic path. Soon the ebb and flow of his reflections fell into a rhythm, dancing to the peaks and troughs of the chant. He was no longer swaying, but surfing the acoustical waves which flooded his senses. At the peaks he experienced a joyous sensation that took him to heights of ecstasy he had never known before. He heard the songs of the lark, the koel, and nightingale merge into one glorious proclamation of the Singularity.

Then came the downward plunge that took him deep into indigo depths, where all was darkness, all a seething mist obscuring his surroundings. Uncertainty and intense melancholy suffused his mind, filling him with a dread that he would never be able to rise again.

But he did rise, again and again; and fell again and again. He oscillated between the two states of being until he could no longer distinguish between the peaks and the troughs. At that critical moment, a blinding light enveloped him and his mind ceased to exist.

δ

Zenad Reality
Italy

Grey clouds piling over the horizon painted the trees in vivid shades of green. The horse in his stall whinnied and pawed the ground impatiently. He knew she was near for he caught her scent even before he heard her voice.

Ruari O'Connor answered his call, walking rapidly towards Quasar, her palomino, who was as bright, as energetic, and as rare as the object found only in the remote areas of the universe. She wore carefully creased khaki breeches, a white silk shirt open at the neck and highly polished riding boots made from soft brown leather. Her auburn hair blazed and her green eyes glinted with pleasure in an oval face. She had escaped the dustings of freckles which usually accompany such hair color, her smooth, creamy complexion stirring envy among other redheads.

She kissed the horse's soft muzzle, running her hands down his back and stroking his neck over and over again. Quasar shook his blonde mane. His pale body quivered with nervous excitement, shooting out golden glints in the afternoon sun.

Ruari walked her horse out of his stall, his hoofs clip clopping over the cobblestones. She had chosen to spend her week's break at her mother's six hundred acre estate where she had grown up and which she loved passionately. The backdrop of hills became shrouded in a purple haze as thunder clouds loomed on the horizon. Weeping willow branches drooped into a river that bisected the grounds, its two banks spanned by an ancient stonework bridge some distance away.

Ruari's father was an Irish adventurer and her mother an

Italian with a long ancestral lineage, and she never failed to marvel at the very successful marriage of two such diverse personalities. Looking at her ethereal beauty, one would be hard pressed to believe that she was a headstrong, hardnosed mathematician and cosmologist who believed what could not be scientifically proven, did not exist. Science and logic were her gods, and she subscribed to the literal interpretation of Karl Marx's view that religion was the opiate of the masses.

But now, all Ruari thought about was riding the palomino. She hated to saddle and bridle the beautiful animal, preferring to ride him bareback so that she and her horse could feel as unfettered as the wind that blew through his mane. As she readied to mount, a groom knelt and cupped his hands. She stepped lightly into the hollowed palms, and threw her leg over the horse, seating herself comfortably on the strong, broad back. She stroked Quasar over and over again, knowing that the sensitive animal was waiting impatiently for her signal to canter across the fields.

The lowering clouds had by now risen above the horizon, layering the sky in dense patches. Pointing to the looming darkness and the brewing thunderstorm, the groom warned her it was unsafe to go riding in this weather. She laughed at his concern and said gently, "You know I've ridden in a storm many, many times, Guido. Quasar and I will be perfectly safe. We'll be back before the heavens break. I have only a few days of leave, and I cannot waste even a minute of it."

With deep misgivings, Guido watched Ruari ride away. He knew it was useless to try and change her mind. Graying and middle-aged, Guido had started life in the estate as a young stable hand and was now responsible for managing all six horses in the estate. He had taught Ruari to ride when she was barely tall enough to sit on her horse, and even then had to contend with her reckless nature. She was a fearless rider to whom a hint of risk and danger always drove her to greater heights of excitement.

But it wasn't her recklessness that worried Guido, for she seemed to lead a charmed life, never having met with a riding accident as far as he could remember. What made him anxious was her oversized ego and deep seated arrogance which lay hidden behind a sweet and innocent face that captivated all with whom she came in contact. But what really troubled him was her occasional malevolent and malicious behavior and the sly and almost evil look that he sometimes glimpsed in her emerald eyes. One of these days she would be exposed, and Guido didn't like to think what chaos might ensue. Folklore professed that long, long ago strange and evil entities co-habited with humans, tainting their DNA with foul traits. Perhaps Ruari was such a hybrid, her genes a throwback resurfacing in a human eons later.

But right now, all was well in Ruari's world as she rode out of the stables. A fresh breeze tousled her unruly curls, for she obstinately refused to wear her hard hat in spite of repeated warnings from grooms and family alike. As soon as they were in the open, Ruari kneed the horse into full gallop. The wind tore through the blonde and red manes which rippled out like the wake of a motorboat speeding through the waters. The exhilaration and freedom was heady wine as horse and rider flew through the air like a spinning pulsar.

Quasar raced forward with Ruari leaning over his neck, fingers entwined in the blonde mane. Her knees prodded him in the direction she wanted to go, but the horse needed no guidance. He knew exactly what his mistress wanted. He would take her over the bridge and across the river to her favorite spot at the top of the rolling hills from where she could see Subiaco spread out like a patchwork quilt below.

The ancient monasteries, the narrow streets, the rows of houses with red-tiled roofs tinged grey with age, the tolling bells of churches, the cypress trees, all evoked happy childhood memories in Ruari. She was an atheist, but that did not prevent her from fully enjoying and appreciating the art and architecture nurtured and encouraged under the Catholic church in Italy.

His nose turned towards his destination, Quasar thundered across the grassy meadows. Clumps of sod flew from under his hoofs as he headed towards the old moss-covered bridge arching cross the river. Since the new road had been built along the estate boundary, this route was out of use, but a creature of habit, the animal stuck to the familiar path.

Horse and rider neared the river as fat raindrops descended from the skies, making the two hundred year old, sunbaked cobblestones of the bridge, hiss and sizzle. Savoring the rain on her upturned face, Ruari was deliriously happy. She spurred him on, and Quasar galloped onto the bridge, hitting the shiny, wet stones in a great clatter of hoofs.

The rain now came down in sheets. Forked lightening rent the sky in two, and seconds later was followed by a deafening thunderclap. The sudden onslaught of light and sound startled the sensitive animal and Quasar reared up in terror. With no reins to clutch and no saddle to break her downward slide, Ruari started slithering down the horse's rain-drenched back. She made a desperate grab at Quasar's mane, but the snorting, frightened animal was vigorously tossing his head to the left and right. Ruari couldn't get a good grip and the few strands of mane she had held on to, slipped through her fingers. She slid off the nearly vertical horse, and fell backwards, hitting her head on the stone parapet of the narrow bridge.

The fall jarred her whole body, sending intense bright flashes pulsating like strobe lights through her head. She receded into unconsciousness, then returned to the edge of wakefulness over and over again. The oscillation between the states of consciousness and oblivion might have continued until she had fully regained consciousness, but fate, or perhaps her karma, intervened.

A second peal of thunder, followed by another flash of blinding light, created an atypical ionization in the atmosphere. The chemical reaction, occurring at the very instant of Ruari's transition from a state of consciousness to a state of oblivion, disrupted her spiritual structure, ejecting her soul out of her body away from Zenad into another Reality.

Ruari's physical body remained in the Zenad Reality, but her mind was sucked into the event horizon of a black hole. It was enveloped in a kind of darkness unknown on earth. No sound or light penetrated this region of spacetime, and she lay suspended in a state between life and death. Perhaps this was purgatory, but then Ruari didn't believe in such things. She didn't believe that after death one endured a state of intermediate existence before being rewarded with a place in heaven or punished by being cast into hell.

Seething and writhing in a no-man's land without any deep-seated faith to anchor her to the Zenad Reality, Ruari drifted into a coma.

δ

Zenad Reality
California

Erlang Shen's astral self wafted upward, weightless, formless like a cloud. The absence of a physical body did not prevent his senses from being fully active. He smelled the ocean, the pines, the palms, the roses.

He glanced down and saw himself sitting cross legged on the stone slabs that bridged a bubbling brook. He recognized it as his favorite spot for meditation. He was wrapped in a black silk robe, a gold embroidered, fire-breathing dragon sprawling across his back.

The sense of sight and smell did not distract him, so Erlang did not feel the need to follow the usual practice of excluding them from his consciousness during his state of reflection. His face glowed pink-yellow in the rising sun which was just becoming visible behind the bushes. His shaven head and ZaZen posture made him look more like a Shaolin monk that he had once been, than the astrophysicist that he was... is,... had been...?

As he floated, Erlang had no perception of passing time, only a feeling of ecstasy, peace and harmony.

In this calm state of being, he continued to observe the scene below and saw the koi swimming lazily in the small, rock-edged pool of his Zen garden which sloped down to the creek. He turned to follow the slope in the other direction towards his house.

Tucked away in a little copse of flowering trees and shrubs, the Japanese style *uchi* had been built by Erlang himself. It stood on the banks of the Los Tracos Creek, just minutes away from Stanford University and its golf course. The tiny house with its sliding, papered doors had a verandah running along its full length. A wind chime hung from a wooden lintel, tinkling now and then in the slight breeze.

The *uchi* had only two rooms. One, where his bedding was rolled up and stacked in a corner, served as his sleeping quarters. The other was the hall, bare, save for an antique scroll hanging from ceiling to floor depicting a red-robed Chinese sage contemplating the full moon. The accompanying poem written in ink and brush strokes ran vertically down one side.

A low lacquer table in front of the scroll held a minimalist ikebana arrangement. A gnarled piece of driftwood spiraled upwards, a single fresh flower nestling in its fork as a reminder of the eternal cycle of life and death. Whenever he came to stay at the *uchi*, Erlang replaced the flower daily. Today it was a creamy chrysanthemum, its curling white petals a stark contrast to the speckled brown of the dry bark.

Erlang was an astrophysicist with a special interest in particle physics. Like Einstein, his dream was to uncover the elusive theory of everything. He and his two colleagues were currently working on the Veil Lifter project which was housed in an obscure little building close to the Collider Experimental Hall. The shabby exterior of the nameless building belied the ground breaking work that was being carried out by his team, and the state-of-the-art technology that was at their disposal. The mathematical model that he and his team had developed was the foundation of the Veil Lifter project which would open the path to harnessing renewable energy from dark matter, ending the ecologically disastrous extraction of fossil fuel, oil, gas, and other forms of energy from the earth's core.

Erlang was assigned faculty housing in the university, and that's where he lived most of the time as it was close to the lab. The *uchi* on the other hand, was Erlang's retreat and on weekends he preferred to come here and indulge in his passion for the meditative experience and search for his inner self. So, not surprisingly, Erlang chose to spend the week's leave that he and his team had been granted, at his *uchi*.

To rest and relax his mind, and so help him get further insights into his research, Erlang explored different schools of meditation. He discovered that deep, inner reflection helped him to detach himself from the complicated thought processes of astrophysics and particle physics, so that free from anxiety and worry, solutions to bottlenecks and structural obstacles in the model surfaced more readily in his mind.

Erlang had studied and practiced yoga, Tai Chi, and Qigong, all of which he had found uplifting. Yet his thirst remained unquenched, and his search eventually led him to explore the Zen experience, the objective of which was "to be in the world but not of it; to occupy the physical world but transcend it mentally, aloof and serene." He learned that Zen masters believed rational intellect obscured the truth and constrained the mind, whereas intuition developed through Zen meditation released the mind to seek out the ultimate truth.

So now, although ZaZen meditation elevated Erlang's astral self into space, an invisible thread still connected him to his body below, through which a stream of worldly concerns continued to flow towards his astral self. Uppermost among these thoughts was a nagging suspicion that there was a glitch in the model which could prove dangerous for the Veil Lifter.

The deadline for the Veil Lifter launch, however, was approaching fast, and Erlang fretted that the modification wouldn't be made in time. The procedure for harvesting dark matter was so complex and potentially hazardous for planet earth as well as the universe, that he and his colleagues had to be hundred percent sure of their calculations before giving the green signal for using the model to launch the Veil Lifter.

The current of reflections carried Erlang back to the start of his day.

δ

Dawn is about to break, and as usual, I spend an hour practicing various martial arts techniques. That done, I kneel before the ikebana and meditate on life and death.

As the sky begins to lighten, the wind chime tinkles melodiously from the verandah. I rise and walk across my tiny Zen garden, down the gentle slope, to the little bridge which is my favorite spot for meditation. I sit cross legged on the stone slabs, my back straight, my posture symmetrical, in preparation for ZaZen, the heart of Zen practice.

As ritual demands, I fold my hands in the cosmic mudra, left palm facing up, resting on my right palm, thumbs barely touching each other. The posture helps me focus my attention inward, towards the self, towards my hara, towards my lower dan t'ien, which Taoism defines as the physical and spiritual center of the body.

I balance myself on the narrow stone slabs, and rock back and forth until I locate my center of gravity and come to rest in a stable position. Following Zen techniques, I close my mouth, let my tongue touch my palate and inhale and exhale deeply through my diaphragm.

As I fall into a natural rhythm, my body begins to relax. My steady breathing fuels my joriki, the spiritual power which guides my mind, allowing it to dive into deep introspection. My preoccupation with internal conflicts slowly dissolve, and my whole being opens up like a flower in sunlight. My joriki merges into my samadhi, the state of intense concentration of energy or qi that eliminates the sense of separation between self and others, and I begin to sense the underlying oneness of all things.

Yet, even as I feel my concentration converge to a single point, my mind wanders, entangling itself in the reeds of anxiety for the looming deadline and the problems with the model. The torrent of distorted and fragmented mental activity begins to drag me away from my inner self. I'm forced to invoke Zanshin to extricate myself out of the quagmire.

I'm aware that Zanshin in martial arts means I must follow through with whatever action I have initiated, even if it is a mistake, and only then must I counteract the error by adjusting my techniques to use the opponent's energy to defeat him. In Zen meditation on the other hand, Zanshin means to push oneself to a point beyond hesitation, using mental energy to break all barriers.

I choose to use Zanshin to disconnect my astral self from my physical body. At once, my worries fade away, and like vapor evaporate into nothingness.

δ

Through ZaZen, Erlang had finally begun his journey towards himself. The sensation was as strenuous as climbing a mountain, for he must rid himself of false beliefs and illusions of the material world. With considerable effort of will and using his *hara*, Erlang once again summoned his spiritual power to acquire *samadhi*. It took several cycles of losing and regaining his *joriki*, before he could reach a state of *samadhi* that remained stable for any appreciable period of time.

As the stability of *samadhi* improved, he was able to use ZaZen to descend deeper and deeper into his mind and body, reaching a stillness he had never experienced even in the most profound depth of slumber. The functions of his organs slowed down and his breathing became more and more shallow, until it appeared that he had stopped breathing altogether.

In this state, he neither actively sought enlightenment, nor rejected delusion, yet his scattered mental energy coalesced, transforming his mind into a still sheet of water where reflections of his thoughts floated unbroken, unfragmented. The tranquility of his mind and body radiated outwards, dampening all sound.

For Erlang, no birds sang, no wind blew, even the brook stopped rippling. Only the teachings of Zen masters suffused his mind, deepening his inner peace and harmony. He had taken the first step on the Way to Awakening, the first step to entering the heart, the intimacy and richness of the moment.

Poised as an archer about to release his arrow, the words of the 18th century master, Manzan Dohaku surged through Erlang's mind: *"Like lightning all thoughts come and pass. Just once look into your mind-depths: Nothing else has ever been."*

The wisdom of Gogen Kigen zenji touched his core being:

"One moment of just sitting is one moment of enlightenment."

Erlang continued to breathe in an unhurried rhythm, exposing himself to unique sensations and the luminosity of the bodymind experience. In this state of near Awakening, he became aware of the impermanence of time and was ready to forget the self, ready to be enlightened.

Along with the realization came a release from the constraints of artificial earthly values, a release that snapped the tenuous thread that connected his soul, his *atman* to his physical body. As his astral self floated away, he understood intuitively that the world around him was both one and part of a larger, all-encompassing Absolute.

δ

Next morning, the gardener found Erlang in a catatonic state, barely breathing and cold as the stones on which he sat. His eyes, wide open, stared unfocused into space, into a Reality that he alone could uncover.

CHAPTER II

The Summons

Waara Reality
Somewhere on Earth

It is early dawn and the sky turns a molten gold, transforming the river into a shimmering ribbon and the fields into a patchwork of green shades and hues.

Ormidtz has already arisen and begun his day. He is on Earth as perceived through the prism of the Waara Reality, and is unaware that a tangential force is about to disrupt the steady orbit of his life, setting him on an entirely different trajectory.

With silver hair rippling down to his shoulders, sleek golden-bronze skin, and gold-flecked hazel eyes, he looks ageless. He could easily be twenty years old as counted in the Zenad Reality, or he could be fifty. Only his eyes reflect the many lifetimes he has experienced. Bottomless as the ocean, they sometimes glitter and sometimes recede into an opacity that give him the look of a blind man.

The Waara Reality is a state of being reserved only for those who have earned it. It is for those who are the most dedicated, the most committed to the Tractate and its code of behaviour. In Waara, just as a butterfly emerges from its cocoon, the human *atman*, man's essential being, begins the process of transmigrating to the stage of pure consciousness. Of all the six planes of existence, it is here that the proximity of the human soul is closest to the Seventh Reality, for it is the penultimate step for unison with the Singularity.

In Waara, humans are at the brink of mastering their rhizomes and the multiplicities of their thought images. The perception of physical wants, needs and desires begins to evaporate, and is replaced by an enlightened existence of immense spiritual power. Here, the layers of darkness that surround a human *atman* fall off like the petals of a dying chrysanthemum, exposing the core of the human soul which is energy in its purest form. This purity rips apart the curtain from a human's eyes to reveal to him the true face of the universe.

The world through the Waara prism is not beset with wars, famines, pain and suffering. It is one where the Earth is in harmony with all living creatures, where an ethical balance ensures the peaceful continuity of all creations – planets, stars, galaxies and other worlds. This perfect harmony arises from the realization that physical reality is essentially unsubstantial; that matter is but a curvature of the space-time continuum. Matter is nothing but energy.

This equilibrium arises from the knowledge that the human soul is but a miniscule droplet of energy distilled from the Singularity, from the Oneness, which is then ejected from the Seventh Reality into the universe to fulfil its destiny – to complete a task as unique as the soul's very existence.

In all the six lower energy Realities, the human soul, sometimes called the essential being, sometimes the noumenon, and sometimes the *atman*, is personified by a physical body which undergoes fragmentation within itself as it experiences the cycles of birth-death-rebirth into these Realities. The human essential being is offered several reincarnations and many opportunities to heal the disintegration of self, and until the healing is complete, and perfection of the noumenon is achieved, it endlessly continues its evolutionary path of birth, death and rebirth. When the soul completes the healing process, and successfully recreates its original flawless and cohesive self, it returns to the Beginning and is absorbed into the Seventh Reality, the Singularity from which it was first spawned.

Like all life forms, a human's plane of existence starts in the Vakin Reality, the primordial uterus of creation, where the universe is awash with pulsating chemical compounds. The world is in its formative stage. Light does not exist. All is swirling darkness. Matter is yet to be created.

Little exists in this vast emptiness – no planets, no earth, no galaxies There are only spinning particles and subparticles which sometimes clash, sometimes merge, sometimes fly away from one another to the edge of space. But always there are the souls, essential beings, waiting like the Higgs boson for matter to cluster around them and sculpt the rudiments of a human being.

For most humans the common transition is from the primordial Vakin to the Zenad Reality, the most perilous of all the Realities. It is in Zenad that humans are first exposed to the enticing *maya* of material wealth, sensual pleasures and corporeal gratification. It is here too, that they experience for the first time the burden of a conscience and the power of free will to choose between good and evil.

They have the option to follow the Tractate and transcend from Zenad to the high energy Realities of Khulon, Naqim, Machim, and Waara, each transcendence bringing them closer to the Singularity. Or, they can choose to ignore the guidance of the Tractate and lead a life that creates a congestion in their evolutionary process, trapping them for eternity in a cycle between Vakin and Zenad.

Some humans who adhere to the teachings of the Tractate, such as monks, religious leaders, priests, and sadhus, often evolve faster, sometimes skipping a Reality, to be reborn in a higher energy state. But it is only the Saints who make the quickest transition from the primordial Vakin to uncovering the Ultimate Truth. Because of their proximity to the Oneness, their bodies become so detached from their minds and souls that they are able to undergo unspeakable sufferings to achieve martyrdom.

As humans evolve, the Universe and the Realities themselves undergo a dynamic cycle of creation, annihilation and recreation, the changes determined by the actions and reactions to choices made by humans. At the same time, the universe and all the Realities are interconnected, and disruption in the equilibrium of any one Reality affects the state of existence in the others.

But among all the Realities, the human soul is most vulnerable in the Zenad Reality. A human's insatiable desire for wealth and recognition is fertile ground for breeding temptations that surreptitiously, covertly, prey on human weaknesses.

Seeds for such disruption have already been sown in the

Zenad.

δ

Ormidtz is aware of all this, for before transcending to Waara, he has transitioned through many lifetimes. In his earlier existences, like most humans, he had been caught in the endless cycle of the primordial Vakin and the perilous Zenad Realities. His desire for accumulating material assets and indulging excessively in carnal pleasures had held him back, hindering him from evolving to higher levels of consciousness that would draw him closer to the Ultimate Truth.

It was only during one of his reincarnations in the Zenad Reality, when he met Megan, that Ormidtz experienced a cosmic transformation that ejected him out of the confinement of the Vakin-Zenad cycle into a path that spiraled upwards to higher and higher states of consciousness, bearing him towards the Waara Reality.

Now his essential being is so dominant, his qi so powerful, that the need of a physical body has become nearly redundant. He is at the brink of evolving into a state of existence where his corporeal needs are in the process of being replaced by an insatiable thirst for the Oneness, the font of all Qi.

At this stage of his evolution, Ormidtz has discovered that he is endowed with the rare ability to recall all that has passed during each of his many lifetimes. He has also learnt that he has the singular power to travel between all the Realities that he has already transitioned. But he has no desire to travel, for in Waara he has found a kind of peace that he has never known before. He does not want to risk moving away from Waara, because he is too close to transitioning into the purest form of consciousness, to merging with the Final Reality, to uncovering the Seventh Reality and the Ultimate Truth. So Ormidtz bides his time in Waara, eagerly awaiting his next transition.

As he waits, he follows a routine that keeps him spiritually and physically strong. Every morning when he wakes up, Ormidtz unlocks his third eye to expose his senses to the Realities of Vakin, Zenad, Khulon, Naqim, Machim, and of course Waara where he is right now. The six Realities have no forms, no dimensions, for each represents a stage of enlightenment, but those few who, like him, have the skill, can locate them whenever they wish. The Seventh Reality, the Singularity, of course remains hidden, for Ormidtz has yet to uncover that Ultimate Truth.

He surveys the Realities to remind himself of the long path that he has already traversed, and the even longer journey that still lies ahead. He strips away the layers of Realities and gazes at what his life had been in Zenad with Megan. He sees the bay glistening in the distance and green meadows carpeted in flowers rising to the very doorsteps of the old shepherd's cottage. He sees the two of them sitting by the fire, sometimes talking, often lost in thought, but always, always happy to be just in each other's company. The quiet scene gives no hint of the tectonic plate shift about to splinter their lives.

Then finding the vision too painful, Ormidtz focuses on other Realities where discipline and commitment to the Tractate guided him through the pitfalls, enabling him to metamorphose into purer forms of existence. His daily sojourn of the Realities over, he shuts his third eye which blends imperceptibly into his brow leaving it smooth and unfurrowed.

He begins his day by tending to a small patch of pristine land which he cultivates to produce what he needs to remain alive until his next transition. Any surplus he shares with his neighbors who are few, because not many can achieve the near-perfect consciousness needed to graduate to Waara. Like the others on Waara, he is alone, no family, no kin, for the journey to the Ultimate Truth is a solitary one.

His few chores done, Ormidtz spends the rest of the day in contemplation and in practicing martial arts which help him hone his qi, the anchor that grounds him safely during his odyssey into deep introspection. Today, as usual, after completing his work, Ormidtz seats himself under the flowering *sheuli* tree, the fragrant, saffron-stemmed white flowers of the nyctanthes arbor-tristis dropping around him like snowflakes.

But synchrony of mind and body eludes him. Today, more than other days, he finds his mind wandering, unable to easily shift into a meditative mode. Images flash through his mind – his past lives, the pleasures and pains caused to himself and to others by choices he had made, by his succumbing to temptations, and by his seeking material gratification over spiritual wealth. He is aware that these actions caused him to be reborn in Zenad over and over again.

It was only in his third lifetime in Zenad that the trauma of meeting Megan and losing her within a short space of time, had fractured the monotonous Vakin-Zenad cycle and opened the portals to states of consciousness higher than that in Zenad.

Megan, with her raven hair and blue eyes, who was his one true love. Megan whom he lost in that lifetime, and whom he never again found in his many reincarnations, in as many Realities. Will he ever forget her? *Does* he want to forget her? He knows these corporeal fetters are obstacles to uncovering the Ultimate Truth. Yet, even now, he is unable to wholly discard these binding chains.

To rein in his wandering thoughts and free his conscious-ness, Ormidtz begins chanting the Tractate out aloud, the cadence rising and falling with every breath. The rhythm stills his mind and as the sun begins to set, he too slowly sinks into a meditative state that loosens his earthly bonds, letting his *atman* float into the unknown.

δ

Time passes. His soul, given the freedom to roam, is on the brink of entering unfamiliar territory.

Then a pulsating, high voltage electrical force jars his reverie.

"Ormidtz", the electrical waves call to him. "Ormidtz, your time has come. You are the chosen one."

Floating in the twilight region between meditation and wakefulness, Ormidtz senses his own thought waves being agita-ted by an external force that pervades his entire being. Ripples intersect the frequency of his thought waves, intimidating yet stimulating.

His consciousness stirs reluctantly, for he had been in profound contemplation that gave his *atman* the freedom and exhilaration to explore the eternal cycles of birth, annihilation and rejuvenation in Space, in the Universe, in the Realities.

The call jolts him awake from a fathoms-deep meditation which had taken him further and further into himself, keeping him connected to Earth only by the most tenuous of bonds. The summons forces him to resurface like a deep-sea diver, rising up through each layer of awareness to finally re-enter the state of human existence in the Waara Reality. He cannot ignore the call for he has recognized it is Thebitz who is knocking on the door of his subconsciousness.

Thebitz is a being of light and fire who materializes in different forms to different people, depending on the human's state of mind. To a baby, Thebitz is the face that makes her chuckle and coo while staring into space. To the dying, he could be the Angel of Death mentioned in the ancient Zenad texts. To another he could be Michelangelo's Gabriel with snow-white wings and golden flowing hair. To an old woman struggling with a heavy burden, he could just be the strong young man giving her a helping hand.

But to Ormidtz, Thebitz is always a flow of energy, a stream of thought impulses vibrating through his being. Ormidtz prefers to personify Thebitz as a *he*, although he knows that Thebitz is not human, and so is neither male nor female.

Ormidtz doesn't like being disturbed during meditation, and asks querulously, "Why do you interrupt me at this crucial stage of my evolution, when I'm so close to initiating synthesis with the Singularity?"

Unperturbed by Ormidtz's annoyance, Thebitz announces unequivocally, "The universe and the Realities are about to degenerate into chaos, and the human species is facing imminent danger of annihilation. You've been chosen to avert this crisis."

"Saving the Realities and the universe is a gargantuan task. I'm but a mere human. Surely it's only the Singularity, the Supreme Reality, the Oneness, who can prevent destruction on such a scale?"

"Maybe, maybe not," replies Thebitz quizzically. "As it usually happens, the crisis has been created by humans, a crisis that is putting the Zenad and the other Realities in a very vulnerable position. You well know that high negativity beings, or the hi-negs as they are called, are always hovering in space, ready to take advantage of any situation which will allow them to increase their presence in the universe. If Zenad is weakened in any way, hi-negs will take over control. It's therefore imperative to avert the catastrophe before it takes place."

"Yes, humans are endowed with the supreme gifts of freedom of thought and freedom of choice, but we repeatedly misuse these gifts to create war, famine, chaos and destruction," says Ormidtz.

"True, but it's not for us to judge," replies Thebitz, unwilling to express an opinion on the miraculous creation called Man.

"You are familiar with the Tractate," continues Thebitz. "So you understand that the Supreme Reality cannot intervene to resolve human conflicts. Such actions will jeopardize the ethical balance of the universe. It's only when humans find solutions to their own crises and problems that a state of equilibrium can be ensured."

"And I'm the human to solve the problem?" Ormidtz asks incredulously.

"You are being offered the chance to stop the disaster before it happens. Otherwise all is lost."

"But how can I, alone, perform this miracle?" asks Ormidtz, inundated by doubts of his own ability to handle such a crisis.

"I've been your guide and mentor through all your lifetimes," Thebitz reminds Ormidtz. "I will not abandon you now. I'll be there whenever you need me."

Ormidtz remains silent and Thebitz continues, "Also, as you well know, the human race will never be abandoned. The human *atman* will, through all eternity, be guided towards the Singularity to become a part of the Oneness, so that the cycle of creation and evolution occurs over and over again."

Ormidtz is familiar with the catechism and the oft-repeated refrain from the Tractate. He still says nothing, willing himself to ignore Thebitz's persuasive arguments to accept the role of savior of a universe in grave danger.

Although he gets no response from Ormidtz, Thebitz perseveres.

"Ormidtz, let me first give you a quick briefing on the situation. In the Zenad Reality, humans on Earth have been trying for millennia to discover the origin of the universe, the meaning of life and the ultimate destiny of man. In the twenty-first century they confirmed the existence of the Higgs boson, the particle which enabled matter to form after space exploded. Encouraged by this success, they intensified their search for a scientific proof of the origin of the universe, the First Cause, the Cosmic Evolution."

This time Ormidtz replies, for he is on familiar ground.

"This search is bound to fail unless scientists accept the fact that there is no single point of origin, no beginning, no end, just the eternal circle. To find what they are looking for, they must first develop theories that explain the seen and the unseen, the perceived reality and the spiritual reality, and recognize that there is no past, no future, only the now. Maybe at some stage they will realize that the three-dimensional world that humans perceive in Zenad is just a hologram of its two-dimensional

Reality."

"Exactly," agrees Thebitz. "Scientists in Zenad call Time the fourth dimension. They created the concept to retrofit all phenomena they observe, thus sheathing the visible and the invisible into the straitjacket of Time. And time and time again their theories run into dead ends." Thebitz chuckles at his own witticism, causing ripples in Ormidtz's wave patterns.

"But man's quest for knowledge has always been his strength, hasn't it?" argues Ormidtz

"Yes, but not when the knowledge leads him down a path which is highly dangerous, both in the material and spiritual sense."

"What do you mean? How dangerous?"

"Let me elaborate," begins Thebitz, relieved that Ormidtz has got over his petulance. "In Zenad Reality, there's a laboratory deep under the polar cap in the northern region of Earth. A team of scientists from all over the world have nearly finalized the design of a project, the Veil Lifter, so named because it will enable them to isolate the elusive and invisible dark matter and black holes."

"Oh, you're talking about the ground breaking work carried out by Ruari O'Connor, Erlang Shen and Ameqran Izem? They developed a mathematical model for harnessing energy from dark matter and black holes to meet the ever increasing needs of humans." Ormidtz was drawing on his formidable memory bank generated over his numerous life cycles.

"Yes, the Veil Lifter is based on that very model. The problem is that none of the scientists in the Polar Lab, as it's affectionately known, are aware of a critical miscalculation in the geodesics of the model. The original architects of the model made a wrong assumption in the model's basic tangent vectors. The error went undetected because the results they got from the trial runs of the model were theoretically plausible. The deeply embedded flaw in the matrices did not surface even during empirical tests because the offending vectors don't impact at the particle or sub-particle level, but at a much broader level – the field level."

"But such results are always expressed in charts, graphs and maps which scientists spend years analyzing. How can that be dangerous?" asks Ormidtz, now more alert having put aside his peevishness at being disturbed during meditation.

"Under normal circumstances, what you say is true," concedes Thebitz. "But as things stand, if the model is applied as is, it will initiate a quantum fluctuation that will plunge the Higgs Field into a lower energy state."

"Under the Chaos Theory, this sudden, discrete change of state doesn't bode well," Ormidtz concludes.

"Exactly. The fluctuation will create a tangential force that will breach the Ocyyst Barrier. All evolutionary processes will grind to a halt, and all fields of thought, the core input and output of creation, will be obliterated. The Realities, which now either abut or overlap, will be torn apart and become isolated from one another. Human souls or *atman*s will lose the ability to transition through the Realities and will never experience the Seventh Reality or be able to merge with the Oneness to discover the Ultimate Truth. Free will and freedom of thought will be eradicated."

Ormidtz frowns deeply at the seriousness of the repercussions, the sine curves of his thought waves squishing together in reaction. He knows that fractions of seconds after the explosion of space during the transitional phase from the primordial Vakin Reality to Zenad, equal parts of matter and antimatter particles were created which began to annihilate one another. For reasons as yet unknown, the baryogenesis process allowed one out of a billion particles of matter to survive.

This anomaly eventually spawned the universe of the Zenad Reality with its humans, other beings, planets, stars and galaxies. Equilibrium was maintained simply because cosmic inflation swept the antimatter particles, pairs to the surviving matter particles, behind the Ocyyst Barrier, a firewall at the edge of space which separates regions dominated by antimatter and hi-neg beings from the rest of positive space.

Now, if Thebitz's prophecy came true and the Ocyyst Barrier were breached, the influx of anti-matter interacting with ordinary matter would annihilate both, releasing high energy gamma rays. The asymmetry of the universe, which paradoxically keeps the universe stable, would be destroyed.

A phenomenal amount of energy would be released, causing the universe in Zenad to implode into a black hole, which in turn would jeopardize the state of equilibrium in every Reality. The Zenad universe would swarm with hi-neg entities that thrive on evil and all things that oppose positivity and goodness, characteristics that define the Singularity, the Oneness. Humans would be subjugated to the power of hi-negs in every plane of existence, and would eventually lose their free will to choose between good and evil.

"The solution is obvious, isn't it?" Ormidtz's thought waves spike in puzzlement. "Get the three original scientists to join the polar team and make the necessary corrections before the project is launched."

"Ah, but therein lies the rub," says Thebitz, not above quoting Shakespeare or other great thinkers from any Reality. "The fates of all three have put them beyond the reach of ordinary humans. Ruari O'Connor, the mathematician and cosmologist, Irish to the bone, insisted on riding her stallion during a thunderstorm. Lightning struck, the horse reared, and Ruari was thrown off. She hit her head against the cobblestones and should have died instantly and transitioned to another Reality, but coincidentally, or perhaps synchronicity was at play, the excess electrical energy in the air altered her ionic balance. She couldn't complete the migration to another Reality with the result that her mind and consciousness transcended into another Reality, while her body remained in Zenad. Doctors are, of course, unaware of what actually took place and diagnosed her condition as concussion-induced coma. Fortunately she comes from a wealthy family, and her comatose body is being preserved in Italy with the help of a very expensive life support system."

"And the other two?" asks Ormidtz.

"Before becoming a physicist, Erlang Shen was a Shaolin monk. He has always aspired to develop, like the god he's named after, a third eye that would let him see the ultimate truth. He mastered the meditative arts and frequently dabbled in out-of-body experiences, believing that trances untether the mind, enabling it to seek mathematical solutions that otherwise remain hidden.

When he ran into a conundrum in the dark energy model, he decided to search for the key to the answer through ZaZen meditation techniques. While in a self-induced trance, Erlang's *atman* was transported into a Reality with a level of consciousness purer than he has ever experienced in Zenad. Now he's unable, or perhaps doesn't want to, withdraw himself from the new Reality.

So to people in Zenad, he appears to have fallen into a catatonic state, staring into space, not speaking, nor interacting with anyone or anything. He has no family, but in the interest of preserving the brain of a genius, the Foundation for Future Growth provided financial support to fly his body to a sanitarium in Nepal that specializes in reversing such conditions."

"And Ameqran Izem? Is he comatose or catatonic as well?" asks Ormidtz, sarcasm creating deep troughs in his thought waves.

"His case is a little more convoluted," parries Thebitz.

Familiar with Thebitz's understatements, Ormidtz waits, terror gnawing his guts as he waits for Thebitz to unfold the complexity of the problem.

"Ameqran, or Izem as he prefers to be called, is an acoustics expert, whose work on the Veil Lifter exposed him to the mystery and mysticism of particle physics, quantum mechanics, and molecular theory," continues Thebitz. "Izem became convinced that the three-dimensional universe is actually multi-dimensional, and that there are many universes, not just the one that humans experience in Zenad."

"Everyone is entitled to his opinion," said Ormidtz prosaically.

"True, but his case is slightly different. Izem was convinced that he would find confirmation of his ideas through the Sufi meditation technique. So he launched himself into *zikr* without adequate preparation, with the result that he went into a dangerously deep trance that transported him into unknown and unfamiliar spiritual territory. Although his exposure was only for a fraction of a second, he was unable to cope with what was revealed to him. He consequently became psychotic and now wanders around shrines talking to himself."

"So he's lost forever?" Ormidtz interrupts Thebitz.

"No," Thebitz assures Ormidtz, the voltage of his electrical vibrations dropping a notch. "The simple answer is that at different moments Izem is experiencing different Realities. So that when at times he appears to be mad, or possessed by evil spirits, or to put it medically, schizophrenic, his mind has actually flitted off to another Reality, temporarily abandoning his Zenad body."

"So what is my task?" asks Ormidtz, not sure he wants to know.

"Your mission is to collect the lost mind, essence or soul of each scientist from whichever Reality it is inhabiting and unite it with his or her corporeal body in the Zenad Reality. You must guide the scientists back to their Zenad levels of consciousness. Once they are whole again, they can amend the flawed mathematical model before the Veil Lifter is launched," explains Thebitz.

"On the other hand," says Ormidtz, "I could try to convince the polar team to abandon their experiment. What would be my probability of success if I chose that line of action?"

"Good question," replies Thebitz, just like any speaker who, faced with a tough challenge, seeks to buy a few seconds to marshal his thoughts. "First, you'll not be able to convince the venture capitalists, who are businessmen and not scientists, and who have poured billions of dollars into the project, that the Ocyyst Barrier exists, leave alone, that it will be breached.

They'll insist that the project be launched on schedule. Secondly, top scientists of the world have staked their reputations and a lifetime of labor on this experiment, not to mention their dreams of untold wealth from the commercial sale of the new technology. They won't agree to abort the project either. So to answer your question, I'd hazard a guess that the probability of shutting down the project is zero."

"But what you are expecting me to accomplish is impossible," Ormidtz protests vehemently. "I'm the wrong person for the task. I'm not brave and I'm not interested in being a hero."

"You have an extensive knowledge database accumulated over several lifetimes and you can travel between Realities. These attributes define you as the chosen one, as the only human who can save the universe," insists Thebitz.

"I don't want to go on a mission where I'll have to regress to the Zenad level of consciousness, the most rudimentary stage of spiritual evolution." Ormidtz continues to resist the idea of launching himself on such a dangerous undertaking. "In Waara my essential being is at the brink of being transformed into pure consciousness, dispensing with the need for corporeal bodies and material goods for survival. If I exit Waara, I may not be able to return. I may have to start my evolutionary journey all over again."

"Those risks are real," agrees Thebitz. "You, of course, have the right to refuse this mission for, like all humans, you are endowed with the gift of free will. But remember, you also have a conscience. Knowing all that you now know, can you remain in Waara and concentrate only on synthesizing with the Singularity?"

"I don't know," Ormidtz confesses. "But what I do know is that I don't want to be once again exposed to the material attractions of Zenad, to become vulnerable to seeking attachments to humans rather than the Oneness. Moreover, I'm quite sure that I'm not fit to carry out the perilous task of saving humankind."

"It's just a point of view, Ormidtz," says Thebitz, softening his electrical impulses to break down Ormidtz's resistance. "One task is as easy or as hard as the other. It all depends on the lenses through which you perceive your mission."

"My lenses tell me that I cannot be successful in this mission," Ormidtz insists stubbornly, impervious to Thebitz's persuasive powers. Paralyzing fear swamps him, drenching him in cold sweat. Beads of perspiration form on his brows and trickle down his temples.

Thebitz makes a last attempt at convincing Ormidtz to fulfil his responsibilities as the chosen one.

"Remember, Ormidtz," cautions Thebitz, "If Zenad is destroyed, all the other Realities will also become altered. Waara may not remain the Waara you know and love."

"I'll take my chances on that." Ormidtz's thought waves fluctuate erratically as he continues to resist Thebitz.

"You are free to make your choice, Ormidtz, but remember that your actions will generate consequences of causes and effects. So choose wisely, my friend."

Thebitz's electrical vibrations degenerate into flatlines.

CHAPTER III

THE MANIFESTATION

Zenad Reality
Bangladesh

Reluctantly, even grudgingly, Ormidtz prepared to transition from Waara to Zenad.

He still did not want to leave the peace and harmony of a near-perfect Earth in Waara, to come to its damaged and soiled version in the Zenad Reality. But after Thebitz's departure, Ormidtz's conscience refused to be quietened. It pricked him, it prompted him, causing him intense mental distress until he could no longer ignore it. He succumbed to the bidding of his conscience. Against his better judgement and despite his misgivings about his own ability to carry out the challenging task, Ormidtz donned the mantle of the savior of Zenad.

But downgrading from a higher level of existence to a lower one was almost as difficult as transitioning in the opposite direction. After some contemplation, Ormidtz decided to draw upon his energy force from the sea of qi residing in his lower *dan t'ien*, for he would need tremendous power to undo his braid of life, the billions of atoms that created trajectories through spacetime to forge his unique identity.

His energy force generated an electric charge that sliced through him like a knife, prying apart the elementary particles that made him who he was. His physical body disintegrated releasing his astral self to transition out of Waara.

While most humans cannot decide or choose the Reality into which their *atmans* will transition after death since it is determined by the acts and deeds they perform in the Reality they are about to leave, it is different for Ormidtz. He has the power to transition into any of the six Realities and he now willed his essential being to cross into Zenad where he was needed to complete a mission.

δ

Ormidtz stood at the edge of the promontory letting his eyes sweep the tree tops below. Emerald, jade, peridot, they stretched as far as the horizon, itself obscured by the misty rain swathing through the trees, and disappearing in wisps somewhere down the hill. The pristine natural surroundings, untouched and undamaged by humans, looked the same perceived through any Reality.

Through a gap in the trees he could see a thin ribbon of a waterfall trickle down the hillside into an unseen underground spring. He felt that, like the waterfall, he was dropping into an unknown abyss, the sensation filling him with deep disquiet. He was on a perilous journey and heading for unchartered destinations with hidden, unrevealed horrors.

For the first leg of his odyssey, since his life braids were already in an unraveled state, Ormidtz had opted to use the subparticle mode of travel. This allowed his essential being to be anywhere, everywhere, or nowhere at all, until his consciousness selected a particular spot where the quantum wave function of his soul could collapse into a single piece of matter with specific physical properties.

In other words, a place where he would become visible to humans on the earth in the Zenad Reality. This mode of transportation between Realities, which enabled him to travel faster than the speed of light, however had its drawbacks. Because of the oscillations of the particle wave functions, there was always a statistical margin of error in quantum relocation. A slight error in theta, and the deviation could be hundreds of earth miles.

Ormidtz had randomly chosen to first track down Erlang Shen, the astrophysicist. Thebitz had provided him with very little data on Erlang, other than the fact that he was in a catatonic state brought on by his ZaZen experience, and that he was being cared for in a sanitarium in the mountains of Nepal. So now he cast his eyes to the right and left, trying to gauge if he had reached his first destination.

A shadow creeping along the hillside caught his attention. It was an old woman making her slow way downhill, bent double under the weight of firewood. She stopped by the dribbling waterfall to catch her breath and slake her thirst. He decided to probe her mind. He could do this easily because she was old and defenseless, unaware of his presence. It was not always as effortless to peer into a person's mind, especially those who were very intelligent and alert. The naïve, the skeptic and the vulnerable were always easy targets.

The woman's mental database told him that he was in the Bandarbans. Where was that?

From his pocket he fished out a small thin card, nebulous yet glinting in the dim morning light. He transferred the woman's thoughts into the card which then tele-flashed the co-ordinates of the location, together with a brief description of the area.

It appeared that he was in the ancient region of the Bengal delta formed by silt deposits of three powerful rivers flowing from the Himalayan mountain range into the sea. Fascinating though the information was, Ormidtz did not spend any further time researching the location. This was not where he had to be. He must find a way out of this place. Unwilling to risk arriving at yet another wrong destination and losing precious time, he abandoned the idea of subparticle travel for more conventional modes of travel.

As he dithered whether to take the right or the left fork in the road, voices floated up from somewhere nearby. He set out to investigate and soon located the source. Two men, seated on a rickety bench, were holding cups from which tendrils of steam snaked up and dissipated into the chill air. Ormidtz caught a whiff of the contents. It was centuries in terms of earth time since his last life cycle in the Zenad Reality, but he could still recall many of the human sensations he had enjoyed. He was sure the aroma was from black tea brewed over woodfire and sweetened with condensed milk, a product that contained no dairy but gave the tea flavor and a golden, creamy color. He looked around to see where the tea came from, and noticed a man squatting over a large flask, a plastic bucket loaded with teacups, packets of tea rusks and a bunch of finger-length, golden bananas.

He sauntered up to the little group. The men looked up to see a tall, lithe man emerge through the mist wearing a safari hat, pilot sunglasses, and a leather jacket. This was a popular tourist spot and the men were used to strangers and foreigners touring the scenic area. They nodded their welcome and smiling made a place for him on the swaying bench. Reciprocating their camaraderie, he bought a cup of tea and a couple of the tiny bananas and sat down on the creaking bench. He reactivated his taste buds that had degenerated over time, and was surprised by the richness of the tea and the sweet tartness of the bananas. Corporeal pleasures were beginning to resurface in Ormidtz.

He had barely finished eating, when a rattle and clank announced the approach of a wheeled transport. A contraption, pock-marked with dents, its flaking red paint revealing the original gray undercoat, wheezed up the road. Headlights speared the dimness of the early morning drizzle as it ground to a halt near the bench. The driver, muffled up to his ears, stepped out for a cup of tea.

Neither the driver nor the passengers seemed to be any hurry. What was the point in rushing through the day? There was plenty of time to do whatever needed to be done to fill one's stomach. It was more important to savor the misty rain on one's eyelashes, to watch an eagle soar high in the sky, to see fish jump in the mountain spring. This was the land of the gods.

Yes, Time, thought Ormidtz, as he later followed the others into the bus, settling into a window seat to gather his thoughts. Time meant nothing in the Waara Reality. Time was created by humans in an attempt to explain phenomena they observed on Earth in Zenad, for unlike Ormidtz, who could perceive all the

Realities simultaneously when he chose to do so, most humans experience only the Reality they are inhabiting at any given moment.

Perhaps it was better that way. For the knowledge of being part of the Singularity, that there is no beginning, no end, just the eternal inhaling and exhaling of the Realities can be exhilarating and joyous. At the same time, it can be deeply disturbing for it casts a tremendous burden on the human soul.

Lost in thought, Ormidtz gazed out the window as the bus snaked down the pot-holed mountain road. He had opted for this form of transport rather than subparticle travel in the expectation that it would help him readjust to Zenad which he had last visited eons ago. Although Ormidtz had experienced Zenad before, he had to strategize carefully, for each Reality was dynamic, every human reincarnation subtly changing its characteristics and properties. From past experience, Ormidtz knew that the Zenad he was now experiencing was not the same as the Zenad of his earlier reincarnations, for his consciousness was now casting it in a different light, in a different form of relativity.

In the middle of his musings the bus came to a stop in front of a Buddhist temple. An open doorway revealed a steep flight of steps flanked on either side by golden balusters. As he stepped out of the bus, a sudden deluge of rain, a common occurrence in the region, soaked him to the skin. Ormidtz stood with his face uplifted to the heavens, savoring a sensation that had receded far into the depths of his memories. Laughing and shaking his head like a drenched dog, he raced up the steps and took refuge under an ornate archway which proved to be the entrance to the temple. In front of him the intricately carved, red and gold wooden temple, reflected in the thin layer of water covering the courtyard, appeared to float in a pool of patterned tiles.

The rain stopped as suddenly as it had begun, and sunrays streaked through the clouds, turning the courtyard into a sea of sunbursts. Ormidtz walked across to the temple where a saffron-robed monk was supervising a *sramanera* clean the altar. The novice, with his clean-shaven head, was no more than ten years old. Ormidtz bowed to the monk and waited at the temple door for permission to enter.

The monk looked intently at Ormidtz and said, "I can sense that you are not of this Reality. You must have come here, or sent here, for some reason. Your red aura shows you are agitated, much disturbed, about something. Enter. Perhaps your essential being will find some peace in the temple."

Slightly flustered at the monk's ability to so accurately read the state of his mind, Ormidtz bowed his thanks and walked into the cool pagoda. He was alone in the temple which was dimly lit by sunlight filtering through the filigree woodwork. The benign features of the bronze Buddha lying on his side with head propped on one hand, cast an aura of tranquility all around.

Ormidtz lowered himself on the floor, adopting the yogic lotus position in preparation to meditate and pray, for every place of worship offered a gateway to the Oneness, if one were but to seek it. He partially closed his eyes and focused his mind on the single syllable Om, but contrary to the serenity that the mantra usually invoked in him, unease pervaded his senses, flooding him with irrational apprehension. As Ormidtz struggled to calm his fears, a shadow flitted over the dragon-shaped crossbar in the courtyard. He heard the monk murmur a greeting. Then silence.

Overtaken by curiosity, Ormidtz squinted through slit eyes. The figure of a woman wearing a long, gossamer dress that shimmered, now in rainbow colors, now fusing into a non-hue, floated rather than walked passed in front of the golden statue of the reclining Buddha. Her gown trailed on the floor as her fine, rainbow tinted tresses, falling to her waist, wafted about her in a mist. He peered at her face, but it was like looking at something through rippling water. Bars of rainbow hues undulated across a visage that now looked Oriental, now African and now Caucasian. As Ormidtz tried to focus more closely, the apparition became invisible as all the colors fused into the colorlessness of a crystal prism. The scent of jasmine flooded the temple.

Once in a while Thebitz chose to manifest himself to Ormidtz in bodily form, and thinking that his mentor had come to his aid, Ormidtz called out, "Thebitz?"

There was no answer. Instead, inexplicably, the hair at the nape of his neck rose like the hackles of an animal under threat. An intense sense of evil permeated his whole body and he shivered in the humid heat, as a piercing sound that only he could hear, tore through his auditory nerves.

Clamping his hands over his ears, Ormidtz screamed silently, "Who is this? Who are you?"

This time he got a reply, an answer spoken softly, alluringly, but borne along a wave of stinging electrical discharges.

"I am Umani. I'm your nemesis and antithesis through all your Realities. I embody all your terrors and all your nightmares. I am Fear Itself."

Heart thudding painfully against his chest, Ormidtz asked breathlessly, "I don't know you, yet I sense the immense hatred you harbor towards me. Why?"

"I am a hi-neg being, created from fire, antimatter and negatively charged particles. I am devoid of anything and everything positive," replied Umani.

"I know that aeons ago high negativity, or hi-neg beings, cohabited with humans, introducing hi-neg traits in their genes which altered the characteristics of their blood plasma. Such negative traits were transmitted over generations, making those affected incompatible with humans identified by high positivity," said Ormidtz, relaxing slightly as Umani's electrical jabs ebbed to bearable levels.

"Yes, that is true, but I'm not such a hybrid. I'm an original, unadulterated hi-neg being," said Umani.

Ormidtz twisted his torso to take a look at this being that claimed to be his nemesis.

"Don't turn around. You will never be able to see me unless I wish it, but you will always feel and sense my presence, as you do now," said Umani.

As he swiveled back to his original position, Ormidtz stole a glance over his shoulder. There was nothing there, just sunrays shimmering through the filigree woodwork of the pagoda.

"But why the animosity against me?" asked Ormidtz.

"Because," said Umani, "you are on a mission that will thwart the reason of my very existence."

"And what is that reason?" asked Ormidtz.

"It is to transform the universe in the Zenad Reality from its present composition of surplus positive matter into one defined by negativity and antimatter," replied Umani. "In such an environment hi-neg beings like myself will thrive and be in control of all Realities."

"How can you convert the composition of the universe?" asked Ormidtz.

"If the Veil Lifter project is launched, its flawed mathematical model will upset the equilibrium that now exists, and will tilt the universe towards higher negativity."

"But this will destroy the balance and harmony of Zenad and all Realities and lead to chaos," said Ormidtz, unable to control the shudder that ran down his spine.

"Exactly," said Umani. "The new equilibrium, which will be skewed towards higher levels of negativity, will create the perfect conditions for hi-neg beings like myself to flourish."

As things fell into place, Ormidtz asked, "So you were behind the synchronized accidents of the three scientists, the architects of the mathematical model?"

"Yes, of course," said Umani. "With them out of action, I'm free to implement my plans for a negative universe without any hindrance. Until Ormidtz, you appeared on the scene. Your mission to unite the three *atmans* with their bodies in the Zenad Reality, so that the scientists can modify the model and avert chaos, has created a minor hurdle in my path. If you want the clash between our two goals to end painlessly for you, you must abort your mission at once."

Umani's electrical charges escalated, once again sending searing pain through Ormidtz's nervous system.

"And if I don't do what you ask? If I don't abandon my mission?" The defiant words carried little weight for the slight confidence he had gained earlier abandoned Ormidtz, and he was unable to hide his fear.

This time Umani replied in a soft, beguiling voice. "You are not a brave human, Ormidtz. Your self-doubt, your uncertainties, your weaknesses, all augment my strength. I feed on everything that is non-positive in you. So in the end I will win and you will lose."

"I was given the choice to save the universe, and I exercised my free will to take on this task. I cannot turn back now," replied Ormidtz, his bold retort sounding hollow even to his own ears.

"Think Ormidtz, think about all that you are about to sacrifice." Umani altered her vibrations from painful stabs to mind lulling concern for Ormidtz's spiritual wellbeing. "Over your many reincarnations you have accumulated a wealth of wisdom and knowledge. You have acquired a level of peace and harmony few human souls have ever achieved. You are approaching the cusp between Waara and the Seventh Reality. You are on the verge of merging with the Singularity that spawned you. All this you are throwing away to make a futile attempt to preserve Zenad, a Reality that you no longer inhabit, that no longer affects you."

"I made my choice and I will complete my mission," repeated Ormidtz stubbornly, in spite of doubts resurfacing to taunt his consciousness.

"Let me offer you another choice," said Umani persuasively. "Once the new equilibrium stabilizes after the Veil Lifter has been launched, no matter what state the universe and the other Realities are in, I will ensure that the Waara Reality remains unchanged for you."

"You have the ability to do that?" asked Ormidtz.

"I can do that and much more," said Umani. "If you do as I

say, I will endow you with the power to absorb all the energies that will be released when the Realities are disrupted. You can use that energy to transform yourself into a black hole of such tremendous intensity, that you will be able to consume the Singularity and metamorphose into the Final, the Seventh Reality yourself. Imagine, Ormidtz, you can then create your own universe, *be* the Singularity. All this I offer you if you just abandon your mission."

"Why are you giving me this opportunity? Why do you not yourself overcome the Singularity and become the Final Reality?" asked Ormidtz, curiosity overtaking his fear.

"I would, but I cannot. I am not human, and therefore possess neither conscience nor *atman*. Only a human essential being has the potential to benefit from the opportunity I offer because he has the freedom of choice."

A pause. Then as if she had lost patience with Ormidtz, Umani hissed, "Take up on my offer or be forever thrust into oblivion and non-existence."

The threat, whispered softly, echoed in Ormidtz's mind long after the sound had faded.

δ

Ormidtz sat motionless as Umani's jarring vibrations receded and eventually ceased. He exhaled and looked around him with new eyes. Everything looked the same. The large brass bell still hung below the dragon crossbar in the courtyard, sunlight still filtered into the temple through the carved filigree of the pagoda walls, the monk still stood at the doorway awaiting visitors.

Yet nothing remained the same, everything had changed forever.

Tempted by Umani's seductive offerings, he abandoned any further attempt at meditation and stood up in one fluid motion. He walked up to the monk and said, "Bhante, who was that woman who entered the temple after me?"

The monk raised an eyebrow, gave an inscrutable smile and replied, "Son, you're the sole visitor to the temple this morning. There was no one else."

Shaken to the core, Ormidtz stepped out into the blazing sunshine. Newly rain-washed, all nature glinted and sparkled. Miniature prisms, raindrops sparkled like diamonds on flower petals, while the river he had seen earlier shimmered its way out of sight.

A flock of raucous brown and mustard mynas settled noisily on a nearby shrub. Hidden among the foliage, a pair of mourning doves cooed their lamentations, while a golden oriole dropped honeyed notes from the high branches of a stately tree.

But Ormidtz saw none of it. Quelling niggling doubts about Umani's trustworthiness, he sat under the tree to give serious consideration to Umani's tempting offer. The hi-neg being promised him an immediate return to the peace of Waara where he could continue to explore new caverns and depths of knowledge in pursuit of the divinity of human consciousness. All he had to do in return was abort his mission.

Continuing to debate with himself, Ormidtz surfed his vast database which confirmed that there was an infinitesimal probability that Waara could remain intact, unchanged, even if the Zenad universe degenerated into chaos. So if Umani spoke the truth about this fact, was it not also possible that Umani could also endow Ormidtz with the power to displace the Singularity and grant him supremacy?

But would Umani keep her word? Could he trust the hi-neg being?

The questions milled around his head, running down dead-end paths in a maze without an exit. He eventually abandoned the useless exercise, and weighed his options. If he continued his assignment, he may or may not succeed in stopping the destruction of the universe and termination of the human species. In which case, he too, would be annihilated, never to return to his hard-won state of consciousness in the Waara Reality.

On the other hand, he could abort his mission, return to Waara, and let Zenad meet its destiny. The second choice was definitely more appealing, for he wouldn't have to face dangerous and perilous situations with uncertain outcomes. It would be a selfish choice but it would assure his own survival against tremendous odds.

Like corrosive acid, his fears and doubts ate away at his commitment to the mission. Ormidtz was trapped within his dilemma and couldn't find a way out. He searched his cosmic consciousness for Thebitz's guidance to resolve his quandary, but he couldn't sense Thebitz's presence anywhere. There was only profound emptiness.

And a resurgence of paralyzing terror.

δ

Spiritually at sea, Ormidtz returned to the stop and boarded the next bus that trundled up, not caring where it took him. He was physically and mentally drained, and as the bus made its way down to the plains below, Ormidtz fell into an exhausted sleep. He was still in deep slumber, when he was shaken awake up by the driver whose gestures seemed to indicate that this was the end of the line and all passengers must get off at the stop.

Fatigue still lying heavily on his shoulders, Ormidtz stepped into the night. Intense darkness and deep shadows increased his sense of disorientation, a sudden notion that he had become blind filling him with overwhelming, irrational fear. Then a flame flickering some distance away, the only source of light in the pitch dark, caught his attention, and he sighed in relief. On nearer inspection, it turned out to be a little oil lamp burning next to an old man begging bowl in hand, sitting under an archway.

Resorting once again to mental probing to pinpoint his location, Ormidtz tapped into the old man's mind.

"What is this place," asked Ormidtz, telepathically.

Not aware that the communication was unspoken, the beggar replied aloud, "You're a *farangi* tourist, I see. Many foreigners come to see this place. I tell them the history and they give me a little something in return."

"I'll buy you a meal, old man," said Ormidtz. "So tell me what you know."

The beggar happily launched into his oft-repeated tale. "This is a shrine built around the time of the Moghul Emperor Aurangzeb. It's dedicated to the memory of the Persian Sufi, Bayazid al-Bastami. The story goes that during his visit to this spot, the Sufi Saint pierced his little finger and wetted the ground with a few drops of his blood as a token of his visit. Later his followers built the mosque here."

Ormidtz did some mental arithmetic. Moghul Emperor

Aurangzeb's time would indicate the seventeenth century in Zenad Reality, but before he could follow the line of thought any further, the old man rattled his bowl and said, "Put a few coins in my bowl and I'll say a special prayer for you at the shrine."

Ormidtz reached into his pockets and handed several coins to the beggar, thinking as he walked on that he, Ormidtz, would need many, many special prayers to help him out of his quandary. He wandered through the archway and saw a group of people jostling to feed giant, soft-shelled turtles surfacing from the depths of a large pond. Ormidtz recalled that according to legend, these turtles were descendants of evil spirits who had created obstacles for Sufi Bayazid al-Bastami from spreading the message of Allah. As a punishment, the Sufi had transformed the evil spirits into turtles and had doomed them to an eternity in the pond. Amused by the story, Ormidtz marveled, not for the first time, at how legends were perpetuated in each Reality to continually assure humans that good always triumphed evil.

Leaving the pond behind and still troubled in spirit, he continued to explore the grounds. He soon came upon an ancient three-domed mosque which he immediately entered in the hope of finding a solution to his dilemma. The white-washed mosque was bare but for some prayer mats lining the floor. A muezzin was readying himself to recite the *azaan* summoning the faithful to the last prayer of the day.

Ormidtz knew the rites and traditions of all religions that had ever been practiced in Zenad, for like the Tractate, each propagated the same concept of the Oneness, the Singularity. So now he knelt on a prayer mat, adopting the Islamic form of prayer. He closed his eyes and let all the sounds, soft and loud, rising and falling, wash over him. The melodic cadences of the azaan petered away, soon to be replaced by the trickle of water as people performed the ritual ablutions at the fountain outside the mosque. He heard the shuffle of people looking for empty spots on the prayer mats inside the mosque. He heard the imam take his place at the head of the group and start to intone the introductory verses of guidance in Arabic. He heard the clink of metal striking the stone floor, and guessed that the beggar he had met earlier had taken the prayer mat adjacent to his.

Alien sounds and smells inundating his senses, Ormidtz heard the beggar ask, "Do you have no faith in yourself, Ormidtz?"

The unexpected question startled Ormidtz out of his dejection into cosmic wakefulness. A whiff of attar swirled around him, and fractionally opening his third eye, Ormidtz perceived Thebitz's familiar aura enveloping the beggar.

"Do you have no faith in yourself?" repeated Thebitz.

"No," confessed Ormidtz, "I have no faith in myself. I'm terrified. I don't want to experience the trials and tribulations ahead of me. I don't want to be the savior of the human species. I don't want to once again suffer the states of fear, uncertainty and doubt about myself that I've endured in my other lifetimes. I just want to return to the peace and harmony that is Waara."

"Who can guarantee that you will find Waara as you left it?" asked Thebitz.

"Umani has assured me of that, but only if I abort my mission and turn back right now," replied Ormidtz.

"Understand this, Ormidtz," said Thebitz, "Umani came into being through a congestion in her spiritual evolutionary process. She is filled with negativity which fosters evil."

"I really don't care," Ormidtz replied. "The task you set me is too terrifying, and Umani is offering me a way out."

"You naive and trusting human," thundered Thebitz. His electrical vibrations tore through Ormidtz leaving him breathless with pain. "Don't you know that Umani is only as strong as you are weak? She is most powerful when you are full of doubts; when your self-esteem is low; when you are at your most vulnerable. Do you not know that Umani exists to create havoc and chaos in all the Realities?"

"That may be so," panted Ormidtz, his agonized screams audible only to Thebitz and himself. "But since Umani is so powerful, she can fulfil her promise to me if I do as she says."

"Ormidtz, Ormidtz," Thebitz cried in despair, the intensity of his vibrations abating a little. "Do you think you will find peace and harmony in Waara when the Seventh Reality is being threatened and violated? You of all humans know that if the soul is destroyed nothing can ever remain the same."

"What am I to do, Thebitz" groaned Ormidtz, holding his head between his hands. "I do not have the strength to do what you ask of me."

"Listen Ormidtz," relented Thebitz, his vibrations now soothing and calming. "Call upon your inner strength, your cosmic consciousness. It has helped you transition through all the Realities, and it will help you now. I know you fear that even if you complete your task, you will not be able to transcend to the purity of Waara, but will have to embark on the arduous spiritual journey anew."

"Yes, that is one of my greatest fears, Thebitz."

"Then I say to you, Ormidtz, that whichever Reality you find yourself in after your mission, if you find it wanting, become the agent of change and transform it into the Waara that you love."

"You demand too much of me, a mere human, Thebitz."

"You are the chosen one, Ormidtz. You can perform this task, no matter how impossible it may seem to you."

"Ameen," the imam concluded the prayer.

"No I'm too weak," began Ormidtz, but realized he could no longer sense Thebitz's presence. There only the beggar kneeling on the adjacent mat, arms wide open to the heavens beseeching blessings of Allah.

Deep in thought, Ormidtz walked out of the mosque towards the arched gateway through which he had entered earlier. As he passed the ancient pond, Ormidtz once again glanced at the soft-shelled turtles floating partially submerged under the dark, algae covered water. Even as he watched, a white shadow flitted over the backs of the turtles and swirled above Ormidtz's head. He knew at once it was Umani.

"I warned you, human, and you paid no heed to my words. Now you will pay the price for your disobedience." The sound was like a thousand cobras spitting venom into the air.

Fear crawling over every nerve, Ormidtz prepared for another subparticle passage to a new destination and unknown destiny.

CHAPTER IV

THE REVELATION

Zenad Reality
Nepal

Lithe and tall, his long silver hair tied back and hidden under a hat, Ormidtz walked with the grace of a panther through the tin shed that served as Jumla airport's immigration office. Once a powerful, independent kingdom, the semi-arid valley in the lower Himalayan ranges of Nepal was now reduced to a destination for just a handful of hardnosed European backpackers, keen to explore the mysterious foothills. The quickest way to reach the tiny town perched 2500 meters above sea level, was by small planes that ran twice a week. The other option, cheaper and favored by the local small farmers and the Himalayan salt traders, was on muleback along steep, winding trails. That was a no-go for Ormidtz. He had already lost time when his first attempt at transitioning from Waara to Zenad had delivered him to the wrong coordinates. He was now in a hurry to make headway in tracking down Erlang Shen and locating his errant *atman.*

Ormidtz strode quickly down the only road snaking away from the air strip towards town. It led to a cobbled square sparsely dotted with vendors whose wilted vegetables and fruits bore clear testimony that the difficulty of access deprived the inhabitants of Jumla of fresh food. He paused and scanned the square, looking for a signpost that would indicate the location of the sanitarium where he hoped to find Erlang Shen whose exploration into ZaZen meditation had ejected his soul into an unknown Reality, leaving behind a catatonic body.

He spotted a freshly painted wooden board with the single word Sanitarium written in large blue capitals, a red arrow below pointing towards one of the three narrow exits off the square. He followed the direction of the arrow and came upon a steep, unpaved path which was walled on one side by rocky crags, the other side dropping several hundred feet down a deep gorge. He peered down to see a mountain river flashing crimson and gold in the setting sun as it eddied around giant boulders, fragmenting the reflections of pine, spruce and juniper that thickly cloaked its banks.

He had barely savored the pristine surroundings, when something came hurtling towards Ormidtz, shattering the peace and quiet. Ever on the ready, his martial arts reflexes immediately came into play and he dodged the missiles even before he laid his eyes on them. Rainbow hues rippling over the shower of stones and rocks sent shivers of apprehension through Ormidtz, for he knew it could be none other than Umani keeping her promise to destroy him.

"Ormidtz," Umani's vibrations were like wind crackling through dry leaves. "Ormidtz, you still have time. Turn back and I will spare you. If you do not heed my warning, you will be annihilated with all of Zenad Reality."

Panting in the high altitude, Ormidtz ducked behind an outcrop of rocks to shield himself from the sharp, flinty rocks which continued to fly at him. Ormidtz resisted starting an argument, and focused instead on the most effective defense to counteract Umani's attack, for his martial arts expertise was of little use against an enemy that had no physical body.

As he crouched behind the outcrop, Ormidtz's peripheral vision caught a glint of light reflecting off metal, and he flashed a quick glance in that direction. The slanting rays of the dying sun outlined a stone-hewn Vishnu, reposing within the Chandannath Mandir, a brass crescent adorning his topknot. Shielding his head with his arms from rocks that continued to rain down in a steady stream, Ormidtz dove through the temple door, coming to rest at Vishnu's feet.

He had gained himself a few moments of respite from Umani's attacks, because cosmic ethics forbade violent acts in any place of prayer and meditation. He used the lull to examine himself and found that his neck was bleeding from a shallow gash, his back and arms felt tender from the bruises the rocks had inflicted, but seemed otherwise unharmed. Assured, he quickly scrambled to his knees and joined his palms in salutation to the Hindu deity Vishnu, the Vedic Supreme God who always wore a cobra coiled around his neck.

He had barely completed his salutation, when a breeze swept through the temple threatening to extinguish the little lamp that burned at the stone altar. It flared redly then settled back to a steady flicker. The scent of jasmine wafted through the mandir, and Ormidtz's hackles rose as he sensed Umani's close presence.

"I warned you in the Bayazid shrine, and now I'm warning you again in Vishnu's temple, return to the Waara Reality. There, you will be safe and you will be able to continue your cycle of cosmic consciousness. Otherwise, when the Ocyyst Barrier is ruptured, and I will see to it that it does, you will be cast into a limbo of unending mental and spiritual discord from which you will never be able to recover."

Umani's threat suffused him with renewed doubts about his choice, for such a fate meant his evolution to higher states of consciousness would be forever disrupted, dooming him to eternal suffering in a spiritual purgatory. In spite of misgivings, Ormidtz forced himself to remain seated in front of Vishnu, and recalling Thebitz's advice, he silently willed his qi to pervade his body and imbue him with an inner strength that would dissipate his fears, harmonize his mind and body, and enable him to continue his mission.

But Umani's hiss tore through the calm that was beginning to envelop him. "You will see me again, very soon, I promise you that."

The lamp flared up as a light wind current circled the room and drifted out the door. Once again Ormidtz sensed he was alone in the temple with the benign god whose uplifted palm blessed all who came to his house.

He listened for a while, and when all seemed quiet, Ormidtz cautiously stepped into the dusk that was beginning to shroud the valley, and continued his interrupted quest. He returned to the path he had chosen earlier and after a short walk, came upon a dimly-lit structure. A plaque embedded in the boundary wall announced that the sanitarium was endowed by the Foundation for Future Growth and that it specialized in treating trauma patients in need of extended periods of rehabilitation and recuperation.

Needing no further confirmation, Ormidtz walked through the open gate and headed towards the main door of the clinic, taking care not be silhouetted against the orange harvest moon creeping up the mountain side. He stopped in his tracks when he saw a nurse walk into one of the rooms in the building. He at once changed direction, and stepped on to a portico, the checkered pools of moonlight and darkness providing him with sufficient camouflage. He found that the rooms arrayed along the verandah were fitted with wide windows overlooking hills and deep gorges, that now lay hidden in mist and smoke rising from the valley below.

He cautiously peered through each window, until he came to a dimly lit sparsely furnished room. The footboard of the hospital bed displayed a clipboard with Erlang Shen clearly printed in large letters. A white enamel ewer and basin edged in blue, sat on a wooden table pushed up against the wall. A nurse, with her back to the window, was filling the basin with steaming hot water, presumably preparing to give her patient a sponge bath. Seemingly sculpted from wood, and little resembling his original self, Erlang sat expressionless on his bed. He stared unblinking into space, as unaware of Ormidtz peering in at the window, as he was of the nurse in the room with him.

Assured that he had found the physicist, Ormidtz squatted beneath the window sill and waited impatiently for the nurse to leave. As he bided his time, he pondered how to enter Erlang Shen's mind and how deep he would have to penetrate to learn where Erlang's essential being was hiding. Under normal circumstances, probing a highly intelligent mind like Erlang's was a daunting challenge. Now, his catatonic mind was an even more elusive target and it would be impossible for Ormidtz to probe it from a distance. He decided that the best way would be to first make physical contact with Erlang Shen and then try to tunnel into his frozen brain. He might be able to uncover a chink, however small, that could provide an entry into the Reality where the physicist's soul had found refuge.

After several minutes had passed, Ormidtz took another quick peep into the room. The nurse had finished bathing Erlang and had settled him in bed for the night. Ormidtz couldn't see the nurse from where he was crouching, but receding footsteps and a door clicking shut told him that she had left the room. He cautiously raised his head higher, checked that the room was empty but for the patient, then gently pushed against the window. It was unlatched and swung open soundlessly on well-oiled hinges. Ormidtz threw his long legs over the sill and still crouching low to avoid casting shadows on the walls, crept deeper into the room.

Erlang was facing the wall, and unsure if the physicist was awake or asleep, Ormidtz crawled to the bed, stretching out his hand to touch Erlang's arm. He had barely made contact with the physicist's palm, when strong fingers clamped over his wrist. Startled, and taken off guard, Ormidtz watched helplessly as in one smooth motion, the catatonic man twirled him over his head and threw him against the wall.

"You fool," said Erlang, but Ormidtz at once recognized Umani's sound frequency. "You fool, I've warned you several times, yet you continue to pursue a mission that you can never accomplish. You didn't know, did you, that even if I'm not endowed with a corporeal body as you are, yet I can possess other bodies that are weak and vulnerable, like this catatonic thing here."

Umani's disclosure stunned Ormidtz. He wasn't afraid that Umani or any other entity would possess his own physical body, or probe his mind, for he was protected by a cosmic shield against such occupation. It was only Thebitz who had the ability to penetrate Ormidtz's cosmic barrier, but Thebitz always remained within the boundaries of ethical codes and never encroached upon Ormidtz's privacy without first seeking permission.

What terrified Ormidtz now was that, with Umani in control of the physicist's physical brain and body, he was faced with a formidable opponent, for Erlang held a Master Level Ten in Shaolin kung fu martial arts. Furthermore, with Umani usurping Erlang's body, Ormidtz's task of extracting information from Erlang's mind became doubly complicated. Now, before he could approach Erlang's mind, he would first have to defeat Umani without destroying Erlang's physical body. Erlang's body had to be preserved in good condition, for once Ormidtz had tracked down Erlang's *atman,* he would have to reunite Erlang's soul with his body, prior to being aroused from his catatonic state.

The pitfalls in his current situation raging through his consciousness, Ormidtz belatedly leapt into the tiger stance. Erlang's rotating body kick came at lightning speed aimed at Ormidtz's lower jaw to rip his head off. Ormidtz swerved but couldn't wholly escape the strike, and Erlang's rock-hard foot landed on his left shoulder. Ormidtz grunted in agony as the joint made a grating sound and his arm twisted into an unnatural position.

Hoping desperately that the bone was only dislocated and not broken, Ormidtz squatted on one leg, and extending the other, swiveled around trying to sweep Erlang off balance without seriously damaging the scientist's body. But Erlang, alert to the feint, flipped backwards and landed on his right foot, effortlessly regaining his balance.

Then, not missing a beat, and with eyes glued to Ormidtz, Erlang stepped forward, cutting off Ormidtz's escape route. Towering over the fallen Ormidtz, he angled his hand to deliver the lethal blow to Ormidtz's jugular. As pale as the white-washed walls of the room, and wincing in pain at each step, Ormidtz shuffled away from Erlang, unwilling to suffer any more pain. He backed into the table, sending the basin and ewer clattering to the floor. Erlang continued to advance threateningly, and cornered, Ormidtz raised his good arm in a futile attempt to ward off the deadly chop.

The blow never came. Instead, he heard a nurse burst into the room, alarmed by the din from a catatonic patient's room. In the ensuing hubbub, Ormidtz dragged himself into the triangular shadows of the niche made by the displaced table and the open door, and lay hidden from immediate view.

The nurse, who had flung open the door, stared mouth agape at the sight of a heaving and thrashing Erlang, for Umani had hastily deposited his body on the bed at the sudden interruption. She couldn't comprehend how a man, who had not made a single voluntary movement in all these months, should now be jerking about so violently. Too shocked to take any action, she shouted for help. A senior nurse ran into the room and quickly assessed the situation. More experienced in inexplicable medical turn arounds in comatose and catatonic patients, she quickly took matters in hand and injected Erlang with a mild sedative. Within minutes Erlang's body collapsed in a flaccid heap.

Furious that the scientist's unresponsive body was now useless as a weapon, Umani relinquished Erlang and snarled, "Next time you will not be so lucky."

Umani swept angrily out the window, her passage marked only by curtains billowing in an otherwise still night. The nurses heard nothing, for Umani's high frequency sound waves were beyond the normal hearing range of humans and audible only to Ormidtz. All that the nurses saw was a pale shadow rippling over the curtains before disappearing into the night.

A careless cleaner must have left the window ajar and an owl or bat had found its way into the room and knocked down the ewer and the basin. It had never happened before, but how else to explain the strange incident? Clucking at such lapses, the junior nurse crossed the room and pulled the window shut.

As the nurse returned to the bed, Ormidtz cringed and quietly squeezed himself further into the wedge of darkness behind the door. But the room was dimly lit, and nurse had her eyes fixed on Erlang. She joined the other caregiver, and they both took their time fussing over Erlang's body, making him comfortable, replacing the fallen things. They anxiously checked and rechecked the window and the bed, and finally departed pulling shut the door behind them.

Exhaling in relief, Ormidtz checked his shoulder. It wasn't broken, only dislocated, and he would have to reset the joint. Moaning softly as each movement sent streaks of agony up his arm, he eased himself to the floor, and lay on his back while he gathered strength and courage to initiate the painful process.

Drenched with sweat from the effort, he placed his left hand on his chest, elbow bent at a ninety degree angle, and with his right arm he first pulled the left shoulder inwards and then rotated it outwards. He gasped in agony, but the bone didn't reset. He took a deep breath and repeated the movements. Nothing happened. He would give it one last try and if he still didn't succeed, he would abandon his mission. It was a perfectly legitimate reason for not having to face Umani again.

He took another deep breath and groaned as the slight movement shot searing fire up his arm, through his jaws and into his brain. Clenching his teeth, Ormidtz once again repeated the motions of rotating his shoulder outwards. This time the joint clicked into place, the sudden release from pain making him lightheaded with relief.

But he couldn't afford the luxury of rest. There wasn't a moment to lose for Umani could return anytime, anywhere. Massaging his sore shoulder, Ormidtz inched his way to Erlang's bed, alert for any unexpected movements from the sedated scientist. Discerning no reaction, Ormidtz tentatively clasped Erlang's palm in his own.

The physical contact of co-joined neural transmissions between the two of them opened up a passage to Erlang's brain, and Ormidtz was immediately thrust into Erlang's conscious-ness. He now faced an imminent danger of being sucked into the molasses-like quagmire of Erlang's sedated mind. Horror stricken, Ormidtz's one thought was to extricate himself from this treacherous trap before he too became catatonic like Erlang.

To counter the lethal and overpowering undertow of Erlang's catatonic brain, Ormidtz first anchored himself to his upper dan t'ian where his spiritual energy was most concentrated. Then, wrenching himself free from the quicksand of Erlang's mind that was adrift between Realities, Ormidtz snatched away his hand, breaking contact with Erlang's body. At once he felt released from the fatal magnetism of Erlang's lost mind.

Once again able to think independently and rationally, Ormidtz realized that directly accessing Erlang's consciousness would expose him to a danger which he wouldn't be able to overcome. He had to find another way to open the door to Erlang's mind. Perhaps Erlang's physical brain, rather than his mind, might prove to be a safer option. In which case, the pons Varolii could be the key.

Since the pons Varolii was part of the brain stem that linked the cerebrum, cerebellum and medulla and contained sensory motor tracts that connected the brain to the rest of the body, Ormidtz could use these tracts to travel through the dense network of nerve cells to reactivate Erlang's brain. Also, since the medulla oblongata controlled the automatic functions of breathing and heart beat throughout a human's lifetime, this part of the brain should remain unaffected by catatonia, medications and sedatives. If Ormidtz penetrated the medulla oblongata through the pons Varolii, he should be able to safely enter Erlang's unconscious self to uncover the Reality into which his soul had transitioned during his ZaZen experience.

It was a high risk maneuver for he could still become inextricably submerged in Erlang's mental quagmire, but he had to take the chance for he had no other options left. Time was running out.

δ

This time, better primed to face the pitfalls ahead, Ormidtz firmly attached himself to his middle dan t'ian, the seat of his inner strength, and waded through the physicist's brain towards the medulla oblongata. Ormidtz penetrated the organ, and entered the murkiness at the base of Erlang's head, but detached from his physical brain, Erlang's mind was difficult to probe, impossible to read.

Ormidtz wandered around in Erlang's dense, spiritual haze until he hit upon a trail. But it led nowhere, ending at a blank wall of neurogenic motor immobility erected by Erlang's catatonia. Ormidtz retraced his steps and went down another passage, then another and another, but they all proved to be dead ends. No matter which path he chose, it didn't allow him to penetrate Erlang's brain and knowledge cache. Exhausted, dejected, and frightened, Ormidtz drifted along Erlang's chaotic thought waves, as lost as Erlang himself.

Then out of the void Thebitz's electric impulses vibrated through his consciousness. "Ormidtz, remember, each human noumenon has a free will. It is present in every Reality."

Thebitz's interference dispelled his stupor, spurring Ormidtz to change tactics. Since he was now firmly ensconced in Erlang's brain, they now shared a common cosmic consciousness. Using this commonality to his advantage, Ormidtz began to transmit powerful thought waves to the scientist.

"Erlang, you are catatonic because your mind is caught between Realities," Ormidtz telecommunicated to the scientist. "But your essential being still resides within you, and you can still exercise your free will. Use it to show me where your soul has taken refuge. Help me to find your *atman*."

No response, no revelations.

Swirling in the murkiness of Erlang's brain, Ormidtz pleaded again, and again, and yet again.

In desperation, he cried out, "Erlang, release me from the purgatory of your lost mind. Point me to the path of discovery, so that you and I can both find redemption."

As long moments passed in dark silence, Ormidtz despaired of reaching Erlang. His despondency approaching its nadir, Ormidtz prepared to exit Erlang's mind, when a faint movement caught his attention. At first it was just a flicker. Then the flicker burst into a spark.

New hope surging through him, Ormidtz ploughed through his dismal surroundings towards the point of light. As he neared, the point blossomed into a nebulous, undulating, shimmering expanse, now approaching, now receding like ocean waves.

His dejection turned into elation for Ormidtz recognized Naqim Reality. He had been there before.

CHAPTER V

THE TRANSITION

Naqim Reality
China

Hark, I hear someone calling. It's just a faint, echoing sigh... I hear Er... laaanggg...then it fades away. Who or what is Erlang?

It's barely dawn, and low clouds still cling to the slopes of the hills surrounding this little hamlet in Henan which I call my home. Terraced rice fields cascade down to the valley below. A soft spring breeze ripples through my clothes, the simple, white tunic of a Shifu, but it doesn't disturb the red fan snugly tucked into my belt. It lightly tousles my long, but sparse head of graying hair as I run my fingers through my wispy beard which straggles down to my chest. It caresses my gaunt, hollow-cheeked face, and flits off to play hide-and-seek with the leaves of grass.

I sit and ponder. Last night I again dreamt the same dream. It's a dream that visits me often. I'm in a place I don't recognize but somehow feel I know well. It's a strange land and I'm living a different life. I have lost something but I don't know what, nor where. All I can sense is that what I've lost is something very important, and that I must look for it. I don't understand where these thoughts come from, nor why. Time and again, they just flit through my mind.

Right now I'm taking a brief rest having just completed a lesson in martial arts. I teach reading, writing and arithmetic in the village school and also instruct the children in martial arts simply because I love the beauty, grace and hidden violence of this skill. Martial arts, practiced for its own sake, can invoke heavenly peace; used in self defensive, it can keep the enemy at bay; but when used as a means of offensive attack, it can create chaos and havoc. This is what I tell the children when I teach them the skills that hone their physical coordination and sharpen their mental acumen.

My students are a small group of boys and girls of varying ages, and I have to adjust the timing of my classes with the work they have to put in to help their families in the fields and to tend farm animals. They are agile and hardy youngsters and I feel pleasure and pride in the potential that one or two have demonstrated in mastering qigong, wushu and kungfu techniques.

My biggest challenge is Bu Zai who is tall and strapping for his age. He's the sixth son in his family for his parents wishing for a daughter, kept on trying. When the sixth attempt also resulted in a male child, they gave up and his mother named him Bu Zai which means No More. She thought it was time to stop chasing an elusive goal. Bu Zai is the strongest among my students, but he is mentally challenged and clumsy of movement. I've given strict instructions to the other children not to tease or bully him, because Bu Zai, in a fit of temper, can hit out and cause serious bodily harm, for he doesn't know his own strength.

Today's lessons included the shingi fist, after which I guided the children through the eight movements which teach them to breathe correctly and stretch different parts of the body. I ended with the eighth movement which jars the body from heel to the head, mildly jolting the internal organs to improve their function and enhance blood circulation.

To calm their young minds and bodies after the rigorous exercises, I led them into a moment of introspection when they sat cross legged with arms extended as if holding a globe between their palms. I urged them to concentrate on their upper dan t'ien by reciting, "The eyes follow the nose, the nose follows the heart." This is the first step in summoning the virtual black spot that hovers between the eyes, and performed successfully, can carry one into a state of nothingness. It is the core of the elusive third eye.

They are, of course, too young to hold that position for long, and I dismiss them after five minutes. They gleefully run off, but not before joining a palm against a fist in a respectful wushu salute, chanting their thanks, "Sheh, sheh, Shifu."

Everyone in the village calls me Shifu. No one seems to know my name, and it perturbs neither them nor me, for I myself cannot recall my own name. I don't have any memories of my parents or where I learnt my martial arts skills. Such trifling details are unimportant to me, as well as to the villagers, for they trust me implicitly. I'm at peace in this place and don't want to make any changes to my life.

As I wait for the sun to rise before partaking my breakfast of rice gruel, I see a nebulous shape forming against the morning mist. Is it a part of my dream? No, it cannot be for I know I'm awake.

I peer intently but the form disappears. I'm about to turn

away, when it reappears, this time a little more distinct, a little more dense. I keep staring in puzzlement as the holographic image appears and disappears, until finally a solid, three-dimensional human figure emerges and stands in front of me. His hair glints in the early light and his odd hazel-green eyes glitter like the sea reflecting sunshine.

I look at him and begin to doubt if I'm awake, or if the vision is real. Yet traditional politeness prompts me to greet the stranger in a normal voice, "Good morning, Xiansheng, welcome to our little village. Did you trek up this morning? You must have started early, the nearest townlet is a two-day walk from here."

I see the stranger hesitate before replying, "Yes, Shifu, I've been travelling a while. I have been searching for you."

Surprised, I echo, "Searching for me? Do you know me? I don't think I know you. Why do you seek me out?"

The stranger doesn't immediately answer my questions. Instead, he casts his eyes around and spotting a little tea stall nearby, points to it and says, "Would you like to have a cup of tea? It's still quite cold right now."

Curious to know what he wants of me, I nod and join the stranger at the simple wooden table and bamboo bench. The shy young girl minding the stall, places before us earthenware bowls, wisps of steam escaping from under the lids. Settling down on the bench, the stranger picks up his bowl, uses the lid to gently sift the furry tipped tea leaves to one side, and takes a sip. He gives an appreciative sigh and I nod my approval. Foreigner he might be, but this laowai knew how to appreciate Mao jian green tea, a specialty of this region.

We sip from our bowls, while I wait patiently for the man to tell me why he has come to see me. As we sit in silence, I notice the serving girl beckon to someone behind us, saying "Here take this, Bu Zai, and go home." I turn to see the boy take the steam bun that the girl had just handed him, and with a big, artless grin, bite hungrily into it.

Following my lead, the foreigner too turns around and smiles absentmindedly at the boy. He then turns back to look directly into my eyes. He takes a deep breath and begins, "I am Ormidtz. I've been assigned a very special task and I need your help to complete it. Please trust me and don't consider me as someone who has lost his mind."

Chinese etiquette requires an exchange of pleasantries before launching into the main topic of discussion. I'm somewhat taken aback by the short and abrupt introduction and excuse him for being an ignorant foreigner who is unfamiliar with Chinese protocol.

After a moment I ask uncertainly, "How can I help you?"

"In the Zenad Reality you are Erlang Shen, a physicist of renown. You're one of the three scientists who developed the mathematical model for harnessing energy from dark matter," comes the unexpected reply from the foreigner whom I now know as Ormidtz. "You are probably unaware that your essential being became detached from your original body in the Zenad Reality and has floated into the Naqim Reality to occupy the body of a Shifu."

His words make absolutely no sense and I just stare at him nonplussed.

"Erlang Shen? Mathematical model? What are you talking about? Who are you? How can you say so confidently that my name is Erlang Shen? I myself don't recall if I ever had a name. Everyone calls me Shifu, and I'm satisfied with the title of Master,

for in this village that is who I am," I cry out perplexed, perturbed.

Ormidtz nods and gives a wry smile. "Yes, it's as hard for me to explain what has happened to you, as it is for you to assimilate what I'm telling you. I will nonetheless tell you how you got here."

"How do you know what happened to me?" I ask.

"How I know it is unimportant at the moment," Ormidtz says dismissively. "What you need to understand is that I've made a hazardous journey through the Realities of Waara and Zenad to search for your essential being, and I've found it here, in the Naqim Reality."

His babble about Realities and essential beings still don't make any sense and he can see it in my eyes. He switches his tactic.

"You will understand what I'm saying if you try to recall your life in Zenad. Try, Erlang, try to remember your team members Ruari O'Connor and Ameqran Izem," says Ormidtz in a coaxing voice. I can see he's very disturbed and agitated for his hazel eyes have turned opaque like those of a blind man.

His deep concern stirs my consciousness and I cast my mind back to my recent dreams. Are these strange recollections actually past memories trying to resurface? Is Ormidtz telling the truth when he says I live in the Zenad Reality, and somehow my atman has found its way into Naqim? I dig into my subconscious but find myself sinking into a void. Fearful of the unknown, I give up the search and start to climb back to the present, when something snaps.

I suddenly feel like a man waking up from a long period of amnesia, from a trance. I take a ragged breath and wonder out aloud, "So they are not dreams or hallucinations. I did work on theoretical physics problems at some stage in my life. Many things which did not make sense earlier are now falling into place."

"Erlang," Ormidtz breaks into my new-found stream of memories. *"I'm sorry to interrupt your thoughts, but there's very little time so I need your cooperation immediately."*

I look at him expectantly, my mind grappling with the flood of remembrances inundating my consciousness.

Ormidtz continues, *"An unexplained and unprecedented series of accidents left you and your team members disabled in one way or another. Under normal circumstances, these events would be allowed to unfold in their own time for external interventions are discouraged by the cosmic consciousness. In your case, however, we're forced to take extraordinary measures in order to avert dire consequences."*

"What kind of dire consequences?" I ask reluctantly, loath to tear myself away from new-found discoveries about my past.

Ormidtz continues to interrupt my reminiscences. *"Now that you have some recollections of your life in Zenad, you know that humans in that Reality are always searching for new sources of cheap and abundant energy to power their extravagant lifestyles. To meet this insatiable need, you and your team developed a mathematical model that enables the extraction of limitless energy from black holes and dark matter."*

"I'm listening," I reply. He has finally got my full attention.

He glances at me and speaks hurriedly, *"The lure of the midas touch has prompted an international group of private entrepreneurs to fund the Veil Lifter Project which is based on your model. The project is operated out of the Arctic Ecosystem Research Center located in the North Pole of planet Earth. Scores of scientists have been working on it for years and they're now ready to launch the Veil Lifter."*

I'm puzzled. *"But that's why we built the model, isn't it?"* I retort.

His impatience at my question barely camouflaged, Ormidtz replies, "Yes, but the problem is that the scientists in the Center are unaware that the model has a fatal flaw. If they conduct the experiment without amending the formula, the Ocyyst Barrier in outer spacetime will be breached."

Ormidtz's words hammer a wedge into the wall that was blocking part of my brain and preventing me from retrieving information stored in that organ. The wedge sinks in deep, widening the crack. Memories of my past life cascade over my senses like a waterfall thundering down a towering precipice. I gasp with the impact of total recall.

"I remember it all," I shout out in jubilation. "I remember that the results from the model appeared plausible to all of us, yet we all had the vague notion that we might have overlooked something important."

"Did you take any action?" asks Ormidtz, hope tangible in his voice.

"Well," I reply, "I remember trying to invert the core matrix, but the resulting geodesics became unaligned. I didn't have time to develop a methodology that would reverse the situation, before we dispersed for our short break."

"So now you understand the urgency and the imminent danger to the world," says Ormidtz, the furrows in his brow deepening as he speaks.

"No, not really," I reply. "What will happen if the Ocyyst Barrier is breached?"

"The ethical balance of the universe and the Realities will be

jeopardized," says Ormidtz, " and high negativity will suffuse the world."

Still unclear about the consequences, I ask, "But how did you find me? How did you get here, to the Naqim Reality as you call this place?"

"Let me explain what happened to you in the Zenad Reality," Ormidtz begins. "As you're well aware, you have always practiced different types of meditation and have dabbled in out-of-body experiments. Your search for uncovering the third eye in your upper dan t'ien led you to the ZaZen meditation technique. Because of your sharp intellect, your very first attempt at ZaZen was so profound that your essential being detached itself from your physical body, and floated away from Zenad into another Reality, the Naqim Reality."

"What do you mean?" is all I can say.

"During ZaZen, your search for the third eye transported only your consciousness into the Naqim Reality, your own body remaining behind in Zenad in a catatonic state," he explains with an exasperated edge to his voice. "The body of a Shaolin monk that you now occupy, is only your perception of yourself in Naqim."

"Then the body you have here, is also a perception of yourself?" I ask.

"In a way, yes," he replies, taking a deep breath. "It may be difficult for you to assimilate the concept, but let me, nonetheless, try to explain it to you. You see, I've lived many lifetimes, each of which has taken me forward towards a state of being where the need of a corporeal body is almost redundant. But to do what I've set out to accomplish, I must appear as a human to other humans whom I will meet during my mission."

"And what is your mission?" I ask.

"My mission is to persuade you to unite your essential being which has sought refuge in the Naqim Reality with your physical body in the Zenad Reality. That's why I had to follow you into Naqim. You must make the correction in the model before the Veil Lifter is launched."

"Did you also experience trauma so that you could enter Naqim?" I'm curious. I must know.

Ormidtz shakes his head and laughs, "No, I'm able to travel between Realities. That's why I was chosen for this mission."

"How did you know which Reality my essential being had transcended to?" I'm persistent for I have to understand this strange phenomenon that Ormidtz says I'm experiencing.

"I located your catatonic body in a clinic in the Zenad Reality. I then probed your mind and through your consciousness followed you into Naqim. I'm therefore able to perceive what you perceive and experience your world in Naqim as you experience it," he explains, this time more patiently.

I finally begin to understand what he is asking of me and without hesitation I outright refuse to do his bidding. "I'm at peace in Naqim, and don't wish to change anything in my life here," I tell him firmly.

"Your life in Naqim is but a maya. It is only temporary," argues Ormidtz.

"In that case," I counter, "If what you say is true, I can end my own life here and be reborn in another Reality where my new existence won't be a maya."

"You know the answer to that, Erlang," replies Ormidtz with barely camouflaged exasperation, "If you kill yourself, cosmic ethics dictates that you will be cast into Vakin, the primordial

Reality. The advancement you made to date in your spiritual transformation, will be forfeited and you will have to restart your evolutionary process from the very beginning, which will again take aeons."

I think for a while, then reply obstinately, "I prefer to take my chances and remain here."

"You do have a free will, so the choice is always yours to make. But you must decide soon, or else the thread of life between your body and your consciousness will be severed, leaving your atman to join the lost souls that wander around, forever seeking a home."

There's an urgency in his voice which I choose to ignore. I get up to walk away, when a sharp intake of breath from the little serving girl stops me.

Ormidtz and I simultaneously hear the swish of a bamboo staff. Both of us duck in reflex, the weapon aimed at our temporal bones skimming harmlessly over our heads. I at once spin around in a defensive stance, and am astonished to see the normally uncoordinated Bu Zai deftly retrieve the staff. He then perfectly balances himself on one leg, and raises the other in readiness for a follow-up frontal kick.

"Why do you not heed me, Ormidtz?" I hear Bu Zai whisper hoarsely, his earlier innocent and guileless smile now a twisted grimace. "Stop now. Return to Waara, and I will spare you and your friend."

Bewildered at Bu Zai's transformation and his strange words, I look towards Ormidtz. His ashen face, terrified eyes and thunder-struck expression do little to reassure me. I watch in stunned dismay, as two more of my students, a girl and a boy, join Bu Zai.

Ormidtz and I, both hesitate to react in self defense, for our attackers are but children. Taking advantage of the delay in our response, Bu Zai leaps up in the air, and points his staff directly at Ormidtz's throat. At the same time, the girl comes flying at Ormidtz, her bent elbow aimed at his middle dan t'ian.

Ormidtz has the quick reflexes of a martial arts expert. He whips around and lifting the bench, hurls it to intercept the staff. Both the bench and the staff shatter on impact. The force throws Bu Zai backward in an arc to land unhurt, but momentarily disoriented, on a grassy mound.

In the next instant, jumping up and twisting his torso in midair, Ormidtz catches the girl's arm between his ankles in a vice grip that dislocates her elbow. The girl drops to the ground shrieking in agony. Ormidtz rolls away from both his attackers.

As I eye Ormidtz's movements, my peripheral vision alerts me that the second boy is cartwheeling towards me. I hold a slight advantage over the boy, for I had recently taught him a move which I suspect he now plans to use to crush my head between his feet. I think quickly and whip out the fan from my belt, flipping it open with a smart crack. The red color and unexpected action effectively distract the boy, his momentary hesitation giving me the time I need. I snap shut my fan and swing it in an arc to deflect the oncoming kick. My movement unbalances the boy, giving me a brief respite from his assault.

In that instant I hear Ormidtz call out, "Erlang, the children are in grave danger. We must end this soon. We must end it now."

In response, I take a flying leap to be closer to him, and back-to-back we turn towards our young assailants. Ormidtz faces Bu Zai and I the other boy, the girl with the dislocated arm no longer a threat.

As Bu Zai crouches low to lash out with his feet, I see Ormidtz sway on one leg, adopting the preying mantis form of defense. I know he is concentrating his qi in his upper dan t'ian, focusing the full energy of his consciousness and shen towards the spot just above his brows. Then with a bellow that echoes through the hills, he releases the power of his qi through a front kick aimed at the base of Bu Zai's skull. Had Ormidtz released the full force of his kick, Bu Zai's head would have split open like an unhatched egg dropped from a crow's nest high up on a treetop. But Ormidtz is in full control. He releases just enough power to knock the boy unconscious who collapses to the ground senseless.

I barely have time to register this, before the other boy leaps towards me, one hand curled into a tiger claw to gouge into my face and eyes. Admiring, in spite of myself, the boy's elegant Hu Zhua moves which I don't remember teaching any of my students, I take up the defensive crane beak position with which I can subdue my attacker without causing too much damage to his body. I create a hook by joining all fingers of one hand, and as he lunges forward, I trap the boy's attacking claw. At the same time, the crane beak in my other hand jabs the boy's solar plexus, and although my controlled thrust barely touches his soft tissues, all breath is knocked out of him, and like Bu Zai, he too falls into a faint.

Danger averted for the moment, I turn to see Ormidtz scoop up the girl and place her on the wooden table in the tea stall. I understand his urgency. He must reset the girl's dislocated arm while the neurotransmitting endorphins coursing through her body continue to dull the pain. He signals to the frightened tea stall girl to prop up his patient. He then tugs at the girl's forearm, relief flooding his face as he hears the dislocated bone click into place. An earsplitting shriek followed by soft sobbing tells me that the girl's pain is abating. Ormidtz gestures to the tea stall girl to take care of the weeping girl, and then turns to the two unconscious boys.

But I'm already ministering to them, gently patting their cheeks and massaging their palms to bring them around. As they begin to stir, I shout for help. The entire attack lasted only minutes, and other than the tea stall girl, no one else is aware that anything untoward has happened. Most of the men are at work in the fields some distance away from the hamlet, and the women are busy with their morning chores.

Now, hearing my frantic shouts, some of the farmers rush back to the village. I ask them to take care of the children, saying they had fainted, but I give no explanation, as I myself am at a loss to understand what had just taken place. The villagers will have to get whatever they can out of the tea stall girl.

Seeing that matters are under control, I ask Ormidtz, "What just happened? How and why did the children behave as they did?"

I watch as Ormidtz tries to control his anger, but his voice shakes with emotion as he says, "Umani is a hi-neg being who, for her own reasons, doesn't wish my mission to succeed. She is an entity of fire and so lacks the physical structure to directly attack humans. I never imagined that she would stoop to occupy bodies of innocent, guileless children to attack us. It's obvious she will stop at nothing to get what she wants."

Unable to follow all that he says, I ask Ormidtz, "How do you know the being is a woman?"

"Because that is how she manifested herself to me," he replies.

"What does this hi-neg being want?" I ask.

More in control of himself, Ormidtz replies, "Although Umani is a creature created from the elements, she has the power to gain control over a human body through the person's mind or consciousness. The more vulnerable the human mind, the easier it is for Umani to take over the body. Innocent children are easy targets and Umani took temporary possession of the children's minds and bodies to use as weapons against us. She knew we would curb our self-defense tactics to avoid hurting the children in any way."

"I see," I say, pretending to understand. I then hazard a guess, "So when the link between the body and the consciousness is broken, Umani can no longer control the human."

"Exactly," says Ormidtz. "Since we made the children senseless, Umani was forced to relinquish the bodies of Bu Zai and the boy. As for the girl, her hysterical crying and misshapen arm made her body useless as a weapon."

Still unable to fully grasp Ormidtz's disclosure, and not quite sure who or what Umani is, I once again just nod.

"You understand now, don't you Erlang, what we are up against?" Ormidtz speaks hurriedly. "You must immediately transition back to the Zenad Reality and reunite your consciousness with your mortal body lying in the hospital in Jumla. I cannot do it for you, for the transition is a function of your free will. No one else can do it for you."

I'm reluctant to leave Naqim and don't quite share Ormidtz's concerns about the mathematical model.

He senses my reluctance, my unwillingness to comply with his request. His hazel eyes flicker grey-green as he bears down on me. He thunders, "We don't have time, Erlang. If the universe and the

Realities are destabilized, Naqim will not be as you perceive it now. Everything will change, and chaos will reign."

Observing my persistent hesitation, he replaces anger and coercion with persuasion. "I cannot force you to return. It must be your own choice to reunite your essence with your body in Zenad."

I remain unconvinced. Who is this stranger who appears out of the blue and asks me to abandon Naqim. How can he be so sure that what I'm experiencing in Naqim is just a maya?

Ormidtz interrupts my thoughts with one last attempt to make me voluntarily do his bidding. "I must leave now to locate the remaining members of your team. Return to Zenad and with your colleagues, find the prescription that will halt the looming universal chaos."

Almost convinced, I'm torn between answering Ormidtz's call to prevent mayhem in Zenad, and my own desire to continue my peaceful existence in Naqim. My senses in confusion, I look up to find Ormidtz sitting cross-legged, already locked in deep meditation. I know what he is doing. During his stressful encounter with the three young bodies he had generated an immense quantity of power, most of which he could not unleash in the fight, for it would have killed the children. Now, to regain his inner harmony and balance, he is storing the residual qi in his zhong or middle dan t'ian surrounding his heart. He is gently thrusting down his life energy until it courses through his Xia or lower dan t'ian below his navel to circulate through his whole body.

I watch Ormidtz, as I relive all that has just taken place. Suddenly all the scattered parts fit together like a jigsaw puzzle and the whole picture is revealed. It's clear to me now, that my dreams are my consciousness telling me that I shouldn't be here. I should be somewhere else. If Ormidtz is right, and Naqim is but a maya, then my subconscious self is urging me to transition to a Reality where I can start the search for a permanent state of peace and harmony. I understand that the only way to do so is to return to Zenad and recommence my search for the ideal existence of higher consciousness. It also occurs to me that I must travel back with Ormidtz for he alone can lead me to my Zenad self.

I finally agree with Ormidtz that I must return to Zenad, but for my own reasons, not to be a hero and save the world. I know what I must do.

Decision made, I adopt the lotus position and like Ormidtz, concentrate in diffusing my unused qi throughout my system. My power begins to drain and my essential being begins to detach itself from the reins of Naqim. As I move into the transition mode, I observe Ormidtz gradually fade into nothingness and I understand that the time has come for my atman to uncondi-tionally relinquish Naqim. The villagers will sooner or later come across the Shifu's inert body, but will ask no questions. They will perform the burial rites and intern his body according to their customs. Shifu appeared out of nowhere and is now gone. That is just the way it is.

As my essential being begins to migrate away from Naqim towards Zenad, I notice a sudden swirl of mist and clouds, a furious stirring of trees and bushes as a shadow flits by that is neither a cloud nor a wisp of mist.

I am drenched in an overpowering sense of fear and terror.

CHAPTER VI

THE DISCOVERY

Zenad Reality
Italy

Craning his neck, Ormidtz stared up at the Monastery of Saint Benedict in Subiaco. Thebitz's cryptic clue that there was a possibility of finding Ruari O'Connor's comatose body in a hospital or clinic in this little Italian town, had eventually led him to this spot. Since Catholic convents and monasteries sometimes ran clinics, Ormidtz was hoping to find Ruari in one of these establishments. He knew it was useless to try eliciting information directly, for no hospital would break doctor-patient confidentiality, more so where Ruari's rich and powerful family was concerned. So he decided to resort to subterfuge to locate her.

Ormidtz glanced upwards again, this time noticing that the monastery appeared to be two churches one perched on top of the other. From where he was standing, a flight of shallow stone steps led to a courtyard with arched corridors branching out in different directions. It was an easy climb and Ormidtz raced up the steps and through the passages, giving scant attention to the walls exquisitely frescoed with scenes from the Bible.

But on reaching the top, he was disappointed to find the place deserted. Perhaps the monks and priests expected visitors and pilgrims to enjoy and appreciate at leisure, the serenity of the church and the spectacular view from the windows; to pray and meditate without any interruptions or interference.

Undeterred, Ormidtz continued his rushed tour of the churches with their richly decorated ceilings and walls, until he found himself at the Grotto of St. Benedict. The saint had spent three solitary years in prayer and penance in this cave. He had survived with the help of a kind-hearted, local priest who had daily lowered a basket of food into the grotto. A statue of St. Benedict, a basket, and a length of rope, all carved from white marble, were reminders of the harsh conditions endured by the saint, a man born and raised in a well-to-do Umbrian family and used to the comforts of life.

Ormidtz was fully aware that time was short, but the hallowed aura of the grotto compelled him to linger and savor the moment a little longer. He leaned against the rocky wall of the grotto, and ever sensitive to his environment, felt powerful waves of by-gone prayers wash over him in benediction. He stood motionless for several minutes, letting the petitions, some joyous, some drenched in pain and suffering, cleanse him mentally and spiritually.

The mystical experience left Ormidtz feeling more optimistic about his mission. He walked out of the church and into an inner courtyard, where a glass doorway with a sign reading "Aperto" invited him to enter. He stepped inside and found himself facing a series of shelves displaying jars of honey, bottles of tisanes, herbal soaps, shampoo, and lotions for the face, hands and feet. There were also liquors made from herbs, blueberry, lemon, and honey. Like the church, this place, too, was deserted.

Ormidtz walked around the shop, examining the different herbal ware available for sale, but none offered him any inspiration on how to proceed in his mission. Frustrated, he turned to leave, when a grey, tonsured head, followed by a pair of twinkling eyes, emerged from behind the counter. The monk's kindly face encouraged Ormidtz to approach him for help. He had a vague plan that if he could spend the night in the monastery, then under the cover of darkness he could search the premises for Ruari's presence.

"Buon journo, padre," he said. "I was passing through Subiaco, and was advised by all to pay a visit to this monastery."

"God's blessings on you, my son," replied the elderly monk. "Welcome to our town. Have you looked around the church as yet?"

"Yes, I have," said Ormidtz, "I am dazzled by the beauty and suffused with the sanctity of this place."

"The monastery has a remarkable history. If you can spare a few moments, you can read about St Benedict's life in that book, there. We have the volume on display so that visitors can appreciate the significance and importance of this church in spreading the missive of Christianity."

As he spoke, the monk led Ormidtz to an ancient, scarred, but well-polished wooden desk on which a creased and cracked leather-bound book lay open at a page showing an etching of St Benedict praying in the grotto. To please the kindly priest, Ormidtz leafed through the volume, once in a while taking a moment to dip into excerpts of the Saint's life history. As he flipped through the book, a section fell open of its own volition revealing an ink sketch of Benedictine monks healing the sick. The illustration gave Ormidtz an idea which he seized with alacrity.

Pointing to the picture, he asked, "Padre, does the monastery still run a clinic or sanatorium?"

The priest glanced at the etching and shook his head. "Several centuries ago, monks living here did help the sick. But things changed over the years, and now I'm afraid we're not enough in number to run a hospital and provide such services." Ormidtz noted the regret in the old priest's voice.

His vague plan dead like a stillborn child in its mother's womb, Ormidtz pondered dejectedly what to do next, when the monk spoke again.

"But if you are in urgent need, Saint Scholastica, our sister monastery, offers some medical services," the padre continued. "Our brotherhood is fortunate that the good nuns can provide us with emergency health care. Most of the time, though, we're able to deal with our minor ailments with herbs from the Garden of Ravens which you must have seen from the terrace, and honey from our own beehives. Ours is but a simple life, following the teachings of Saint Benedict."

His emotions oscillating from despondency to elation, Ormidtz pretended to scan through the rest of the book, reverently closing the back cover and running his hands over the soft, old leather. Turning to the monk, and concealing how important the answer to his next question was, he asked, "Padre, it's getting late. Is it possible for the abbey to provide me with a room to stay the night?"

But the priest again shook his head apologetically. "I'm sorry, my son, but we don't have any facility for housing tourists. Only a handful of monks are resident in this monastery, and the few extra cells we have are reserved for pilgrims. You could look for a *pensione* in Subiaco town," he added helpfully.

"Before coming here, I already searched for a place to stay the night, but couldn't find a room," Ormidtz replied. "But don't worry, padre, I'm sure something will turn up."

Grateful to the monk for inadvertently providing him with the clue to his next step, Ormidtz bought a jar of golden acacia honey and a bottle of lemoncino from the shop. They might come in handy as gifts for other such services rendered.

Swinging the bag of purchases, he made his way down the steps to the bottom of the hill in search of the convent dedicated to Saint Benedict's sister.

δ

Machim Reality
Vatican City

The pale lunar moth fluttered, then came to a rest against the ornate grill of the ventilator set into the wall one level below the high altar of Bascilica San Pietro in Vatican City. Sunlight streamed in through the glass panes, arching over the mammoth main doors of the Basilica, heart of the Catholic church and residence of the Pope. The rays glanced off the Baldacchino di San Pietro, its four helical, Solomonic columns holding up an enormous bronze canopy. The baroque masterpiece, the work of

Italian sculptor Gian Lorenzo Bernini, sat over the tomb of Saint Peter, itself built atop ancient Etruscan burial grounds.

The caroming rays sneaked in through the ventilators, compelling the moth to wing its way into the duskier depths of the Bascilica. The little insect glided deeper into the womb of the three thousand year old necropolis where the conquering Romans, like the Etruscans before them, had interred their dead. Here and there, terra cotta and marble sarcophagi were pushed up against the walls. Urns, which once held ashes of cremated Greeks and Romans, nestled in niches hewn into the stone walls.

The translucent moth, looking ghostly in the near dark, indifferently crawled up the ancient micromosaic plaque chronicling Hades' abduction of Persephone. It then fluttered down, coming to rest on the lip of a burial urn.

δ

Zenad Reality
Italy

A short distance away, Ormidtz could see the looming bell tower of a convent, the encroaching twilight casting purple shadows that intensified the mystery of his surroundings. He wound his way through the narrow streets of the town until he found himself in front of the monastery of St Scholastica. Its imposing gates were tightly shut, but a stout rope hung by the door with a sign in Italian reading "Please ring for service."

He obeyed and jerked the rope vigorously. The faint sound of a bell deep inside the labyrinths of the convent, gave him hope that someone may eventually come to answer the door.

After several minutes of waiting, he heard soft footsteps followed by a scraping sound. A small spy door set in the middle of the solid wooden gate slid open, revealing the fresh face of a young novice.

"May I help you?" she asked gently.

Ormidtz reasoned with himself that the serious nature of his mission justified the means by which he got results. So quashing his twinges of guilt for not being wholly truthful to the young woman, he smiled and said, "I do apologize for disturbing you, Sister. I'm looking for a bed for just one night. I couldn't find anything in town and was told your convent may be able to help me."

He knew that convents often ran *pensiones,* and was hoping that St Scholastica would be one of them. Luck favored him. The novice confirmed that they sometimes put up travelers, but she wasn't sure if any of the cells were available for the night. She asked him to wait and sliding shut the spy door, pattered rapidly away.

Ormidtz sat down on the marble bench placed thoughtfully alongside the gate. A small fountain spouted fresh spring water and Ormidtz refreshed himself, praying fervently that the novice would successfully locate him a cot. Time was fleeting but there was little he could do except pace impatiently in front of the massive gates. It was some twenty minutes before he heard bolts being withdrawn and saw a low door, cut into the main gate, swing open. The smiling novice invited him in saying, "You are fortunate, signore. A pilgrim due to arrive today was delayed and her cell is available for just this one night."

Wondering if Thebitz had anything to do with the delay,

Ormidtz gratefully thanked the novice and ducked his head to follow her through the doorway. She led him down arched corridors which ran alongside rows of flowering bushes and hedges. She came to a stop in front of a well-polished wooden door, deep scars and scratches the only testimony to its age. The novice stood aside, and Ormidtz once again stooped to pass through the doorway and enter the tiny room. Whitewashed walls, a simple cross hanging over the cot bed, and a night table holding a lamp and a leather-bound bible, created a surprisingly welcoming and cozy atmosphere.

"I have to leave now, signore, the vespers are about to begin. All of us in the convent have already eaten so I will bring a tray to your room as soon as I can."

Not wishing to trouble the nun any further, Ormidtz was about to refuse the meal, when he recalled how his taste buds, reactivated after aeons, had awakened the long forgotten pleasures of the sensation of flavor and texture of food on his tongue. He wanted to revive the feeling, so changing his mind, said, "I really don't want to bother you, but I've not eaten anything since breakfast."

"It's no trouble, at all signore," replied the novice. "I'll bring your supper soon."

True to her word, in less than twenty minutes, there was a knock on the door, and Ormidtz opened it to find the novice holding a tray covered with a crisp white napkin. He quickly relieved her of the burden and placed it on the table saying, "*Molto gracias, novizia.* I just want to let you know that I will turn in as soon as I have finished supper. I will not tax your kind hospitality any further and will leave the convent at dawn."

"You are very welcome, signore. When you have finished

eating, you can place the tray outside the door," she replied. Then added, "Before you leave in the morning, you can have some breakfast which is served at the refectory at six o'clock. It's in the outer courtyard just past the sanatorium. When you are done, please come and get me so that I can show you out. I'll be in the vegetable garden behind the refectory."

Ormidtz was pleased that the novice had inadvertently provided him with essential information, and that he didn't have to resort to subterfuge to discover where the medical facility was located. He didn't want to deceive the good nuns more than was absolutely necessary, but neither did he want to stumble around in the dark trying to find Ruari, if she was at all here.

After the novice left, he shut the door and sat down at the table, unashamedly and wholeheartedly looking forward to his meal. Under the napkin was a rich minestrone soup of vegetables from the convent's kitchen garden, no doubt. An aroma of oregano and other herbs assailed his nostrils, making his mouth water. He reveled in the reawakening of his long forgotten sensory reactions to the sight and smell of good food.

The soup was accompanied by a warm ciabatta roll, its crust dusty with white flour. A thoughtfully provided cruet of translucent green olive oil allowed Ormidtz to alternate spoonfuls of minestrone with chunks of ciabatta generously dipped in oil. He finished every last bit of the simple meal, relearning and remembering that a human body in the Zenad Reality needed its nutrition.

By the time he had sopped up the last drop of minestrone with the remnants of the ciabatta, darkness had overtaken twilight. Soon the haunting notes of Ave Maria echoed through the corridors, seeping into his cell through the cracks in the ancient door. Always awed by the power of music to stimulate spirituality in humans, Ormidtz, without reservation, exposed his inner self to the cadences of the hymn. The ethereal melody transported him into deep meditation which led to an introspection that he hoped would rejuvenate him body and soul to meet the challenges of the task that lay ahead.

Late into the night, the intense darkness and quiet of the monastery paradoxically nudged him out of his mentally suspended state. He sat unmoving for a moment, reassuring himself that nothing was astir. Satisfied that all was quiet, Ormidtz swung himself out of the bed and stood up, his head nearly hitting the low ceiling of the cell.

He tiptoed to the door, its well-oiled hinges making no sound as he swung it open. He stepped into the corridor, its arches now framing a starry but moonless night. The shadows cast by the buildings helped camouflage his presence, but they also obscured his path, leaving him little choice but to grope his way around in the starlight.

Recalling that the novice had said that the refectory was in the outer courtyard and the sanatorium was next to it, Ormidtz headed down the corridor away from the direction he had taken with the novice to reach his room. He kept to the shadows as much as possible, sidling along the walls of the sleeping quarters. He was making slow but steady progress, when a barely audible rustle from a bush covered in white margaritas forced him to a standstill. Ormidtz stood rooted to the spot, waves of panic crashing over him, as he waited for Umani's assault. A moment or two later, a brindle cat padded out from under the foliage, its mottled fur making him almost invisible in the semi-dark.

Exhaling in relief, but annoyed at his own paranoia over Umani, Ormidtz continued along the corridor until he turned a corner and found himself stepping into a square courtyard. In spite of the darkness, the refectory was easy to spot for its door stood slightly ajar, a faint sliver of light partially revealing long, scrubbed tables laid ready for breakfast.

His eyes swept past the refectory and fell on a building barely visible in the gloom. He repositioned himself to get a better look. The structure seemed more modern than any he had seen so far, and was, in all likelihood, the sanatorium. Dim light passing through a glass-fronted entrance door cast a dull patch of gold on the ground, illuminating parts of the azalea hedges which bordered the perimeter of the double-storied building.

Ormidtz sprinted noiselessly towards the door, crouching behind the bushes to avoid detection. He tried to peer through the glass panes, but was too far away to see anything clearly. Dropping into a military crawl he wriggled his way to the lit doorway, and still prone, cautiously raised his head to peer into the room. He was rewarded with the sight of a desk prominently displaying the sign "Duty Nurse." A recently vacated office chair swung in slow arcs. Desperately hoping that the duty nurse would take a longish break to fetch a drink or snack, Ormidtz decided to grab this opportunity to covertly gather some information on Ruari's whereabouts.

Hunched over to make himself as inconspicuous as possible, he quickly opened the entrance door and crouch-walked stealthily into the room. He stood up and warily surveyed his surroundings. All was still, all was quiet. He crept up to the nurse's station and rifled through a pile of papers lying on top of the desk. They turned out to be just duty rosters, yielding no clue to Ruari's presence.

Rigid with tension but breathing rhythmically to maintain a steady heartbeat, he explored the room with his eyes. A slight flutter drew his attention to a cork board hanging on a wall next to the desk. A sheet of paper was thumbtacked to the board, a closer inspection revealing that it was a list of patients and their rooms. He leaned forward to read the names, when he heard footsteps striding confidently down the corridor towards the nurse's station.

Trying to still his palpitating heart, Ormidtz made a split second decision. No matter the risk, he wouldn't leave without confirming Ruari's presence in this clinic. Nervous sweat ran into his eyes, as he ignored the footsteps and continued to scan the sheet.

The footsteps, now about to enter the duty station, came to an abrupt halt as a cry rang out from the far end of the corridor. The footsteps paused, then turned and hurried back the way they had come. Breathing more easily, Ormidtz ran his eyes rapidly down the list, finding Ruari's name at the bottom, a dotted line leading to a room number which began with a two. It could only mean that she was on the upper floor.

Ormidtz barely had time to dash out of the entrance door as the footsteps returned, marching down the corridor towards the duty station, presumably having satisfactorily dealt with whatever had caused the cry. The nurse reached her chair and sat down at her desk unaware of any disturbance or anything amiss among her papers.

But with the nurse at her desk, Ormidtz couldn't hope to

reach Ruari from inside the building and needed to find an external access to the upper floor. A fire escape was perhaps the answer, for the clinic was sure to have one, even if it was part of an ancient monastery. A quick tour of the perimeter revealed an ornate, wrought iron spiral staircase at the back of the building. Ormidtz streaked up the steps, two at a time, coming to a standstill at the landing door. He forced open the lock and held his breath waiting for a strident burglar alarm to shatter the quiet of the night. When nothing happened, he exhaled a sigh of relief and stepped through the doorway.

That was a mistake. A high intensity electrical charge surged through him, throwing him against the wall. He was unprepared for the assault, for under normal circumstances, any emanation from Ruari's comatose mind would have had little effect on him or on any other human. But he had forgotten that in order to locate her he had fully exposed his own consciousness towards Ruari, making him highly vulnerable to her distorted mental emissions.

As realization struck, he immediately threw a defensive barrier around his senses to absorb most of the shock. In spite of the block, he couldn't escape the agonizing pain of the taser-like blast that tore through him, but he shrugged it off, now certain that Ruari was behind one of the doors on this floor.

As his Zenad body re-adjusted itself after the shock, Ormidtz tried to analyze what could have happened to Ruari. Thebitz had said that a thunderstorm had been raging when her head hit the cobblestones, throwing her into a state of oscillation between wakefulness and coma. In that case, Ruari's semi-comatose mind in self defense, could have generated a powerful electromagnetic field. At the same time, although the probability of occurrence was extremely low, the electrical discharges in the thunderclouds could have caused a reversion in her system stimulating her *atman* to behave like an elementary particle in entanglement with another particle. If so, the *atman* would have the ability to radiate out at a speed faster than light. Detached from its human anchor, and therefore highly vulnerable, her *atman* could have coalesced into a new form, or have occupied any living thing in any of the six Realities.

But where and in what form, were secrets Ormidtz would have to prise out from Ruari's comatose mind.

His pain subsiding to a tolerable level, Ormidtz made another attempt to locate Ruari. He took a tentative step towards one of the doors lining the corridor, then realized, too late, that his defense barrier had dissipated and had lost its potency. He was immediately sucked into a swirling vortex of insane turmoil from which he was unable to extricate himself. He knew he was trapped in the event horizon orbit of the black hole of Ruari's coma. Pinned to his spot near the door, Ormidtz broke out in cold sweat. He was in unchartered territory; in a dangerous situation. He could be crushed out of existence at the dense core of Ruari's coma and there was no escape route.

As the vortex spiraled downwards, it stretched Ormidtz's body like an elastic band, the distance between his head and feet increasing exponentially, his muscles, tendons and bones snapping, cracking, breaking apart. He could withstand the excruciating pain only by separating his consciousness from his physical body which he knew to be nothing but a maya, a perception, a projection of his brain in the Zenad Reality.

He went into a spin. Time and space merged as the orbiting radius became smaller and smaller, creating an immense pressure that compacted his elements into zero mass. As the black hole swallowed his body, Ormidtz reverted to his astral self and drifted into the unknown.

δ

Machim Reality
Vatican City

Its proboscis quivered. The lunar moth felt a faint vibration like a baby's breath. Its wings fluttered nervously, uncertain if danger lurked, or whether it was just an errant breeze that had wound its way into the Etruscan burial grounds. It crept into a darker corner of the niche.

δ

Ormidtz floated in spacetime, for a few seconds, for eons, who could say?

He couldn't tell when his surroundings began to alter, when the pitch darkness paled into a greying mist. When matter lost its density and his spinning velocity decelerated, so that the centrifugal force lost traction, dwindling to lethargic swings in preparation for arriving at a position of rest.

He drifted aimlessly in this nebulous state, until his physical body, like matter adhering to the Higgs boson, once again began to envelope his essential being. With it came a welcome calm as his inner harmony surfaced, anchoring him to the Reality into which he had been ejected.

Ormidtz wallowed in the semi-darkness, waiting for his

body to become fully functional. As he bided his time, his eyes were drawn to a pinpoint of phosphorescent light in the far distance. Checking to confirm that the reassembling of his human body was complete, he half swam, half waded towards the faint beacon, tearing through the clinging, clammy fog-like substance swirling around at the exit point of the vortex of Ruari's comatose brain.

Soon his feet touched solid ground, and he found himself at the mouth of a dusky, dimly lit tunnel. The miniscule beacon still winked in the distance, and he began to walk towards it, hoping to discover who or what had guided him to this spot.

δ

The moth felt air currents invade its space and fluttered out of the niche, seeking sanctuary elsewhere.

δ

The faint light suddenly blinked out. His target no longer visible, Ormidtz groped in the semi-dark. The narrow passage-way that he had just traversed, seemed to have ended in a T-junction, tunnels with rough stone walls stretching out in both directions into the unknown. His guiding light still not visible, he lingered at the point of divergence, reluctant to explore unfamiliar territory, getting lost and losing precious time in the process.

As he dithered, he heard a faint rustle coming from the tunnel branching towards the right. Not wishing to lose the only sign of life, he hurriedly followed the sound, disturbing a lunar moth in its uneven passage up the rough wall. Hearing the noise, the moth immediately took flight.

Convinced that this was the light that had guided him out of the viscous debris at the exit of the black hole, Ormidtz quickly pursued the translucent, glowing creature. In his haste, he stumbled on the uneven floor, stubbing his toe against a sarcophagus, invisible in the gloom. Limping slightly from the impact, he set out to chase the elusive insect fluttering ahead of him.

As his eyes adjusted to the dimness in the tunnel, Ormidtz felt more at ease in his new surroundings. He strode swiftly through the tunnel, barely glancing at the walls made from ancient blocks of stone. The occasional mosaic murals also escaped his attention. It was only when his eyes fell on burial urns embedded in niches, that he recognized his location. He realized with a start that he was in the ancient Etruscan burial grounds which lay deep below Saint Peter's Bascilica, the symbol of Catholicism.

Why or how did Ruari find her way here? Was the moth really leading him to Ruari, or was he chasing a will-o-the wisp? Where was Ruari's *atman*?

Questions flooded his mind, giving him no clue to the direction he should take, until a soft whisper, lighter than a spider's silk, caressed his ears.

"You who pursue me, who are you?" said the voice.

Half fearful it might be Umani, yet half curious, Ormidtz asked, "Who speaks? I see no one. Where are you?"

In response, a soft, furry moth's wing brushed his face. He fingered the faint, powdery residue on his cheeks and was immediately bathed in joy mingled with pathos and nostalgia.

Long forgotten emotions stirred within him, rekindling human passions and sentiments.

Bewildered and elated at the same time, Ormidtz asked, "Who are you?"

A sigh, as soft as a baby's breath, tickled his lashes. "I'm an essential being, a lost soul trapped inside this lunar moth."

"Why do I feel I have known you all my life?" asked Ormidtz.

"I do not know the answer to that," came the whispered reply.

"Why are you here? How did you get here?"

"I do not know."

Ormidtz took a moment to decide what to do next. He thought to himself, "I'm sure the lunar moth's phosphorescent wings was the pale beacon that guided me here. For some unfathomable reason, it's helping me find Ruari."

Recalling the feelings that arose in him from the powdery deposit of the moth's wings, Ormidtz took a shot in the dark.

He asked tentatively, "Are you Megan?"

"Perhaps."

"Or are you Ruari?"

"Maybe. I don't know, I have no name."

Ormidtz reflected on the non-answers, then said, "Little lunar moth, I've come to the conclusion, and I don't think I'm wrong, that you rescued me by showing me a way out of the morass that is now Ruari's brain. I don't understand how it happened, but the *atman* you are sheltering belongs to someone whose karma is inextricably bound with mine one way or another."

"Whose *atman* is hidden in me?" the moth asked. "You

mentioned two names."

"If the situation were different, I would want it to be my Megan's soul," said Ormidtz, his voice husky with anguish and desire. "But right now I have to locate Ruari's essential being, and I hope that it is she whom you are sheltering."

"Who is Megan?" asked the moth.

"It is a tale that would take too long to tell," said Ormidtz, "and we have very little time."

"Then tell me who is Ruari, and why do you seek her?" said the moth.

Ormidtz could barely make out the outline of the lunar moth as it sat with flattened wings against the wall. "If you are harboring Ruari's *atman*, and I believe you are," he said, "you must help reconcile her soul that is within you, here in the Machim Reality, with her body that is lying comatose in the Zenad Reality."

"So we are not in Zenad right now?" asked the moth.

"No, we are both in the Machim Reality, a state of being which is at an evolutionary level higher than Zenad. I transitioned through this Reality in another lifetime, so I recognize it," said Ormidtz.

"How did Ruari get here?" asked the moth.

"It is a strange tale. In Zenad, she went riding, fell off her horse, hit her head and slipped into a coma. At the time of the accident, a thunder storm created bizarre atmospheric conditions which caused her essential being to be ejected out of her comatose body and into the Machim Reality, where her soul found a safe haven in you," explained Ormidtz in one long breath.

"You could be right," replied the moth. "It happens now and

then that a lunar moth becomes a temporary home to a soul in transition."

"Yes, I'm convinced that this is what happened to Ruari," agreed Ormidtz.

"I sympathize with you and hope you succeed in your mission, but I want to remain in Machim. I feel it is my destiny, my karma, to end my days in the Etruscan burial grounds," replied the moth.

Frustrated and anxious at the slow progress of his mission, Ormidtz nonetheless painstakingly explained to the little insect, "There is a lot at stake, little one. The Zenad Reality is in grave danger, a danger that is also a threat to the universe and to all the other Realities."

"I don't understand," came the whisper.

"You are holding Ruari's soul, so if you communicate with her, you will learn that she, Erlang Shen, and Ameqran Izem developed a groundbreaking mathematical model," said Ormidtz.

After a moment's pause, the moth replied, "Mathematical model? No, the soul has no memory of it."

"Try, Ruari, try," said Ormidtz trying to awaken the mathematician's *atman.*

Several moments passed before the moth spoke again, "Wait, I do recall something vaguely, but it was a very, very long time ago."

The whisper began to fade.

"Ruari, don't leave. Listen to what I have to say." Ormidtz spoke almost harshly. "The Veil Lifter project based on your model, is about to be launched soon. The project team is unaware of the fatal flaw deeply embedded in the model. If the experiment goes ahead without the necessary modifications, the universe and all the Realities will fall into chaos. Peace and harmony will be lost forever."

Silence.

Then a soft flutter. "You have appealed to my conscience, and I feel I should help you. But I do not know how to return to my body in Zenad."

"I can show you the way," said Ormidtz, triumphant that he had got through to Ruari. "But you must exercise your free will to transition back to the lower energy Zenad Reality."

"My conscience tells me to help you, but why should I trust you?" came the doubt filled question.

"Think back, little one," said Ormidtz, "when you touched my face with your wings, did you not feel that you knew me once? That we've met somewhere, sometime? Maybe in another world, another Reality?" Ormidtz's voice was hoarse with emotion.

"Yes, for some reason I do feel I know you, yet I do not remember you." The moth fluttered in agitation.

"Our lives are entwined in some way but I don't know how or why. There's no time to try and understand this attraction between us, but please just trust me and return with me to Zenad." Ormidtz cried.

"I do not understand all that you say, but I feel I should do as you say. Show me the way to Zenad," came the whispered reply.

Grateful that the lunar moth trusted and believed in him enough to willingly transmigrate back to Zenad, Ormidtz cupped his hands, offering the holder of Ruari's soul, a safe and protected passage to the tunnel exit. The moth quivered and in a draft of air coasted towards Ormidtz. Suddenly it changed direction and swooped away, arcing over his head. Ormidtz swung around in surprise, his eyes following the moth's sudden change in trajectory.

The reason soon became apparent. A cowled Franciscan monk was walking down the narrow passageway holding a flickering candle. His grey habit billowed out behind him, a white cord belt with knotted ends girding his waist. Rosary beads clicked in tempo with his footsteps.

The moth was flying towards the candle flame in a hypnotic trance. Why do moths find flames irresistible? Are they aware they are flying to their death, yet do it anyway? No one knows the answer, perhaps not even the moth itself.

Momentarily paralyzed, Ormidtz stared in horror. If the moth got caught in the flame and burned to death, Ruari's *atman* would seek another Reality. Perhaps he would be able to eventually track her down, but he did not have the time to start another search for Ruari's *atman*, nor was he certain that he would survive the ordeal of another journey through the black hole of her brain.

As the candle flame danced seductively, the monk cupped his palm around it protecting it from getting extinguished. The sudden movement distracted the moth, and it missed the flame, coming to rest on the priest's hand.

Angry with himself for his slow reactions, Ormidtz called to the monk, "Padre, please wait."

But the priest didn't slow down, instead he threw a glance at Ormidtz over his shoulder and increased his pace. The vicious and evil expression on the priest's face turned Ormidtz ashen with fear as he realized that Umani had usurped the good monk's body. In spite of his fear, Ormidtz was now convinced that the lunar moth was sheltering Ruari's essential being, for he knew that Umani would do everything in her power to prevent Ruari's soul reuniting with her body.

Ormidtz lost precious moments rooted in indecision as the moth crawled over the monk's hand, drawing closer to the flame. He weighed his options. He could try to remove the moth from Umani's grasp which may damage its body, and release Ruari's *atman* into the unknown. Or he could try dousing the candle, which should arrest the moth's fatal journey. The first would involve violence which Ormidtz was reluctant to use. Although he knew that it was Umani, yet respect for people of the cloth from any religious order, ingrained in him over eons, inhibited Ormidtz from directly attacking the priest. So Ormidtz chose his second option.

But Umani seemed to have already read his mind. She preempted Ormidtz, springing up and placing the candle on a protuberance in the rough wall. The ledge was several feet off the floor, and Umani stood sentinel below, blocking Ormidtz's access to the candle and any chance of putting out the flame.

Temporarily conceding victory to Umani, Ormidtz searched for a way to prevent the moth from reaching the candle. He noticed that the insect had abandoned the monk's hand and was creeping along the wall towards the flame flickering on the ledge. Seeing that the insect still had a little distance to cover, Ormidtz leapt up and cupped his hand against the wall, trapping the moth.

He scooped up the insect, intending to put it somewhere out of harm's way, when a brick, dislodged from the ancient wall, came hurtling towards him. He put up his hands in reflex and dodged. The brick missed his head but grazed his knuckles, the impact forcing his loosely fisted hand holding the moth to fly open. The freed moth once again headed towards the flame.

Nursing his slight but painful joint bruise, Ormidtz took a few steps backward until an obstacle blocked his retreat. A quick look told him that the lip of a burial urn was scraping the back of his neck. He reached behind him and removed the urn from its niche, all the time keeping his eyes fixed on Umani, the moth and the candle.

He swung the urn over his head and tossed its contents towards the candle, hoping the sand and debris deposited over the centuries would snuff out the flame. But he was standing at an awkward angle and failed to generate sufficient force behind the toss. The incomplete parabolic arc ended with the sand dribbling harmlessly to the floor.

Umani retaliated immediately. The priest twirled swiftly, his long skirt creating a draft that blew dust particles into Ormidtz's eyes and dislodged the moth which fell to the tunnel floor. Blinded, Ormidtz dropped to his knees, and through a mist of tears saw the moth struggling to once again fly to its death. Ormidtz pounced and deftly scooping up the moth, thrust it into the now empty urn. He turned the urn over and placed it, mouth down, inside an uncovered sarcophagus where the moth would remain safe for the moment.

He didn't notice the spider lurking in the darkest corner of the marble coffin, quivering in anticipation of an easy meal.

With the safety of Ruari's soul temporarily off his mind, Ormidtz turned to face Umani. A click and a swish were the only warning sounds Ormidtz received, before a blow from the string of wooden rosary beads split open his cheek. He barely made it to his feet, when the rosary came at him again, thrown like a lasso to rope him round the neck like a calf at a rodeo. This time he saw it coming, and Ormidtz caught the string of wooden beads and pulled hard. The chain snapped, scattering the beads on the rough floor.

Undaunted, the monk untied his cord belt, twirled it over his head like a whip, and lashed out at Ormidtz. In spite of such vicious attacks, Ormidtz still couldn't bring himself to lay a hand on the priest. Instead he jumped back, trying to put himself beyond the range of the rope. But as he retreated, Umani advanced, repeatedly hurling the thick cord at Ormidtz until with an ominous zing the cord hit Ormidtz on the forehead, singeing a deep furrow over his brow. Ignoring the stinging pain, Ormidtz lunged forward to grab the rope which he wound round his forearm and yanked hard to throw the monk off balance.

The monk released his hold on the cord and Ormidtz pulled it free. He swiftly coiled it tight and aiming at the candle still sitting up on the wall, Ormidtz unleashed the cord to its the full length, sending it snaking towards the flame. The cord failed to reach the candle, a surge of oxygen from the resulting airflow making the flame flicker more intensely. As Ormidtz rapidly recoiled the rope in preparation for another try at extinguishing the flame, the monk leapt forward locking his bare hands around Ormidtz's neck in a death throttle.

But Umani was fractionally too late. Ormidtz had already flicked the cord at the brittle, charred end of the wick which was clearly visible against the blue heart of the flame. The wick disintegrated, the flame died, and the candle dropped to the floor.

The distraction caused Umani to momentarily relax her grip

around Ormidtz's neck, which was sufficient time for Ormidtz to extricate himself from the stranglehold. Gasping and coughing, he crawled away, groping his way towards the sarcophagus, hoping that the moth was safe. He plunged his hand into the sarcophagus to retrieve the moth and felt the hairy legs of a spider scuttle over his arm. The unexpected presence of a predator arachnid in the sarcophagus sent terror spasms through Ormidtz. He hurriedly upended the urn, fearful of what he might discover.

His tremulous breath of relief to find the moth still inside the urn turned into a sigh when he discovered that one of its wings showed a ragged tear. He gently picked up the bruised and inert insect and placed it against his breast, hoping the warmth of his body and the beating of his heart would revive it. Then he turned and ran. He kept running, unsure how long he would be able to protect the moth from Umani's murderous fury.

Ormidtz sped down the tunnel, the monk's footsteps pounding after him. He stumbled and fell, then got up and continued to run. He did not stop. He stubbed his toes against invisible objects hidden in the shadows, but he did not stop. He ran until he could run no further, then breathless and ashen faced, he turned to confront his nemesis.

Ormidtz was dumbfounded. The Franciscan was walking swiftly away from him, towards a lighted archway in the far distance. Relieved but stunned at Umani's inexplicable retreat, Ormidtz searched for a clue as to what could have caused the monk to depart so hurriedly. He saw that he was in a small clearing at the center of which stood a glass case displaying a purple velvet bundle. The surrounding aura was pure, calm and peaceful. This had to be a sacred, sanctified spot, for only such a place could block Umani's evil powers. This must be the reason why Umani was forced to walk away.

Grateful that he and the moth had temporarily escaped Umani, Ormidtz took a moment to relax. Wondering what to do next, he felt a flutter against his chest. Overjoyed that the carrier of Ruari's soul had been resuscitated, he knelt near the case, and gently holding the moth in his palms, whispered, "Ruari, you must now find your way back to Zenad. You know the way. You just have to want it deeply and sincerely. Remember, the fate of the universe hangs in balance, and you are one of the few who can avert the impending disaster."

The moth sat passively on his open palm, its pale green wings tinged grey, perhaps from the dust in the sarcophagus. Murmuring reassurances, Ormidtz breathed gently on the moth, hoping his qi would energize the little creature into action.

For a long while it lay very still. Then, luminous wings gleaming in the semi-dark, the exhausted moth zig-zagged drunkenly through the air to settle on the glass case. It began to creep down the side of the case, its hairy legs barely finding traction on the smooth glass pane. It slowed to a stop, lost its hold, then slid to the bottom edge of the case. It was dead before it dropped on the dusty floor. Ormidtz saw with dismay that its pale green wings were marred by more dark streaks which he had failed to notice earlier.

As sadness filled his heart, a breeze soft as a kiss, caressed Ormidtz's cheek, and he knew Ruari's *atman* had found release.

CHAPTER VII

THE FRACTURE

Zenad Reality

India

A tsunami of sound buffeted Ormidtz, grating his most sensitive nerves, invading his deepest being.

The raucous onslaught quickly ebbed, and as his auditory senses acclimatized themselves to the strange sound waves, they metamorphosed into joyous music in unfamiliar chords and harmony. Ecstatic sermons in a profusion of little known tongues washed over him, now overwhelming, now receding to a faint whisper. But beneath the joy and ecstasy ran an under-current of unfulfilled desires, of despair, of death, of lost souls seeking sanctuary. The conflicting auras of hope and despon-dency seeped through his every pore, reminding him that there was accumulated vital energy in this place of sanctity, and the needy had but to drink from that well.

Ormidtz had come to the Sufi Saint's shrine in Ajmer in the hope of finding Ameqran Izem, the last of the three scientists who had created the model for the Veil Lifter. Chasing Thebitz's vague clue that a disoriented Izem was haunting shrines of Sufi Saints in the hope of rediscovering his inner self, Ormidtz had journeyed across the earth visiting shrines of Jalal al-Din Muhammad Rumi in Turkey, of el-Mursi Abul Abbas in Egypt, of Shaikh Aamadu Bàmba Mbàkke in Senegal, and of many others in as many countries. But in none of them, had he found any indication of Izem's presence.

It was only here, at the shrine of the Sufi Saint, Khawaja Muinuddin Chisti in Ajmer, India, that Ormidtz had his thought waves intercepted by vibrations that could only be emanating from Izem. For Izem was an expert in the theory of sound and acoustics, and unconsciously or subconsciously, he would choose to communicate through this medium.

δ

Khulon Reality
Ethiopia

The gaunt monk, as burnt and stark as his surroundings, carefully lowered himself down the rope, one fist below the other, until he reached the bottom. He did this several times a day because the thick hemp cord hanging from the roots of an old, gnarled tree on the high plateau above, was the only access to the ancient Ethiopian Orthodox Tewahedo monastery carved into the rocks.

As his feet touched the ground, the monk felt a little disturbed and edgy. Something was different today. He couldn't place his long, bony finger on it, but he sensed that the aura around the church was not the same as yesterday.

He pulled the several meters of white cotton swathing his body a little tighter, and set off over the arid, stony ground, muttering to himself prayers in the archaic Ge'ez tongue. He had been called to read the last rites over a dying old woman in a village some ten miles away. Walking long distances was no great challenge for him. Here, everyone walked to wherever they had to go. This did not bother him in the least. No, it was something else, something else entirely.

Under the blazing hot sun, a shiver ran down his spine. He was frustrated for he felt troubled by a sensation he couldn't define. He decided that after the evening services were done, he would delve into himself to try and trace the source of the terror.

δ

Zenad Reality
India

Surrounded by a sea of people, Ormidtz stood pondering the best way to locate Izem. Although he had never set eyes on any of them before, Ormidtz had identified Erlang Shen and Ruari O'Connor through the clinics that ministered to their needs. But in Izem's case, Ormidtz had no inkling what Izem looked like, nor could he be sure that Izem was actually here.

He toyed with the idea of conducting a broad, sweeping mind probe of those around him, which would be the quickest way to locate the scientist, but immediately rejected the idea. Ormidtz was unwilling to destabilize his inner harmony by again exposing himself to the seething raw emotions of people in agony, people who had come to seek succor from the Saint. It was too painful, too torturous.

Undecided, he turned to a man standing nearby and asked, "Sir, have you by any chance recently seen a foreigner visiting this shrine?"

The stranger shrugged and said with a laugh, "Many foreigners visit this shrine. If you have his photograph, someone might recognize him. As for myself, I've just arrived today and can't help you much." Then pointing to an elderly man whose back was turned towards them, he added, "But you could ask that *khadim*, he's a caretaker of the shrine, and he might have seen your friend."

Nodding his thanks, Ormidtz hurried up to the *khadim* and coughed discretely to attract his attention. The *khadim*, who had been talking to a small group of local people, turned around with a frown which transformed quickly into a wide smile when he saw it was a foreigner. Foreigners were always welcome for they could easily be preyed upon to make donations to orphanages supported by the shrine. Of course, no one actually followed up to see if the donations reached their destinations, so some of the low level *khadims* milked such sources to augment their meager salaries.

With such possibilities racing through his mind, the *khadim* rubbed his hands obsequiously and asked, "Sahib, would you like a tour around the shrine? There are many things to see. Besides the Saint's tomb, there is the crypt of his daughter, Bibi Hafiz Jama, and the vault of Moghul Emperor Shah Jahan's daughter, Chimni Begum."

"Perhaps another day," replied Ormidtz, trying not to sound too dismissive or disinterested in local history. "Right now, I was wondering if you could help me find someone. A friend came here a few days ago to attend the death anniversary of the Saint. I haven't heard from him since. Have you seen him by any chance?"

"What does he look like?" asked the *khadim*. "This is a very popular place of pilgrimage. Many people come to this shrine so it's hard for me to tell if he was here."

Ormidtz floundered to answer the very reasonable question. Then basing his guess on Izem's name, he said, "He... um... looks kind of a mix of Central Asian and North African heritage."

A cagey look quickly replaced the *khadim's* fawning. He knew at once whom Ormidtz was talking about, for he had seen shades of African nomadic tribes in the man – the dusky complexion, the sharp nose and prominent cheekbones. Although some people from his own region had similar facial characteristics, the *khadim* could easily tell them apart.

But right now, he was unwilling to share any information with Ormidtz, because in exchange for a generous fee, he had allowed the uninitiated Izem to take part in a *zikr* meditation event. He could get him into serious trouble over this, particularly since Izem was a *farangi*.

In an effort to salve his conscience for succumbing to the temptation, and accepting the fee, the *khadim* had told himself that since he was ignorant of the *tariqa*, the inexperienced Izem would at best, be able to penetrate only the lowest levels of introspection. He had never imagined that the act of *zikr* would have such a disastrous effect on the *farangi*.

The memory made him shift uneasily from one foot to the other as he wondered how much he should confess to this man seeking his help. Then, seeming to make up his mind, the *khadim* glanced in both directions to make sure that no one was within earshot, and said, "Sahib, many come to this holy place, so it is hard to remember any one person. But I did see several foreigners visit the *dargah* recently."

"Are they still here?" asked Ormidtz.

"I'm not sure, Sahib, but I think they may have left," was the *khadim's* untruthful reply, for he knew that Izem, confused and lost after his ordeal, was still loitering in the premises.

Then anxious to escape Ormidtz's scrutiny, the caretaker walked away rapidly, apologizing to Ormidtz over his shoulders. "I'm sorry, but I have to go now. The time for prayers is close."

Ormidtz stared at the retreating back, convinced that the man knew something about Izem which, for some reason, he didn't want to share with him. Ormidtz didn't believe the *khadim's* claim to ignorance, and was fairly certain that the scientist was nearby. His conviction gained credence with himself, for although the static caused by the audio interference in the environment prevented Ormidtz from isolating the source of the sound vibrations pervading his senses, he was now sure they could only be emitting from Izem.

Realizing that the shifty *khadim* wouldn't be of any help, Ormidtz scanned the crowd searching for inspiration. His eyes fell on a Hindu sadhu clad in saffron robes, his matted, red-brown dreadlocks and skeletal frame testament to lack of nutrition from long periods of fasting and starvation. Three white stripes streaked his brow. Could that be Izem?

Ormidtz gently probed the sadhu's mind, searching for a clue. He found that the ascetic's mind, while deeply spiritual, lacked the logical and coherent thoughts of a scientist. No, this couldn't be Izem, he must look elsewhere.

But Ormidtz's exploration of the sadhu's mind hadn't gone unnoticed. The ascetic's extra-sensory perceptive powers had alerted him to an alien interference in his body. The sadhu instinctively turned towards Ormidtz, then gasped. His eyes widened in terror as beads of perspiration burst through his chalked forehead. He backed away, pointed an accusing finger at Ormidtz and screamed, "You're a being not of this Reality. I see several layers of aura surrounding you. Who are you? Why are you here? Why did you enter my mind? Stay away from me, I'm not ready to depart from this world as yet."

Ormidtz glanced around quickly, hoping no one had heard the sadhu, for the last thing Ormidtz wanted was to draw attention to himself. It was wishful thinking. Several men loitering nearby, pressed closer to learn what the hullabaloo was about.

The sadhu pointed to Ormidtz and again shouted, "This is not a man. He's a demon from hell. He is stealing my mind. Get rid of him, get rid of him now, at once, before he eats all our brains."

Like any shrine, this dargah attracted all kinds of people, from those genuinely seeking help from the Saint, to those who are frustrated, disgruntled and disillusioned with life. Often unemployed, they just hang around the premises for an opportunity to pick a pocket, or steal an unattended bag or briefcase. For them, any distraction was welcome because it brought some excitement into their lives and took their minds off their troubles.

And now, a group of idlers quickly took up the chant. "An evil spirit, a demon is amongst us!"

"A wicked djinn," screamed a voice shrill with fear. "Call the mullah, quick. That stranger must be exorcised immediately."

"It's the devil in human guise," screeched someone else, giving goosebumps to anyone within earshot.

As pandemonium broke loose, Ormidtz turned and fled. It was futile to try and explain anything to this terrified, unruly mob. He ran across the vast courtyard, darting under covered porches and scrambling through narrow archways, until he arrived at the main gates of the shrine. Pausing under the massive portals, he looked to his right and left, desperately searching for a place to hide before he was lynched by the crazed crowd.

As the thunder of pursuing feet came closer and closer, Ormidtz heard a whisper, "Come here. I have a place where you can hide."

Ormidtz looked down to see an old women squatting on the steps of the dargah. He dropped to his knees and stared into dead, milky opal eyes. Still out of breath, he rasped, "Ma, was it you who spoke? Can you help me?"

The woman leaned forward and held his head between her hands. She traced Ormidtz's eyes, nose and mouth with her thumbs, then nodded, "I knew you would come."

"Can you help me?" repeated Ormidtz.

"Yes, I can and I will. Do you see the hut just outside the main gate? Go inside and wait. There is someone else in there, but you don't have to worry about him. You will be safe. No one will look for you inside a blind old beggar's shack."

A few steps took him outside the massive, arched gate where he at once spotted a lean-to fabricated from a length of discolored tarpaulin, its tattered ends draped over wooden poles. He dashed inside, oblivious to the scent of roses pervading the dim interior, unappreciative of the cramped but neat and clean abode. Only too glad to have escaped the maniacal mob, he squatted on the earthen floor and pulling his knees to his chin, tried to stifle his panting and slow down the thumping of his heart. He vaguely registered the presence of another person, but following the blind beggar's advice, he paid no attention to the shadowy figure hunched up in the corner muttering to himself in an unfamiliar tongue.

From his safe haven, Ormidtz heard shrill, panicky voices at the main portals of the shrine. Nervous, he crept further inside the tiny hovel, shifting into deeper shadows. He found himself pressed against the other occupant's forearm, the contact sending audio frequencies vibrating through Ormidtz to which he paid little heed, for the noise and chaos from the mob outside filled him with dread. His entire attention was focused on avoiding a confrontation with the terror-stricken crowd.

As minutes ticked by, and there was no sign of the commotion abating, Ormidtz grew edgy. He must return to the shrine to continue searching for Izem, but he couldn't pass through the main portals where the mob was still milling about. There had to be another path and he was certain the old woman could show it to him.

As the din subsided a little, Ormidtz cautiously raised the tarpaulin flap which served as the hut's door, and stuck his head out, looking for his savior. It was a big mistake. Someone from the crowd noticed the movement, recognized him, and shouted to the others, "I've found him. I've found him. He's hiding in the beggar's shack."

Ormidtz ducked back inside and sat rooted in fear. Shouting

and screaming, the crowd rushed towards the hut, intent on destroying the demon amongst them. Men empowered by the righteousness of the devout, surged forward to crush the evil fiend.

In spite of being aware that his mission would be seriously jeopardized, but unwilling to face the mad crowd, Ormidtz prepared to transition himself out of the Zenad Reality, when the melodious sound of adhan rang out. The call to prayer drowned out the cacophony, casting a mantel of peace over the bedlam. The frenzy came to an abrupt halt as the crowd and everyone in the vicinity responded to the summons. Dropping whatever he was doing, each shuffled off to perform the ritual ablutions mandatory before every prayer.

Rescued from the edge of disaster, Ormidtz waited until he was sure that the mob had dispersed, and all he could hear was the assuring murmur of everyday life. As the adrenalin dissipated from his system, he became aware of strong acoustical waves buffeting his inner senses. He realized he was still squashed up against the other occupant, an ill-kempt man with a three-day growth darkening his chin.

Peering into the sunburnt face, Ormidtz asked hesitatingly, "Izem?"

"Who asks?" came the reply.

"Izem, is that you?" Ormidtz asked again.

"I know no Izem," the man replied.

"He has no memory of who he is," the blind woman's voice came from the entrance of the shack. "I found him wandering at the shrine, ignored by everyone. I brought him to my shack and have looked after him the best I could."

"Who is he, then?" asked Ormidtz.

"I don't know, but he could be the man you're looking for, the man you call Izem," replied the woman.

"Why do you think he is Izem?"

"Just put it down to intuition," she said with a smile.

"Do you know what happened to him?"

"I know a bit, and can guess the rest," the woman began with a sigh. "Son, there are many people in this world who are spiritually troubled and wish to understand the meaning of life. They read a lot, acquiring theoretical knowledge about the different paths to the ultimate truth. They think that knowledge is sufficient preparation for setting out on that hazardous journey."

"There's nothing wrong in that, is there?" Ormidtz protested mildly.

"You're right," she said. "It's always good to explore and search for the truth, but it's also important to know the correct techniques for conducting such a search. Otherwise one can put oneself in great jeopardy. Take your friend here. He had little or no knowledge of the *tariqa*, the way of the *zikr*, yet three days ago he insisted on participating in a gathering held at the dargah. He offered the *khadim* a lot of money which the ill-paid caretaker couldn't refuse, and allowed him to join the *zikr*. As it often happens with the uninitiated, at the conclusion of the *zikr*, he fell into a deep faint."

"He seems to have recovered from his fainting spell," Ormidtz commented, glancing at the shadowy figure still rocking and murmuring to himself.

"Most of the time people recover from their faint and go back to leading normal lives. But your friend woke up a day later and could remember nothing, not even his name. Since then he has been drifting about in a delirious manner, chanting in a tongue none of us understand."

"What happened during the *zikr* to put him in such a state?" Ormidtz asked.

She nodded knowingly. "It happens now and then, that the act of *zikr* transforms a person when he becomes enlightened and reaches the zenith of spirituality. But more often, the process of deep meditation exposes the inner self to forces beyond human control. In such a state one's essential being, as well as one's physical self, become vulnerable to outside elements."

"Izem became vulnerable to what elements?" Ormidtz asked.

"Was Izem in the habit of practicing meditation?" she asked without answering his question.

"He's a scientist and his research in particle physics led him to seek the connect between science and spirituality," said Ormidtz. "This in turn made him look for meditation practices in the east."

"That might explain it," said the beggar woman with a sigh.

"Explain what?"

"Although your friend didn't know the *tariqa*," she continued as if Ormidtz hadn't spoken, "His experience with other methods of meditation had thrust him into a state of enlightenment that he was ill prepared to absorb. The trauma made him lose control of both his physical and his spiritual self, creating a vacuum within himself. I think that vacuum was filled by a djinn. Your friend is now possessed."

"A djinn? You mean a being of fire? How can you be so sure that he is possessed?" asked Ormidtz fearful of having to deal with more complications.

"You see, the powerful aura that this holy shrine projects into space attracts many spirits, both good and the not-so-good. Humans can seldom see these spirits, but some of us who live here, can clearly feel their presence. Since your friend lost control of his inner self, he became spiritually susceptible and a djinn took the opportunity to usurp your friend's powers."

"Do you think it's possible to talk to the djinn?" Ormidtz asked in a low voice, wondering why he was whispering. "It might tell me where to find Izem's soul."

"Well, you could try," said the blind beggar. "If the djinn wants to, he will answer your questions, but it depends on whether it is a good or a bad djinn. The bad ones don't always answer truthfully and enjoy causing trouble and mayhem."

Ormidtz decided to take the chance and shifted around in the cramped space to face the possessed man. "Izem," he called out, "Izem, I must talk to you."

"Why do you keep calling me by that name? I do not know who Izem is."

In exasperation, Ormidtz cried, "If you are not Izem, then who *are* you?"

"I am a free spirit. I answer to no one."

"But spirits don't have human bodies. So I ask again, who are you?" Ormidtz asked more boldly.

"I'm Zepar, the djinn of sound. I visit shrines during important events such as a birth or death anniversary of a saint or holy man. Many humans come to the shrines during these times, and if I am lucky, I can take over a mind and body."

Ormidtz heard a sharp intake of breath and turned to see that the old woman had turned ashen.

"What?" he whispered.

"Zepar is a Duke of Hell. He's as evil as Shaitan, his master, the Devil," the old woman replied, fear making her words almost unintelligible.

"Are you sure he's the devil? Zepar said he is affiliated with sound. What does it mean?" asked Ormidtz.

"It means that Zepar can manipulate sound to control a human spirit," she replied. Then after a pause added, "On the other hand, if you know how to do it, you can use sound to bring Zepar under your control," the old beggar said in a trembling voice.

"And how do I do that?" asked Ormidtz.

"I do not know, I do not know," moaned the woman, covering her face with her hands and rocking back and forth in terror.

With no new information available to him, Ormidtz turned back to the man he believed to be Izem, and asked, "Zepar, why are you occupying Izem's body?"

The djinn appeared to be in a mood to enlighten the ignorant human.

"*Zikr* is a very complex form of meditation," he said. "Many humans are keen to perform devotional meditation, without considering the risks they face when crossing spiritual boundaries where the soul is barely tethered to the body. This man, whom you call Izem, hadn't learnt the technique to filter out external elements when the act of *zikr* throws his mind's door open to all and sundry. I was passing by and when I found him to be well trained in the science of sound and acoustics, I immediately seized his mind and body for he was a perfect match for me."

"What do you want from Izem's body?" asked Ormidtz, hoping to find a way to liberate Izem from the djinn's possession.

"We djinns are made of fire and cannot experience what humans experience. So it's always entertaining to be in a human body now and then," answered Zepar.

"How long will you occupy this body?" Ormidtz asked,

"Why do you want to know that?" countered Zepar.

"Because it's imperative that I reunite this man's body with his lost *atman*. Izem is one of three scientists who can avert the impending destruction of the universe."

"Destruction of the universe?" Zepar asked. "What do you mean?"

"The Veil Lifter, a flawed project, is about to be launched. Izem and his colleagues can make the corrections which will prevent the disaster. Otherwise Zenad, the other Realities, and the universe will be destroyed. The ensuing chaos will threaten even the Singularity."

"Hmm," pondered Zepar. "Destruction of the Realities and the universe. Are you sure the Veil Lifter can do that?"

"Let me tell you something that might convince you," Ormidtz replied.

"I am listening," said Zepar.

"As a djinn you are familiar with the Realities, and can therefore appreciate the sacrifice I'm making to avert the catastrophe," said Ormidtz. "I was in Waara Reality when I was asked to take up this mission. I forfeited my Waara lifetime, which had taken me eons to achieve, to return to Zenad. I took the huge the risk of dropping from the high energy Waara Reality to one of the lowest energy levels, because it is only in

144

Zenad that I can help turn the course of events that can spell the spiritual end of mankind."

Zepar was quiet for a while, then said, "Few humans can transcend to the Waara level of consciousness, and since you have succeeded, I hold you in great esteem. If you have sacrificed everything to return to Zenad, then you must truly believe that the Veil Lifter is a threat to the universe and the Realities." A pause, then he added, "You do realize that you may never find your way back to Waara?"

"I was fully aware of the risks when I made my choice," said Ormidtz, not wishing to be reminded of the dangers of his mission and the sacrifices he was making. "It was difficult for me to refuse, because I'm the only human who can travel between Realities and probe any human mind for intelligence that will help me in my mission."

"So what do you want from me?" asked Zepar, after a brief pause.

"I need you to depart so that I can enter Izem's mind to locate where his essential being is hiding."

"Entering his mind is not going to help you much," said the djinn.

"Why not?" asked Ormidtz.

"This man's essential being is not inside him at all. It slipped out when he was in the throes of *zikr*. That's why he was so extremely vulnerable and I was able to enter so effortlessly."

"But where has it gone?"

"I don't know." Izem shrugged. "His *atman* could be inside a newborn human or even a dying man in any of the Realities. Who knows?"

"But you will nonetheless withdraw from Izem's body?"

Ormidtz insisted.

A smile twisted Izem's lips as Zepar replied sardonically, "I may or may not vacate his body. I enjoy experiencing life through a human body."

Turning away from Ormidtz, Izem rocked back and forth, muttering what sounded like gibberish under his breath.

δ

Khulon Reality
Ethiopia

Gnarled and twisted like the old dead tree standing one-legged on the wasted land below, the monk at the edge of the rocky plateau sat lost in thought. The monastery behind him cast long shadows in the afternoon sun.

Why does my head buzz as if a honeybee is flying inside? Why do I feel as if I'm part of two worlds. Is my time near, and the Lord calls me to him? But I feel no peace. Only a strange turmoil, as if a tidal wave is about to sweep over the shores of my mind.

δ

Zenad Reality
India

For the lack of other options and in spite of the djinn's evasive reply, Ormidtz once again tried to reach Izem's inner self. Wary of his conscious or unconscious acoustical onslaughts, this time he approached Izem with great caution, as in the stifling heat of the lean-to, he held Izem's head firmly at the temples, and gently probed the scientist's mind. While partly relieved at being spared the pain, Ormidtz was disappointed to receive only faint acoustical echoes, for it meant that he wasn't being able to access Izem's awareness. He tried again, this time circling inside Izem's head to penetrate deeper into his mind, but no matter which path he took, a sound barrier blocked him in every direction.

Frustrated, Ormidtz cried out, "I can't reach him. And if I can't reach him, how will I find his *atman*?"

"What do you see inside his head?" asked the old woman.

Ormidtz was momentarily startled for he had quite forgotten the blind beggar. "There's a wall in his mind which I can neither scale nor breach. I have so little time left, what shall I do?"

The old woman said nothing, instead began to rummage through a bundle by her side. She found what she was looking for, and handed it to Ormidtz. It was a small copper cylinder with one end sealed with ash-peppered wax, the small object hanging like a locket on a length of black string.

"Tie this amulet around Izem's neck," she said. "I think Zepar has erected the barriers to prevent you from discovering his location and liberating Izem. The amulet holds a special prayer that will weaken Zepar, but not for very long. So you must act quickly before Zepar recovers his strength."

Ormidtz peered into the blind woman's eyes, searching for a clue to the source of knowledge she had revealed on such deep, spiritual matters. As he looked into her cataract-ridden filmy eyes, he suddenly recalled that when he was running from the mob, she had not only offered to help but had also said that she had been waiting for him.

"Who are you, Lady?" asked Ormidtz in a voice filled with awe.

The woman smiled. "I'm just a blind beggar spending the last days of my life in this holy place."

"No," replied Ormidtz, not believing her dismissive answer for a moment. "I'm convinced that you are a Sufi who has reached the highest tier of consciousness. You're wholly detached from worldly affairs and oblivious to your material surroundings. That's how you knew I was coming, and that's how you know how I can reach Izem's *atman*."

She neither confirmed nor denied Ormidtz's observation, instead cried out, "Beware, son, yours is a perilous journey, fraught with danger."

She turned to leave, and Ormidtz caught a glimpse of her third eye visible only to the initiated.

δ

Ormidtz leaned forward and tied the amulet around Izem's neck, the man acquiescent, oblivious to his surroundings. Ormidtz waited for some sign of external transformation in Izem, but there was no manifestation of any change in him. The beggar woman had already left, so he had no one to give him any further advice. Doubtful that the amulet had had any effect on Izem, Ormidtz made another attempt at penetrating Izem's mind.

This time he was instantly swamped by a tidal wave of sound. Apparently the amulet had done its work. A weakened Zepar could not prop up the sound barriers, allowing Ormidtz to directly pierce Izem's now defenseless consciousness. Waves of diverse lengths, pitches and cadences deafened Ormidtz, destabilizing his inner balance, disrupting his mental harmony. He retreated hastily, quickly detaching himself from Izem's turbulent mind. He had to find a way to circumvent those deadly acoustics, for any direct approach would place both their lives at serious risk.

Searching unsuccessfully for alternative routes to Izem, despair surged through Ormidtz, sapping him of his spiritual strength. As he struggled to overcome his despondency, he heard footsteps approaching the shed. Fear overtook despair. Was someone from the mob returning to look for him?

Kneeling, he lifted the doorway flap and peered out cautiously. He saw a pair of gold-thread embroidered slippers come to a halt at the entrance of the shack. At the ankles swung the hem of a floor length gown sewn with seed pearls and sequins. Why was she here? Was she a pilgrim wanting to meet the Sufi beggar? Or was she the beggar woman in a different guise? Ormidtz sat still, hoping the stranger would think no one was home and leave.

But the slippers stood still, and anxious to return to Izem, Ormidtz took the risk and stuck his head out the doorway to find a heavily veiled woman standing a short distance from the hut. Ormidtz's fears turned to elation as he sensed Thebitz's familiar electrical impulses radiating from her.

"Izem is empty of himself. It's true that Zepar occupied the void, but in the process he created a complex tangle of uncontrolled thought waves. These can be very painful for anyone trying to break into Izem's consciousness," announced the veiled woman.

"Thebitz", cried Ormidtz overjoyed to find his mentor miraculously by his side. "Thank you. You've come to my aid."

"I've told you many times Ormidtz, that I will stand by you whenever you need me." Thebitz's electrical impulses flickered through Ormidtz's thought waves. "You have little faith in me, and even less in yourself."

"You're right, Thebitz, as always," said Ormidtz. "Now that you've explained what is going on inside Izem's head, tell me how to reach his consciousness. You know well, that's the only way Izem can guide me to his *atman*."

"Your false humility doesn't fool me," Thebitz replied sternly. "But we'll discuss that later. Now let us deal with the matter at hand. If you want to enter Izem's mind, you must deconstruct the wave-particle duality in his brain. Apply quantum erasure theory under Einstein locality conditions to erase Zepar's information path. It is the route through which Zepar entered Izem. This will disentangle Izem's quantum system, allowing you to locate his essential being."

"How do I do that?" Ormidtz exclaimed, stepping out of the hut to face Thebitz. But all he saw was the retreating back of the veiled woman.

The woman halted, cast a look over her shoulder and said, "The erasure theory is usually applied to optics, but you can also apply it to acoustics. Try it, it's possible."

Then she was gone, her silken gown billowing out like the sails of a schooner, her brightly embroidered slippers twinkling in and out from under her hem.

δ

Ormidtz returned to the hut and rifled through his databank for information on quantum erasure theory. He gleaned several facts from the files he managed to retrieve. First, under quantum theory, elementary particles could be in more than one place at any given time; they could be anywhere, everywhere, and nowhere. They sometimes behave like particles and sometimes like waves, depending on the observer's consciousness. It's possible that these elementary particles could experience quantum interference if they emanated from the same source or if they had the same or nearly the same frequency. Also, when elementary particles chose an ejection trajectory, their interference pattern wasn't always discernable. On the other hand, if the information path of the trajectory were erased, the interference pattern immediately became visible.

Now, since Izem and Zepar were both inhabiting the same location, he could think of them as particles waves in a state of entanglement. Therefore, Ormidtz reasoned, one way to isolate Izem from Zepar would be to erase the information path that Zepar had taken when he had invaded Izem's mind. The erasure would expose the interference pattern of their two waves which would allow Ormidtz to separate Zepar and Izem.

Not very confident that his complicated logic would work, yet desperate enough to try any tactic, Ormidtz tentatively probed Izem's mind. This time he took the precaution of enforcing at the very outset, Einstein's locality conditions to the scientist's acoustical structure, thus preventing communication between erasure and interference of the particle and the wave system.

The procedure was successful and the connect between Izem and Zepar was disrupted, allowing Ormidtz to effortlessly float into Izem's consciousness. All he had to do now was gain access to Izem's memory cache to pin point the location of his soul.

To do that, Ormidtz first chose to penetrate the left frontal lobe of Izem's brain, probing the Broca area which is normally associated with speech and language. The throbbing and turmoil in this part of Izem's brain were strong but not overpowering. Now adept at manipulating the particle-wave interference mechanism, Ormidtz partially neutralized Izem's acoustical vibrations by ramping up his own, so that, while Izem's sound waves still buffeted Ormidtz's senses, they had lost their potency to immobilize him.

Ormidtz immediately set about isolating the patterns of pitch and frequency which would help him identify the system photons in Izem's brain. As the photon patterns emerged, they indicated that Izem was a linguist and an expert in many languages. Ormidtz easily recognized the threads for Arabic, Russian, French, Spanish and English. But amongst them all was an unfamiliar strand that intrigued Ormidtz for he couldn't immediately place the dialect.

He accessed his own colossal database, digging deep to find something similar. No, the alien strands in Izem's photon patterns didn't quite match the peaks and troughs of Amharic. Ormidtz continued and compared them to Ethiopian Semitic. No, that wasn't it either. Perhaps he should search for an obscure, obsolete language. Ge'ez, could it be Ge'ez? Yes, the waves were congruent with a hundred percent match rate.

He fleetingly wondered why Izem had mastered this ancient tongue known to few and now only used in liturgical language of the Ethiopian Orthodox Tewahedo Church, but didn't spend too much time on the puzzle. He picked up the Ge'ez string and followed it, hoping it would lead him to Izem's soul.

δ

Khulon Reality
Ethiopia

A light breeze stirred up little patches of dust in the landscape, making the length of rope swing gently in short arcs. It was late afternoon and a man, clearly a pilgrim, stood at the bottom of the plateau, waiting to climb up to the Ethiopian orthodox monastery. That long piece of rope was the only access.

A monk squatted on top of the plateau, watching the pilgrim grab the rope and hoist himself up. A moment later he heard a thud followed by a sharp cry of pain. The monk wasn't surprised. Other than the acolytes and priests, few people succeeded in shinning up the rope to the monastery at first attempt. The climb was a test to see how committed and determined a pilgrim was to reach the monastery. The monk shook his head sadly as the pilgrim limped away. He hoped it was just a badly bruised leg.

The monk walked to the ledge and tested the rope to make sure it was still strongly knotted around the tree stump at the top of the mesa. He was astonished to find there was only a short length of the rope left, its edges badly frayed. How did an almost new rope become frayed so soon? He would check it out later, but right now he must fetch the new rope that had recently been donated by a farmer from a neighboring village. He must replace the broken rope at once because some acolytes were due to return to the monastery soon.

δ

Zenad Reality
India

Ormidtz rode the Ge'ez waves through Izem's brain, surfing a stormy sea that had neither shore nor horizon. He plunged deeper into Izem's mind, stripping away layers of consciousness, searching for the quantum optical gateway that would lead him to the secret hiding place of Izem's essence. But nothing surfaced, nothing at all.

Ormidtz again searched for the gateway, and again and again, but each time had to exit without finding the all-important opening.

Exhausted, frustrated, Ormidtz appealed to Izem wherever he was at that instant of time. "Show me, Izem, take me to your place of refuge, to your sanctuary."

There was a faint response, but Ormidtz's nerves, taut to the point of snapping, failed to immediately register the miniscule change in the amplitude of Izem's wavelength.

Then out of nowhere the old beggar woman's voice rang out, "If you wish to gain the advantage, you must first relinquish power."

Her words echoing in his ears, Ormidtz forced himself to reduce the tension binding his system, making him more receptive to external forces. More relaxed, he could now discern interference cutting into his own electrical vibrations, altering their composition. As his system became more sensitive to the new frequency, Ormidtz began to notice more changes in his environment. The magnitude of Izem's wave crest had amplified by a factor of two, which could only be possible if the super-position of quantum interference had been initiated by Izem himself.

Ormidtz had asked, and Izem had complied. But now terror gripped Ormidtz as the rapid magnification of their combined wavelengths propelled him towards a quantum leap into a new Reality. Ormidtz suddenly realized that the interference could cause his physical system to behave like photons, the elementary particles of light. If that happened, the photons associated with him could cross his own initial trajectory from Zenad and place him simultaneously in two different Realities. This splitting of direction could plunge him into an abyss from which he may never escape. But it was too late to change direction. He had chosen to follow the Ge'ez string and must now accept the consequences.

His faith in his choice bore fruit. Ormidtz didn't have to face a split in the direction of his trajectory, for Izem had successfully availed of the hybrid path-polarization technique to block communications between erasure and interference. He had taken Ormidtz with him, and transitioned safely into Khulon, their new Reality.

Just as a quantum particle appears, and within a nanosecond disappears, to reappear at a different location, not as a particle but in the form of a wave, in the same way Izem and Ormidtz disappeared from Zenad to reappear in Khulon in forms so altered as to be unrecognizable in the Zenad Reality.

δ

Khulon Reality
Ethiopia

The aura and the ambience of the new Reality was familiar to Ormidtz for his reincarnation and evolutionary passage had transported him to Khulon in another lifetime. In spite of that, he didn't recognize the location where the quantum leap that he had taken with Izem as a last resort for finding Izem's essential being, had brought him.

In unfamiliar surroundings, he now stood at the bottom of a rocky mountain with a group of pilgrims and tourists, listening to a tour guide extol the wonders of cave churches in Ethiopia. So Izem had steered him to the cradle of an ancient civilization, to the land of Solomon and Sheba, the land of rock monasteries, and the resting place of the Arc of the Covenants as claimed by the guide. This was a land where high plateaus exposed by eons of soil erosion dotted dusty, arid expanses. This was a land where ancient, intricately carved granite obelisks stood like tall, narrow buildings complete with windows, doors and locks. This was the land of the archaic Ge'ez language.

The guide pointed to the top of the mesa where a cave monastery was barely visible. It was the destination for the little group, the only way to the crest being a zigzag path across the steep rock face. Ormidtz noted an occasional niche which provided a hand or a foothold to ease the climb, but any progress up the steep incline would depend entirely on the physical fitness and the determination of the climber.

The guide led the way, leaping across the rocks like a mountain goat. The others followed, gasping and panting, slipping and sliding, until they hit the level ground at the top.

After giving them a few minutes to catch their breath, the guide waved them towards a low and narrow doorway, obliging anyone entering the church to make obeisance and pay homage to the holy spirits that dwelt within.

The group gathered together in a spacious, centuries old hall carved into the rock, the cool interior a welcome change from the heat and dust outside. The rough-hewn walls were covered with primitive art frescos depicting the lives of saints. Here and there, niches and ledges held piles of human bones, stained dark ivory by the patina of age.

The spiritual aura in the church was palpable, and Ormidtz allowed it to pervade every element in his body. He found the aura to be as strong as that he had sensed in the Sufi shrine in Agra, and in the Benedictine grotto in Subiaco.

But he couldn't detect Izem's presence. Why had Izem led him to this monastery?

Puzzled and distracted, Ormidtz only half listened to the guide's lengthy litany about the Ethiopian orthodox church and its history, letting his eyes explore his surroundings. He noticed a short passage leading away from the hall towards the interior, and stepped forward to take a closer look.

The guide, who kept a close eye on his charges immediately called out, "Sir, you cannot go there. That path leads to caves reserved for hermit monks who pray and meditate in solitude."

"Do tell us more about the hermit monks. They sound fascinating," a tourist with an Australian accent urged the guide.

"Hermit monks lead a very austere life," replied the guide obligingly. "Once they enter a monastery, they never leave the premises. They communicate only with God Almighty and have no interaction with human beings. Their basic needs are provided by other monks and acolytes, but even they seldom lay eyes on the hermits. Food and clothing for each of them are usually left at the mouth of his cave, which the hermit monk collects at his own convenience."

"What happens when a monk passes away? Are they left inside the cave?" asked another curious tourist.

"When a hermit monk dies, his body is prepared for burial and then laid to rest in rock catacombs which form part of the church. After several years, the bones of the most saintly amongst them are collected and placed in open tombs in different parts of the church," explained the guide.

"Oh yes," the tourist said, "We did see some of them in the hall."

"We have seen all that we can in this church, and it's time to leave," the guide announced. "We will visit another monastery tomorrow."

The group of tourists, chattering and shuffling towards the doorway, created enough of a diversion to give Ormidtz opportunity to slip unseen into the short passageway he had seen earlier.

He darted down the path and stepped into space.

δ

Half-paralyzed from shock, Ormidtz slithered down the rough cliff face, his scream of terror carried away by the wind into the arid landscape where none could hear it. As he crashed into protruding edges of rocks, he tried not to think about his shattered bones when his body would hit the hard ground below. To reduce the impact of the trauma and dull the ensuing pain, he twisted his body towards the cliff face and began to detach his mind from his body.

Just as he was about to embark on his meditation, his descent was abruptly slowed. A branch of dry brush, its roots clutching a large rock like the tentacles of an octopus, had broken his fall. Ormidtz grabbed at the flimsy outgrowth to arrest his fall, but lack of soil nutrition and the dry desert air didn't provide the spindly plant a strong anchor to the rocky face of the cliff, and Ormidtz found his lifeline dangling in his hands. With nothing more to interrupt his fall, he continued to plummet, jagged ends of stones, sharp as flints, slicing open his skin, and streaking his face and hands with blood.

"Why did you bring me here, Izem?" Ormidtz groaned. "Where are you?"

Even as his anguished cry escaped into the air, Ormidtz crash-landed on a wide ledge at the mouth of a cave. Relieved to be on solid ground and anxious to get away from the terrifying cliff edge as quickly as possible, he scrambled into the dusky cave on hands and knees. Inside, he gingerly lifted his battered and bruised face to find himself looking directly into something red and beady glittering in the dark. The light disappeared as mysteriously as it had appeared, leaving Ormidtz to wonder if he had seen a small animal with reflective eyes, or was it his imagination and he was hallucinating after his fall. On the other hand, like the lunar moth, the glowing red lights could be a beacon leading him to Izem's essential being.

Ormidtz peered into the gloom, but there was no longer any sign of the shimmering red light. The cave didn't appear to be very deep and seemed empty, making him wonder if it was worth exploring. Just then his ears caught the sound of clawed feet clattering against stone, and he decided to follow the noisy signal, groping his way through the dimly lit cave.

After taking a few steps into the cave, he came to a sudden halt as he felt the sole of his right boot step on something soft. Peering hard, Ormidtz barely made out the silhouette of a monk completely draped in white, the ends of his robe pooling out in a circle behind him. The monk was seated on the rocky ground, his back towards the mouth of the cave, and facing a crude stone altar adorned with a simple wooden cross. Once he realized that he had inadvertently stepped on the monk's robe, Ormidtz hastily removed his foot, apologizing under his breath. The monk appeared to be in deep meditation and totally unaware of Ormidtz's intrusion.

About to retreat out of the cave, Ormidtz again heard the scraping of clawed feet against the stony ground. He glanced down to see a rock hyrax staring at him with red, malevolent eyes that looked frighteningly familiar. The rodent scuttled up his arm, digging its sharp claws into his shoulder and back. Ormidtz cried out in pain, and twisted around in an effort to brush the animal off his back. He made a grab at it making his attacker squeal in fright.

As the creature perched on his back, a harsh, grating voice whispered, "You are once again saved, because you are in a sanctified spot where I'm unable to deliver any deadly harm to you. But I warn you, abort your mission and return to your Reality. You still have time."

"Why can't you leave me alone, Umani?" Ormidtz said in fear and frustration, "I cannot, will not, give up now. I have found Erlang and Ruari. I know I will also find Izem."

"You will not find Izem here, nor will you find him

anywhere else." And the hyrax scaled down his arm, its sharp talons tearing into Ormidtz's flesh from shoulder to elbow.

"You will fail, you stubborn human. You are naive and ignorant of the scope of my powers," hissed Umani and was gone.

As blood seeped through his fingers, Ormidtz realized that Umani was right about one thing. Izem was not here. He shouldn't therefore waste any more time in this monastery, but look for Izem elsewhere. But where?

Undecided where he should go next, Ormidtz turned towards the entrance of the cave and started to crawl out, when he sensed, rather than saw, a slight shift in the monk's meditative posture. He glanced over his shoulder to see the hermit looking at him, the cross held up in benediction.

"Search for the monastery with the hanging rope," a gravelly voice spoke in Ge'ez.

Ormidtz whispered a grateful thanks, "Yekeniyeley, Abune," and crept silently out of the cave.

δ

It was a calm day and with no wind blowing, there was little dust in the air. A long, slow mule ride had brought Ormidtz to the foot of yet another mesa. He had spent several Khulon days trying to locate the monastery-with-the-hanging-rope where, according to the hermit monk, he would find Izem. With the help of locals, he had visited many cave monasteries, some placed in the bottom of ravines, some at the top of mountains, but none had any rope hanging from it. This, the last monastery on his list, had a church spire protruding from a rocky crest, and a thick new rope hanging from the top to the ground level. This had to be the place and Izem had to be here.

Jumping off the mule, Ormidtz grabbed the end of the access rope and hoisted himself up the nearly smooth side of the cliff, trusting that he wouldn't be overtaken by vertigo and nausea before reaching the top. As he pulled himself up, one hand above the other, he noticed the occasional notch hewn into the rock which helped him get a foothold in the more treacherous sections. He was halfway up the tor when a sudden gust sent the rope swinging like a pendulum. His hands gripped the rope tightly, knuckles pale blobs on his tanned skin, as his body hit the sides of the tor in brutal lunges, tearing open his earlier wounds. He shut his eyes to overcome his fear of heights, having no doubts that Umani was behind the unusual upsurge of air on a windless day.

If a familiar fear crept up his spine, he also felt elated. Umani had pursued him here, so he must be on the right path. He must be close to Izem.

But his elation was short-lived. The now freely bleeding gashes left Ormidtz weak, his sweaty palms loosening their grasp of the rope. Bleary eyed and light headed, he let go and crashed to the ground. The rope somehow detached itself from its mooring around the tree, and slithered down the cliff face to end in a coil at the foot of the mesa. As his vision cleared, Ormidtz saw a dark silhouette peering down at him from the mountain top. Immobile and vulnerable, he cringed, waiting for another attack by Umani.

Seconds passed. When there was no sign of imminent danger, Ormidtz struggled to his feet and looked up.

"I must come to the monastery," he called to the silhouette.

"I can't climb up because the rope has become detached, and the rock face is too sheer for me to scale."

A reedy voice replied from above, "It's very strange. This morning the rope broke for no reason, and now the rope got detached by itself. Nothing like this has ever happened before, but don't worry, son, I can help you. I have a spare rope, old but strong. Here it comes."

Black with age, long strips of hide knotted together snaked down the face of the rock. Ormidtz grabbed it with both hands and making sure it was strongly anchored above, once again attempted the ascent. He pulled himself up, steadying himself by pushing his legs against the rock. His weakness from the reopened wounds and vertigo again threatened to overtake him. He hung motionless, unable to move. A moment later a slight tug from above reminded him that he wasn't alone. There was someone waiting to help him.

Giving himself a mental shake, Ormidtz swung inwards and attached himself to the rock wall with his fingers and nails. As the rope lost some tautness, the monk pulled upwards, partly neutralizing Ormidtz's gravitational drag. Dizziness and pain slowed the climb, but the push and pull strategy worked, and he felt himself rising. He reached the top and collapsed, his blood and sweat mingling with the dust.

When he could breathe again easily, he rolled over on his back and through a haze, saw a gaunt, ebony face with concern-filled eyes bending over him. By the traditional white clothing and the cross round his neck, Ormidtz guessed the man to be a priest of the Ethiopian Orthodox church, and felt deeply guilty about what he was about to do next.

Mentally apologizing to the unsuspecting monk for the

intrusion, Ormidtz gently probed the priest's mind to search for any knowledge about Izem that it might have cached, knowingly or unknowingly. The solemn surroundings and the kindly face looking down at him, created an aura of safety and sanctuary so that Ormidtz didn't feel the need to take any extra precaution when entering the priest's mind.

He had misjudged. He had barely made contact with the upper layer of the priest's consciousness, when debilitating, high pitched sound interference assaulted his auditory nerves. Too weak from the assault to breach the highly potent firewall, he fell back exhausted but optimistic.

He was absolutely certain that he had tracked down Izem's essential being.

δ

Khulon Reality
Ethiopia

Who is this stranger asking for help? Why does he gaze into my eyes that way? I do not know him and yet I do. He floods me with unfamiliar memories, thoughts and feelings. My ears ring, and a thousand bees buzz in my head.

Lord, is this a burden I will have to carry for the rest of my life? Is this a test of my faith?

Oh, oh, the pain is unbearable. I'm being torn in half. I'm being reborn.

Who am I?

δ

Khulon Reality
Ethiopia

Ormidtz peered deep into the priest's eyes, hoping to uncover Izem's presence. Surfing through the vast database of his memory, he concluded that two things could have happened when Izem's *atman* sought shelter in the priest's body. Either the trauma of Izem's invasion had created a split personality to cope with the phenomenon of two *atmans* vying for residence in the same body at the same time. Or, Izem's incursion had afflicted the elderly monk with gaze-evoked tinnitus. Such a disorder affects coordination between the brain's auditory and visual systems, often causing ringing or buzzing in the ears. Ormidtz decided that the latter condition best explained the firewall in the monk's brain.

Unwilling to risk another assault from the deadly acoustical firewall, Ormidtz decided that indirect contact with Izem's consciousness might be a safer option. He cast around in his mind for an alternative way to detach Izem's *atman* from the monk's body. His reasoning led him to one option, one option only, and an option which he was extremely reluctant to apply.

But he had no choice.

δ

"Abune," said Ormidtz, sitting up to face the priest. "Father, you have spent many lifetimes doing good deeds, which is how you have reached Khulon, a Reality with higher and purer consciousness than Vakin, Zenad and Machim."

"I don't understand what you mean, stranger," replied the

priest.

"I know it's difficult to grasp what I'm saying, Abune," replied Ormidtz, "But please bear with me and I will try to explain the situation."

"Go ahead, my son, I'm listening," said the monk.

With a deep sigh, Ormidtz continued, "Izem is a scientist from the Zenad Reality. He was experimenting with a method of meditation with which he was unfamiliar. He couldn't control the process and the trauma of the raw experience ejected his soul out of his body. Since souls can traverse all Realities, his *atman* took refuge in your body, here in Khulon Reality."

The monk accepted the explanation calmly. Then as if it were an everyday occurrence, he asked, "Is that why I feel so much pain, so much confusion?"

"Yes, Abune," said Ormidtz gently. "When Izem usurped your body with your soul still inside it, you became afflicted with the blight of gaze-evoked tinnitus."

"Is that why my ears ring and bees buzz in my head?"

"Yes, Abune, those are the symptoms."

Then after a pause Ormidtz added, "I need your help Abune."

"I see in your aura that you are deeply troubled and that you are continuously battling fear and despondency," said the monk, sadness and sympathy in his voice. "Tell me, how can I help you?"

"It is not I alone who seeks your help, Abune, but the entire universe and all the Realities," said Ormidtz. "Dangerous elements are out to destroy the human race. Izem is one of the few humans who can help to avert the disaster, but to be able to do that, his soul must return to Zenad immediately and reunite with his body."

"What can I do to help you?" repeated the priest.

"Abune, you are a good and kind man, and I wish I didn't have to ask this of you, but the existence of humankind in all Realities is at stake. It's for this reason alone that I have to ask you to make a great sacrifice," said Ormidtz.

"I'm listening," said the monk, unperturbed, tranquil.

"Right now, there are two souls inhabiting your body – yours and Izem's," continued Ormidtz. "To allow Izem's essential being to return to Zenad, your *atman* must be released so that your body shelters only one*atman* – Izem's. For this to take place, you must unloosen your *atman* from its earthly bondage which means your body must die in Khulon. This will permit Izem to exercise his own free will to transition back to Zenad and unite his *atman* with his body."

"Son," said the monk. "I've lived in these rock caves for more than half a century. I have spent hours, days, years searching for the meaning of life and why it was my destiny to lead this ascetic existence. Today the Lord has answered my questions. Do what you must, and do not mourn for me. I'm at peace and ready to meet my Maker."

The priest's deep faith and devotion endowed Ormidtz with the spiritual strength he needed to complete his difficult task. He stretched out two fingers and pressed hard on the monk's carotid artery. The blockage of blood flow to his brain sent the priest into deep, irreversible coma, freeing the monk's essential being to transition into another Reality – to a higher energy Reality, Ormidtz was sure, for Abune was a true believer.

δ

The monk's body lay crumpled in a fetal curl as dusk stroked the desert, sweeping across the plateau. Ormidtz worked quickly to connect with Izem's essence for without the anchor of the monk's body, Izem's *atman* could easily flit away elsewhere, into another body, into another Reality.

Holding the monk's head between his hands, Ormidtz called, "Izem, are you there?"

There was no response. Had Izem's soul also escaped with the monk's departure?

Pushing back the panic threatening to swamp him, Ormidtz whispered, "Izem, the world needs you. You must return to Zenad. You must save the Realities and protect the Singularity."

More silence.

Ormidtz shook the monk's limp body. "Wake up Izem, you must wake up."

Nothing.

Then moments later faint, disjointed vibrations rippled through Ormidtz.

"Who calls me?"

"Arouse yourself, Izem, we have very little time. You must join Ruari and Erlang in Zenad to prevent universal catastrophe."

"I don't understand. Your words create more imbalance, increase my state of confusion."

But the vibrations, though garbled, were stronger, and Ormidtz felt more hopeful.

"Izem, we have no time. I will explain everything soon. Right now, you must immediately merge your essential being with your physical body lying in a shrine in the Zenad Reality. Hurry."

"Zenad? Shrine?" The communications were steadier and more robust. "I begin to remember. Yes, I was performing *zikr* when I was hit by an intensely powerful ray of light. It blinded and bewildered me, at the same time it made me ecstatic. I was sure I had died and seen heaven."

"It *is* a kind of death, Izem," said Ormidtz, "because the shock of your experience ejected your essence into the Khulon Reality where an Ethiopian monk was deep in prayer and self-introspection. During such intense meditation a person's body and soul are very vulnerable, and your *atman* found a haven in the monk."

"Am I still within the monk?" asked Izem.

"Yes, and you're in a very delicate situation. There were two souls entwined in the monk's body which is a cosmic anomaly. To resolve this, one soul had to be released," said Ormidtz.

"So whose soul was let go?" said Izem.

"Abune, the holy monk, sacrificed his life so that his soul could transition into another Reality, freeing your essence to do what must be done."

"So what must be done?" asked Izem.

"I must guide you back to Zenad where you can be reunited with your body. Only then can you and your two other colleagues, Ruari O'Connor and Erlang Shen amend the mathematical model before the Veil Lifter project is launched. Otherwise the universe and humans are doomed."

"Veil Lifter. Ruari. Erlang. Yes, just before we left on our separate vacations, I recall we had a discussion that, although our results were good, there was something not right with the model," Izem's thoughts coursed through Ormidtz. "We agreed we would work on it on our return."

"Yes, yes," said Ormidtz, now impatient to get Izem moving. "Hurry Izem, you must return to Zenad now."

"How do I do that?" asked Izem uncertainly.

"Exercise your free will," Ormidtz's urgent transmissions sent electrical tingles through Izem. "It will guide you back to your corporeal body which is lying in a beggar's hut in Ajmer."

"How do I do that?" Izem asked again.

"When I sought your help in Zenad, you had used the medium of hybrid path-polarization to lead me here. Retrace that path and it should take you back," said Ormidtz.

"I do recall it. I think in order to retrace that path, it'll be more effective to use superposition of quantum interference to increase the frequency of my essential being. The surge in amplitude should be sufficient to put me on the trajectory to Zenad," said Izem.

"Yes, that should work," agreed Ormidtz.

Several seconds passed. Ormidtz could no longer sense any vibrations emitting from Izem.

"Izem?" he asked.

No answer. Just a faint throbbing against his eardrums like those that happen during fluctuations in air pressure.

"Izem?" Ormidtz called nervously, now deeply concerned that he had lost Izem.

"I... hear... you...," came the reply. "I... I think I'm... on the right trajectory... I... I... have initiated my transition..."

Izem's vibrations faded away, and Ormidtz sat back in relief.

Now Ormidtz must also return to Zenad, but he had to do a few things before he left. He picked up the frail body of the monk from the dusty ground and carried it into the church. He laid it reverently in front of the simple altar, hoping that one day the bones of this holy man would come to rest in one of the open tombs reserved for saints.

Ormidtz then returned to the edge of the mesa. A crescent moon hung low in the indigo sky as a million stars refracted their light through the dry, desert air. He initiated his own transition to Zenad, unsure if he had averted the looming crisis.

CHAPTER VIII

THE BOULDER

Zenad Reality
The Arctic Tundra

The wind howled, sweeping powdery snow into Ormidtz's eyes. Visibility near zero, he tried to examine his surroundings. There was no sign of habitation, just fat snowflakes floating down in deafening silence. The permafrost seemed to stretch unendingly around him, broken in the far distance by what appeared to be hills, or could perhaps be a coniferous belt camouflaged by the incessant precipitation to imitate snow-capped mountains. He couldn't tell.

Thebitz had told him that the Polar Lab was located at the edge of the Arctic Tundra and the Taiga, and he had programmed his transition accordingly. But instead of shifting from the arid, rocky Ethiopian desert in Khulon Reality, to the Polar Lab in Zenad Reality, he found himself caught in a blizzard in this icy wasteland. He must have again made an error in his theta estimate, and now had no clue where he was or if he was anywhere near the Polar Lab.

The sub-zero temperature was already turning his extremities to ice. He wouldn't last long in these freezing conditions and must find shelter soon. His physical body could be seriously hurt, delaying the completion of his mission and he didn't want that to happen.

He chose a random direction and started to tramp through the deep snow, staggering now and then when the terrain beneath the thick blanket of snow became too rough. He lost count of time and slogged through the knee-deep, cold, white powder, one step at a time, until exhausted he fell to his knees and didn't have the strength to stand up again. He lay prone and within minutes hypothermia crept through his body.

As he sank into blissful darkness, his last thoughts were, "Did the scientists make it to the Polar Lab?"

CHAPTER IX

THE GATHERING

Zenad Reality
The Polar Lab

The small chartered plane taxied to a halt at the runway terminus. The co-pilot hopped out and pulled out the small flight of steps for the three passengers to alight. The sky was heavy and overcast with grey clouds, little streams of mist puffing out of every nostril testament to the frigid air.

Pulling her fur coat tightly around her, Ruari was the first to step out, walking gingerly on high heeled boots on the frozen tarmac. Behind her came Izem, quite at home in this weather, having being raised in the extreme climates of the steppes of central Asia. Erlang brought up the rear, his shaven head encased in a massive fur hat, earflaps snugly tied under his chin.

They were led by the ground crew to the arrival hall, each scientist carrying a small bag of personal belongings, as they didn't expect to stay long at the Polar Lab. The well heated arrival hall was a welcome contrast to the chill outside, and the three colleagues directly made their way to the refreshment station to defrost themselves with hot drinks. Steaming mugs in hand, they sauntered over to comfortable looking chairs, waiting for the call to board the helicopter which would carry them to their final destination, the Polar Lab.

Once settled, Erlang and Izem became engrossed in their own thoughts, so it was only Ruari who noticed the sudden rise in the wind and the flurry of snowflakes rushing past the wide windows of the hall. The howling of the wind rose in a crescendo, attracting the attention of everyone in the hall. The three colleagues looked at each other in perplexity, for there had been no weather forecast or warning about a snow storm. Where did the howling wind come from then?

Their consternation increased as they saw a uniformed man, ID card flapping against his chest, approach their little group.

"I'm Captain Rick Holland, in charge of this heliport. I know you are expecting to be flown by helicopter to the Polar Lab," he said looking at each of them in turn.

They nodded wordlessly.

"I'm sorry to inform you," Captain Rick continued, "but due to the freak blizzard, all helicopters are grounded."

"Does that mean we are stuck here?" asked Ruari bluntly.

"When will the storm be over?" asked Erlang.

Captain Holland tried to calm their fears but it didn't help when he said, "It's impossible to predict how long such blizzards last. It can be anything from 30 minutes to 24 hours. Weather here is very uncertain."

"But we have no time to waste," said Izem, "We have a deadline to meet at the Lab."

"I know you are on a very urgent mission," said the Captain, "and so I've made alternative arrangements. I've already informed the Lab of your predicament, and they have sent someone to pick you up by car."

"I don't believe it!" exclaimed Ruari impatiently. "How long do we have to wait?"

"In this weather, if they don't face any breakdowns or other hazards, they should be here in about a couple of hours," said the Captain.

Ruari threw up her hands in typical Italian fashion, and shedding her hat and coat, slumped into a sofa for the long wait.

"I really am sorry," said the Captain, "but the weather is beyond my control. The attendant will bring you some sandwiches and fresh coffee soon." He nodded his farewell and returned to his office to try and disentangle the snarl in his flight schedules.

When the sandwiches had arrived and the three were alone once more, Izem took a sip of his coffee and mused reflectively, "To continue our earlier discussion in the plane, don't you find it strange that all three of us met with accidents simultaneously. Was it a misalignment of planets, or just plain coincidence?"

Ever ready for a scholarly debate, Erlang said, "Rather than calling it a run-of-the-mill coincidence, I would label it synchronicity or a meaningful coincidence. You'll recall that the legendary psychotherapist Carl Jung described synchronicity as events connected by causal lines. He also drew parallels between synchronicity and the theory of relativity, quantum mechanics and cosmology. Why even the Nobel laureate physicist, Wolfgang Pauli, delved into the mysteries of synchronicity."

Before Izem could respond, Ruari interrupted impatiently, "Coincidence, synchronicity, planetary misalignment, they are all hocus pocus, all nonsensical ideas that we need not waste our time with. Instead what bothers me is why the Inter Galactic Security Force thinks there is an error in our mathematical model. What do they know about cosmology, quantum physics and astrophysics?"

"Well," began Erlang, unperturbed by Ruari's rudeness. Both he and Izem were familiar with her lack of interest in anything spiritual, believing in only that which could be proved scientifically. "The briefing that we got from the Inter Galactic Security Force before we headed out here, was very professional you will have to agree."

"Yes," agreed Izem. "The man and the woman who briefed us understood our methodology perfectly and knew exactly what the model could achieve."

"Moreover," continued Erlang, nodding in agreement, "If you remember, before we broke up for our ill-fated vacations, I had mentioned to both of you that I had a nagging feeling that I have overlooked something in the equation. That's why I resorted to ZaZen meditation in the hope of pinpointing the error. But fate, it seems, had other plans," he ended ruefully.

"What exactly happened to you, do you remember?" asked Izem.

"I remember initiating the ZaZen meditation process. I also remember entering an euphoric state and having an out-of-body experience. After that everything is blank. I was later informed that the ZaZen experience was too intense for me and had cast me into a catatonic state. While I didn't die but remained alive, I couldn't connect with anyone around me. Apparently, I just sat staring into space, seemingly into another world. I was fortunate that the Foundation for Future Growth took up my case and sent me to a clinic in Nepal, where I believe I was very well looked after, although I, myself, have no recollection of my stay," said Erlang.

"How did you come out of your catatonic state?" asked Ruari.

"I really have no idea and there was little time for me to find out. All I know is that a couple of days ago, I found myself back in bed in my *uchi* in Stanford. That very day, I received an urgent summons to report to the Polar Lab as the Veil Lifter was about to be launched."

"And you, Izem, what happened to you?" asked Ruari, curiosity driving away her sullen mood.

"My tale is as strange as Erlang's." replied Izem. "I went to India to experiment with the *zikr* form of meditation. While performing *zikr*, I remember a blinding light and a feeling of extreme elation before everything went dark. I was later told that I had fallen into a faint, which apparently is not uncommon during *zikr*. I don't know what else transpired, but like Erlang, a couple of days ago I found myself back in my faculty housing at the University. I too received my marching orders to get to the Polar Lab asap, and had no time to find out the details of my recovery."

"My story is far less strange than either of yours," volunteered Ruari. "I fell off my horse, hit my head on a stone bridge, and not unsurprisingly, slipped into a concussion induced coma. My family admitted me to an excellent hospital in Subiaco. As often happens with comatose patients, I came out of my coma one fine day, perfectly hale and hearty to the relief of my doting parents. So there is no mystery behind my coma and recovery. Then like you, I was summoned to the Polar Lab."

"Well," said Erlang, "The series of odd accidents has delayed the project considerably, whittling down the time left to launch the project. We'll have to work fast to isolate the error."

"Why is it so important to find the error?" asked Izem. "After all, if the project fails, all that will happen is that uncovering the bottomless pit of cheap energy will be delayed or will remain a distant dream."

"Come to think of it," said Ruari, "the Inter Galactic Security Force never gave us any good reason for the urgency in finding the error."

"Izem is right," agreed Erlang. "I don't see any catastrophe occurring even if there is a mistake. Nonetheless," he added, "we are scientists and should not be satisfied with sloppy work. We should look for the error as soon as we get to the Lab. After all, we should try to be hundred percent sure that the project will not trigger any negative impact."

"If we ever get to the Lab in these weather conditions," grumbled Ruari, adding, "And all said and done, I'm confident that I didn't make any mistakes in my calculations."

"Sometimes one can't see the tree for the forest," said Izem, wagging his head in mock sagacity.

Ruari's unladylike, derisive snort was interrupted by a blast of cold air as two young men rushed through the heliport lobby door.

Paul and Raj, already covered in a thick layer of snowflakes during the short path from the car to the entrance of the waiting room of the heliport, whooshed in as the door slid open. Shaking themselves like puppies to dust off the flakes, the two men looked around the waiting room. People were sitting, standing, eating or sleeping, depending on the individual mood.

"There, in that corner, the red head, the monk and the Central Asian guy. Do you think they are our trio?" asked Paul.

"Don't be so disrespectful," admonished Raj. "They are the creators of the mathematical model for harnessing dark energy from black holes."

"Yes, yes, I know," said Paul, "But do you think they are our passengers?"

"Since all the others in the room are sitting alone or in pairs, and they're the only threesome, I would say that there is a high probability that they are our party," replied Raj in a sarcastic tone.

In agreement that the threesome was their quarry, the two men approached the small group. Paul, with marine-cut blonde hair, pale blue eyes, and slightly overweight, turned towards the woman and said, "We are from the Polar Lab. Are you...?" He petered off, dumbstruck by the flashing green eyes of the red-headed beauty.

"Yes," laughed the red head, used to such reactions from men, but nonetheless pleased. "I am Ruari O'Connor, and this is Prof Erlang Shen and Dr Ameqran Izem. I'm glad that you finally arrived. I'm so tired of waiting. We've been stranded here for several hours because all flights have been cancelled due to the blizzard."

"I'm Paul, and this is Raj," said Paul, pointing to the lean young man with longish black hair, black eyes, and a dusky complexion. "When the Lab learnt of the cancelled flights, they sent us to pick you up. We are astrobiochemists and the youngest members of the team. We're therefore assigned all kinds of additional tasks."

"Not that we at all mind coming to pick you up," added Raj

hastily, for Paul sounded rather rude he thought.

"We're very grateful that you could come," said Erlang. "I understand that the only way to the Lab is either by helicopter or by car."

"Well just any car won't do on this terrain. We have a hummer," said Raj, "And we must be on our way soon, for we have a sizable distance to cover."

The group headed out the door, and with little luggage to hamper them, were soon seated in the heavy transport. Raj took the wheel, and Paul dove into the passenger seat. The others settled themselves in the back seats, the hummer being spacious enough for everyone to sit comfortably.

Visibility was extremely poor, and although Raj knew the way to the Lab as well as he knew biochemistry, he drove slowly and cautiously. The Veil Lifter was due for launching and he didn't want to cause any accidents that could further delay the project.

After they had covered a few miles, Paul turned towards the three scientists and said, "Raj and I are responsible for a very specific section of the Veil Lifter, and so we know very little about the overall model. Could you tell us something about it? That is, if you aren't too tired," he hastened to add.

"We are researchers and teachers. I'm only too happy to talk about it," said Izem, "as are my colleagues, I'm sure."

There were nods from Ruari and Erlang.

"Moreover, it'll help to pass the time," said Erlang.

Izem led the discussion saying, "You do know that the model for the Veil Lifter is based on astrophysics, cosmology, quantum mechanics and particle physics? Theories with which both of you are familiar, I'm sure."

"Yes," agreed Raj from the driver's seat.

"Being astrobiochemists, you also know that space is expanding and undulating like ocean waves," Ruari added.

"No arguments there," said Paul.

"To put it simply then, our hypothesis is that these expanding and undulating movements create the dark energy that we are trying to harness," said Ruari.

"But there's an alternative theory that defines space as a cosmic gene pool or *totusmateria*," Erlang couldn't help but interrupt. "This cosmic gene pool comes in two forms, differentiated and undifferentiated. In other words, one form is matter and the other has no particular form. This theory also postulates that those atoms that form matter remain cohesive through sound waves, so that if the sound waves stop, then the atoms dissolve back into the *totusmateria* gene pool to re-emerge when conditions are right."

Izem, the acoustics expert, elaborating on the concept, added, "The implication is that the universe was created when sound passed through a black hole generating a style of sound very much like Bach's Fugues."

"And you have used this theory to develop your model?" asked Paul somewhat confused by the digression into theories unrelated to mainstream physics.

"No," laughed Ruari, "That was just an aside. Erlang is into Zen meditation, and loves to explore the unexplorable. Izem dabbles in Sufi meditation techniques. They both like to show off their esoteric knowledge."

"Sorry, no more digression," said Izem. "To return to the model, we generally accept the theory that nanoseconds after the explosion of space, matter and antimatter particles were created and immediately began to annihilate one another. This baryogenesis process allowed one out of a billion particles of matter to survive, an anomaly that eventually spawned the universe with its humans, other beings, planets, stars and galaxies."

"We know there is asymmetry between matter and antimatter. But what caused the asymmetry? Why did only one particle of matter in a billion survive? Why do the laws of nature not apply equally to matter and antimatter?" Paul shot out a series of questions.

Izem chuckled, "Those are the mysteries of creation which science has yet to fully solve, Paul."

"And related to all this is dark matter and dark energy," said Erlang, bringing the discussion back on track. "Dark matter, or supersymmetric particles to give them their proper name, are invisible to humans because they neither interact with electromagnetic force, nor do they absorb, reflect, or emit light. These supersymmetric particles, together with matter that is visible to us, make up only a quarter of all matter in the universe."

"The remaining seventy-five percent of matter is made up of dark energy," added Ruari. "Now dark energy is evenly distributed in spacetime and does not have any local gravitational effects. Instead it creates a global repulsive force that accelerates the expansion of space. That's why all planets and galaxies seem to be moving away from earth."

"Don't forget the cosmic rays in this equation," said Erlang. "High energy protons from outer space collide with nuclei of atoms in the upper atmosphere creating more particles, the major part of which are pions."

"Yes, as astrobiochemists we're aware that as they decay, pions emit negatively charged particles called muons. These particles have very weak interaction with matter so that they can travel through the atmosphere to penetrate below ground," said Paul. "Just think, muons could be bombarding our heads right now and we are totally unaware of it."

The burst of laughter in the car was abruptly cut short as the hummer slewed to a sudden stop.

"There's a boulder in the middle of the road," shouted Raj, peering through the swiftly falling snowflakes. "Where did it come from? It wasn't there when we set out."

"If you were driving any faster, we would have hit that mound and turned turtle," cried Paul as his seat belt pulled him backwards, pinning him to the passenger seat.

"I can hardly see in this blizzard. I couldn't but drive at snail pace," retorted Raj. "Come help me move it to the side of the road. We still have quite a distance to cover before we get to the Lab."

"What's going on?" asked Ruari from the backseat.

"There's a boulder in the middle of the road. We cannot skirt it, for driving off the road is dangerous. It is rough terrain and covered in snow as it is now, it's even more treacherous. I don't want to end up in a deep rut in this blizzard. I think Raj and I will be able to remove the rock, then we can continue on our way," said Paul.

The two young men hopped out of the rugged vehicle and jogged to the lump in the road. They moved fast to retain their body heat in the freezing temperature.

Paul who reached the mound first, yelled back at Raj, "Hey, this is not a boulder. It's a man."

"What?" Raj yelled back. It was hard to hear over the whistling wind.

"This is a man, and he's still alive," Paul said in a more normal decibel as Raj caught up with him.

"Why on earth is a man walking around in this weather? This area is out of bounds. How did he get here?" Raj asked, not expecting any answers.

"Shouldn't we just get him out of the cold and inside the car?" Paul said, peering at Raj through the pelting flakes.

"We should, but it will be breaking the security protocol," said Raj hesitatingly.

"We can't possibly leave him here," said Paul. "Come, help me pick him up. We can solve the security problem later."

Raj and Paul picked up the frozen body and deposited it on the rear seat of the hummer. They covered it with a pile of blankets, hoping the warmth would revive the person. Right now that was all they could do.

Back inside the vehicle, Raj turned to his three other passengers and said, "The boulder turned out to a half-frozen man. We don't know who he is and why he was wandering around in this area which is off-limits to anyone not connected to the Lab. Faint though it is, he still has a pulse, so we decided to take him with us."

"Isn't that a breach of security protocol?" asked Izem.

"In a way yes," agreed Paul, "but we will let the Lab deal with it. We just can't leave him out here to die."

There was a general murmur in the car, but it was unclear if everyone agreed with Paul and Raj.

"We must be on our way," said Raj getting behind the wheel. "It's getting late and the blizzard is not letting up. Are all of you okay at the back?"

"More or less," said Ruari. "Since my accident I have

occasional headaches, but nothing to worry about."

"Interesting," exclaimed Izem. "Since my experiment with *zikr*, I feel dizzy at times. I also have strange dreams."

"What kind of dreams?" asked Erlang.

"I dream of places I've never travelled to, but which seem familiar. I also seem to be two people with two very different lives. Very odd," replied Izem.

Erlang too had similar dreams, of having lived another life, but he wasn't keen on sharing his experience with the others. An introvert by nature, he jealously guarded his privacy, and now just commented, "I see."

"Dreams aside, I'm a bit concerned about the stranger you picked up, or rather rescued," said Ruari, addressing Raj and Paul. "I'm sure Professor Shen and Dr Izem share my apprehension. After all, the Veil Lifter is a sensitive and highly covert operation."

"Dr O'Connor, I understand your concern, but I assure you, Raj and I are capable of dealing with him, if he gives us any trouble," said Paul. "By the looks of him, he was in the snow for some time and it will be a while before he's capable of functioning normally."

"I hope so," said Ruari doubtfully, snuggling deeper into her fur coat.

δ

Voices, seemingly from a long distance, washed over Ormidtz. Names floated out to him, O'Connor, Erlang, Izem. The names were familiar. Where was he? He stirred and opened his eyes.

"Where am I?" asked Ormidtz, his voice barely audible to the three scientists in the bench seat in front of him.

"Your rescuee is awake," Ruari called out to Paul.

"Oh, that's good news," said Paul turning around to look at Ormidtz who was sitting up, still wrapped in blankets. "Are you feeling better, sir?"

"I'm still quite cold, but I think I'll be okay. How did I get into this vehicle?" asked Ormidtz.

"You're very lucky to be alive. You not only escaped frostbite and hypothermia, but you also escaped being run over by Raj, here," said Paul, his mood lighter now that it was clear there wouldn't be a dead stranger on their hands.

"You were lying in a heap in the middle of the road, nearly obscured by the blizzard," said Raj as an explanation to Paul's earlier accusation. "Who are you, sir? Why were you walking outside in this blizzard?"

"And not even properly attired for this weather," added Paul, pointing to Ormidtz's light leather jacket.

"I was on my way to the Polar Lab when my transport broke down," Ormidtz improvised.

"That's odd. We didn't see any abandoned vehicle on the way, did we, Paul?" Raj said glancing at Paul.

"The visibility was so poor that I completely lost my way," Ormidtz interrupted hastily, before more inquisitive questions could be fired at him. "I've been walking for quite some time, and can't tell you where I dumped my transport."

Not fully satisfied with Ormidtz's answer, Raj said, "You said you were heading for the Polar Lab? Are you a scientist? I don't think we were expecting four of you at the Lab."

"So the three names I heard were not auditory hallucinations," Ormidtz thought to himself, jubilant that the three scientists had not only found their way back to Zenad, but were on their way to the Polar Lab.

"No, I'm not a scientist. My name is Commander Ormidtz from the Inter Galactic Security Force that oversees cosmic stability," said Ormidtz, passing down his shield and paper credentials to Paul. The cover was a result of Thebitz's ingenuity to explain Ormidtz's presence at the Lab. "The Polar Lab is about to launch a major experiment, and I'm additional resource to ensure that security is airtight during the operation."

Handing the IDs back to Ormidtz, Paul said, "Very pleased to meet you, Ormidtz, and relieved to hear that you are a member of the security force. When we picked you up, we were worried about breaking security protocol. At the same time we couldn't leave you to die out in the cold."

"I am indebted to you for that," said Ormidtz, hoping that he sounded suitably grateful for the rescue, for he knew that while he could be badly hurt, maimed, or crippled, he wouldn't, couldn't, die in Zenad.

"It was fortunate that we turned up at the right moment" said Raj. "I think now that we know who you are, we should introduce ourselves. I'm Raj, and this is Paul. We're astrobiochemists at the Polar Lab. The three other passengers are experts in mathematics, cosmology, particle physics, and astrophysics. They are Dr Ruari O'Connor, Professor Erlang Shen, and Dr Ameqran Izem, world renowned for their expertise on dark energy and dark matter."

Ormidtz looked intently at the three faces turned towards him in acknowledgement. He had penetrated their inner selves and travelled through their minds, but Ormidtz did not have a clear idea of what the three scientists looked like until now. He had never seen Ruari's face because, before he could reach her bedside in the clinic in Subiaco, he had been sucked into the black hole vortex of her comatose brain. He had seen Erlang in the clinic in Nepal, but in his catatonic state, Erlang's features were cast into a mask that resembled more his face as the Shifu in Makim Reality, than what he looked like in Zenad. As for Izem, when Ormidtz had eventually tracked him down, he was in such a disheveled and ill-kempt state, that perhaps even his mother would have had difficulty in recognizing him.

"Please call me Ruari," said Ruari, green eyes flashing as she smiled at him, an escaped tendril of copper hair nestling against the fur hat enveloping her head. He caught his breath. She was astonishingly beautiful.

"I'm Ameqran Izem, but prefer to be called Izem," Izem said, stretching out a hand to Ormidtz.

"Then you must be Professor Erlang Shen," said Ormidtz, turning to look at the scientist. Erlang's penetrating black eyes disconcerted Ormidtz, sending for some unexplained reason, a shiver of nervousness down his spine.

"Pleased to meet you," said Erlang in a formal tone, with a faint incline of his shaved head.

None of the three gave any indication that they recognized Ormidtz, or had met him before. Ormidtz didn't expect them to, for he knew that they would remember nothing of the recent events and the encounters they had had with him. He also knew that although he was pivotal in uniting their essential beings with their corporeal bodies, he himself had little knowledge of their personalities and behavioral patterns.

"This freak snow storm has created havoc with our

schedule," said Izem. "We should have been picked up by helicopter, but the plan was scrapped due to the weather. Instead we have to be ferried in this hummer. I believe we still have many miles to cover."

"I'm afraid that is correct," said Raj. "So make yourselves comfortable, and if you are hungry, you will find food and drink in the cooler at your feet."

As the passengers all settled in for a long ride, Paul spoke to Raj in a low voice, "I tell you, Raj, that Ormidtz fellow is an alien."

Raj shrugged, "You have such vivid imagination, Paul."

"That imagination has often helped me think outside the box, and solve problems," retorted Paul.

"I'll give you that," conceded Raj.

Still whispering, Paul added, "Did you notice his eyes?"

"What about them?" asked Raj. "You are a fine one to talk with your own odd, pale eyes."

"But his eyes glitter in a very strange way. He's not of this world, mark my words," Paul pronounced theatrically in *sotto voce*.

Raj grunted his disbelief and silence soon descended in the car as each became lost in his or her own thoughts.

δ

The Inter Galactic Security Force may be right about a glitch in the model which could cause havoc in the universe. Just before the three of us met with our accidents, I remember having a nagging doubt that we had overlooked something in the algorithms. Now I can't recall what it was. I don't know if I want to pinpoint the mistake, nor am I sure that I even want to prevent the destruction that the Veil Lifter is supposed to cause. For I feel the disaster will help to hasten my transition into a new life of higher consciousness and take me to the place that I dream of every night, that place of peace, quiet and harmony. I won't look for the error. I'd rather let kismet take its course.

δ

I don't know why everyone keeps harping about the error in the model. I'm sure there is none. I don't think we are bound to act on the Inter Galactic Security Force's advice. After all, they are not scientists, and know nothing about cosmology or quantum physics. On the off chance that there is an error, it will cost me my reputation and I will lose all funding for my upcoming projects. I'm willing to gamble that nothing will go wrong. I will not search for the error.

δ

I wish my hallucinations would go away and I would stop feeling as if two people live within me. It's hard to concentrate when parallel thoughts run through my mind simultaneously. I wish the buzzing in my head would stop. I hope the others will make the corrections in the model and avert any disasters because I'm very confused and can't think logically.

δ

I really believe Ormidtz is not of our planet. His golden bronze skin is not out of a bottle, and his strange eyes are not created from contact lens. He seems young and old at the same time. Something is definitely odd here. He scares me.

δ

Visibility is not improving, and I can't increase speed without risking skidding and an accident. I'm getting tired, and hope that we can reach the Lab safely. Ormidtz does seem a bit weird, but I think he's a nice guy. I hope we don't get into trouble for taking him aboard. Another ten miles, and we should be home.

δ

The team is together and the first phase of my mission is complete. I hope these scientists understand the seriousness of the situation and will resolve the anomaly in the model. The Ocyyst Barrier must not be breached at any cost. Hi-neg beings cannot be allowed to dominate the Realities. If they do, it will lead to an implosion of the universe and mankind's positive spirituality will be destroyed.

CHAPTER X

The Reincarnation

Zenad Reality
The Polar Lab

Situated fifty feet below the treacherous surface of the Arctic Tundra, just at the edge of the Taiga in the northern polar region of earth, the Arctic Ecosystem Research Center was an architectural wonder, possible only because of advancements in laser technology that allowed the permafrost to be pierced without ecologically damaging the natural balance of the, until now, uninhabitable wasteland. The site was carefully chosen to preserve secrecy and security, the nearest town being several hundred miles away. Access to the Center, known affectionately as the Polar Lab, was either by helicopter or by a roughly hewn path meandering through coniferous forests. Only those who needed to be at the lab ventured to undertake the arduous journey.

The nature of research being conducted in the Center was jealously guarded, the name of the institution providing the necessary cover. The project, funded privately by a handful of multi-billionaires across the world, was kept shrouded in mystery, only a few people outside the Center being aware of what was being attempted in this formidable region.

Snug and warm, and well protected from the ravages of the icy winds whistling across the snow covered wasteland, Ormidtz sat at a table in the cafeteria which was situated at the topmost tier of the building. The remaining four levels extended below ground.

The cafeteria was at surface level, and was the only part of the complex with windows which overlooked the surrounding snowscape of powdery white stretches dotted with pines, spruce and firs. No animal life ventured into this snowy desert, though once in a while, a couple of anoraks jogged past the window, and sometimes a cross-country skier could be espied, poling his way across the flat terrain. These were staff enjoying some fresh air and exercise during their break, and before once again getting ensconced at their stations in the various labs.

The soundproofed walls of the cafeteria, built of light but highly durable material, were wallpapered with sunlit, bucolic scenes designed to lift the spirits of the hardworking and highly stressed people working at the Center. One wall was dedicated to several TV screens tuned to different sections of the Center while another displayed a detailed map of the complex.

The floor plan of the Center showed a red flag with the sign Shelter at the top left hand corner. Emergency Exits from each floor led to the Shelter, which served as the panic room for the staff in case of explosions, nuclear fallouts and any other major accidents. The cafeteria, conference rooms, and gym, together with all the living quarters were at Level 1. The rooms in the living quarters branched out from a narrow corridor running the length of the building.

The next tier below, Level 2, housed the support laboratories, where preliminary research and tests were carried out. Below that was Level 3, the heart of the Center where the most sensitive experiments were conducted, while Level 4 was the nerve center and home to the principal computer system. It was under heavy security twenty-four hours a day and accessible to only a few, authorized personnel. At Level 5, in the nethermost regions of the complex, sat the Particle Collider atop miles of underground tunnels snaking through the surrounding area like leviathan monsters.

Except for the sleeping quarters, the entire complex was on sound enabled, close circuit TV. Everyone who worked at the Center had triple-checked backgrounds and privacy was sacrificed for the safety and security of the scientists, their equipment and their work. No one objected for everyone was fully aware that the trailblazing experiments to harness energy from dark matter, if successful, would bring them untold wealth and fame. On the other hand, if the Veil Lifter failed, their lifetime of labor could evaporate like snowflake on a child's tongue.

But they were not deterred by the thought of failure. Dedicated to their work, the scientists soldiered on, not resting until their hunger for answers was sated, and then, when craving for knowledge gnawed anew, seeking new frontiers to explore and conquer.

Thinking it prudent, Ormidtz walked over to the wall and studied the floor plan of the Polar Lab, effortlessly memorizing the details. He then helped himself to a cup of tea from the beverage station before seating himself again at his table.

He took a sip of tea and let his eyes sweep over the bank of ccTVs. At Level 3, a score or so scientists, singly or in groups, were concentrated around computer stations, intent on analyzing the disgorgement on their screens. The hum of machines could be heard over the ccTV, interspersed with low voices discussing, confirming, rejecting, and arguing over complex mathematical results. There were men and women of various ages, some very good looking, some less so, but all brilliant in their area of expertise for they were handpicked from among the best on earth.

From the scientists, Ormidtz's eyes travelled to a large panel made of some luminous material that hung suspended from the ceiling and exhibited spectra of galaxies several billion lightyears away. His eyes then slid below the panel down to the array of paper-thin computer monitors which blinked intermittently as codes for mathematical formulae, equations and geodesic matrices streamed like endless tears.

Another bank of monitors displayed three-dimensional images which were being transmitted from different regions of space. On one screen Ormidtz recognized the deep red, brightly glowing pulse of a supernova. On another spurts of blinding blue sparks followed by utter darkness signaled gamma ray emissions. If he looked hard, he could even spot very faint images of galaxies at the extreme edge of space. All this was made visible through highly sensitive radio and optical tele-scopes, technology that surpassed the archaic Hubble Telescope.

His eyes swept upwards again to clearly labelled giant screens, placed high up in four corners of the room, each reporting the status of the project in partner labs in China,

Switzerland, Australia, and Chile. The central and most prominent screen ran readings from the Particle Collider humming contentedly at the lowest level of the building.

Before he could further continue his armchair tour of the complex, he was interrupted by rapid footsteps entering the cafeteria. Ormidtz looked up to see a man with tousled hair, wearing horn-rimmed glasses and an harassed expression, coming towards him with both hands extended.

"Welcome to the Polar Lab. I was told I would find you here. Ormidtz, isn't it? Oh by the way, I'm the Project Director for the Veil Lifter."

Ormidtz smiled at the Director's informal and easy going nature, and taking the proffered hands in his own, said, "Yes, I'm Commander Ormidtz from the Inter Galactic Security Force. I was about to come down to the lab to introduce myself."

"I'm on my break and thought I could get to know you a little over a cup of coffee," said the Director.

"Allow me," said Ormidtz in a somewhat formal tone, as he stepped to the beverage station. "Any particular choice?" he asked. The station boasted a wide range of freshly brewed coffee as well as black, green and herbal teas.

"Thank you," replied the Director. "Kona green coffee please."

He poured a steaming cup and asked, "Cream? Sugar?"

The Director shook his head. "Just black, please. I consider it sacrilegious to contaminate such superior brew with milk or sugar. It destroys the flavor."

Handing over the cup, Ormidtz nodded, "I couldn't agree more." Then cocking an eyebrow at the Director, joked, "I can see you're looking for a quick adrenaline rush. If so, you're on the right track. Green Kona is very potent."

"I know," said the Director. "I need the caffeine to keep me going. I've been able to sleep for only a few hours in the last few days, and don't expect the situation to improve before the launch."

A tea drinker, Ormidtz refreshed his cup of lapsang suchong, the smoky fragrance of the tea competing with the strong coffee aroma. He seated himself across the table to face the Director. At such close quarters, Ormidtz could see that the Director's smile didn't quite reach his eyes and his casual approach seemed a little forced.

But then the man was under tremendous pressure and was obviously running on caffeine-generated energy. Ormidtz reminded himself not to jump to conclusions about someone he had just met for the first time. He must curb his paranoia of seeing Umani behind every face and every pillar.

After a couple of appreciative sips of his coffee, the Director took a deep breath and said, "I'm very pleased that our security system is being augmented by you."

"Thank you, but why do you feel it is necessary to boost your security system?" probed Ormidtz. "Have you recently observed anything out of the ordinary?"

"I'm not sure what's going on," confided the distraught Director. "Uncanny incidents have played havoc with our very tight schedule. Our window of opportunity for launching the Veil Lifter, initially quite ample, had been whittled down to the last seven days of this month. It will be another twenty years before a similar confluence of favorable conditions will enable launching of such a project."

"What kind of strange incidents?" asked Ormidtz.

"Well, first we find a helium leak in the collider here at the Polar Lab. Such a leak is of course possible, but not very probable under our vigorous system of checking and crosschecking every step we take," said the Director. "Fortunately we were able to take care of that problem quickly enough, but immediately after that we discovered a major flaw in the structural design of the collider. It's beyond my comprehension how the team could have overlooked such a slipup in an essential part of the architecture. We lost several days modifying the design."

"Were any of your scientists recently replaced? Or did you bring on new people?" asked Ormidtz, digging for clues for possible sabotage.

"No. It's out of the question to induct anyone new at this stage in our program. We still have the original team that has been working together for the last ten years. Everyone here knows exactly what he or she must do."

"Were there any other incidents?" asked Ormidtz.

"Unfortunately, yes," said the Director with a sigh, gulping down more coffee. "An earthquake damaged sensitive equipment in our partner lab in China so that their electrical system had to be reinstalled. That ate further into our schedule, so instead of a week, we're now only twenty-four hours from launch time."

Ormidtz shuddered mentally. The series of possible, but highly improbable, occurrences, all falling within a very tight timeline, had Umani's signature on it.

"Then again, added to all that, is the flaw in the mathematical model which Erlang, Izem and Ruari must modify before the

Veil Lifter is launched," said Ormidtz in a slightly questioning tone.

"Um, yes," the Director replied doubtfully. "That's what we were told, but I'm not very convinced that the model has any error in it."

"Why is that?" Ormidtz asked, his voice rising in consternation for he recognized that the Director was in denial, and was refusing to acknowledge that there might be additional complications in the Veil Lifter.

Then taking control of himself, he continued more calmly, "When I was prepping for this mission, the Inter Galactic Security Force showed me documents that proved there was an error in the assumptions of the model's basic tangent vectors. This oversight, apparently led to a critical miscalculation in the model's geodesics."

The Director looked intently at Ormidtz. "You're from the security department," he said, "Yet you speak like an expert in the field. How is that?"

Realizing his mistake, Ormidtz back pedaled furiously. "The Veil Lifter is a groundbreaking project with wide ranging implications for the universe. If it fails, it could destroy humankind, earth and even the galaxies. So to ensure maximum security, the Inter Galactic Security Force insisted I complete a crash course on the project details." Then he added as further explanation, "I have a photographic memory, so I remember all I learn."

"Yes, we too were briefed about the flaw, but I'm not convinced that there is one. Nor do I think we face any danger," the Director repeated, waving a hand, dismissing Ormidtz's concerns.

"What makes you so sure?" asked Ormidtz, keeping in check his fear and frustration at the Director's stubborn attitude.

"I'm sure because we've conducted endless tests which by now would've highlighted discrepancies and defects in the model if there were any," the Director said with exaggerated patience.

"You could of course be right," conceded Ormidtz. "On the other hand, I'm sure you will agree that it's entirely possible that the errors could have gone undetected, because the tests were performed within a simulated environment that gave you theoretically plausible results."

"The results have been proven to be both empirically and theoretically correct," the Director insisted forcefully, visibly annoyed that a layman would presume to argue with an expert in the field of particle physics.

But too much was at stake and Ormidtz refused to back down. "Even empirical tests will fail to expose the deeply embedded flaw in the matrices, if the delinquent vectors, instead of impacting at the particle or sub-particle level, interact at a much broader level. In fact the repercussions can be at the field level, which is most likely the case here," he argued.

The Director glared irritably at Ormidtz. "I don't have time to continue this meaningless debate with you," he said curtly. "I have to go now."

Deeply disturbed at the Director's ambivalence towards locating the flaw in the model, Ormidtz stared at the Director's receding back. Could Umani have somehow engineered the various mishaps to compress the window of opportunity, drastically reducing the time available for amending the mathematical model? Was the Director, consciously or unconsciously, being manipulated by Umani to ignore the dangers?

Filled with unease, Ormidtz turned back to the ccTV panels on the cafeteria walls to monitor the progress of the three scientists he had rescued. He was just in time to see Ruari and her team settle down at their computer stations. Her exquisite profile was clearly visible, and even at this distance he sensed a strong attraction, the same allure he had felt when he had held the lunar moth in the Etruscan burial grounds. He couldn't explain the magnetism then, nor could he put a finger on it now. All he knew was that Ruari reminded him of someone he had known, a long, long time ago, in another lifetime, in another Reality.

He took his eyes off Ruari and gazed out the window at the snowscape. As he often did, he once again let his mind wander back to the days of bitter anguish and rapturous joy.

δ

I remember my Megan. I remember how I watched her transition into another Reality while I had to bide my time in Zenad. I know that when we next meet, if we ever do, she will recall nothing, and will not recognize me. But I, I who remember every lifetime that I've ever lived, will know who she is and will recall everyday of our briefly shared destiny.

But will I be able to recognize my Megan if she is encased in another body, or takes another form?

The more I think about it, the more certain I feel that Megan's essence had taken sanctuary in the lunar moth. That is why the little insect guided me out of the treacherous black hole of Ruari's comatose mind and into the passages of the Etruscan burial grounds.

Even now our bond remains unbroken. It remains strong.

δ

Ormidtz was jolted out of his daydreams by the click of high heels on the stone floor of the cafeteria, left uncarpeted so that mud and slush dragged in by snow-encrusted wet shoes and boots could be easily cleaned.

"Hello Ormidtz," Ruari greeted him flashing her infectious smile. "I thought I would take a break. The stress and anxiety in the lab is so intense that you could cut it with a knife. I feel it might trigger an emotional short circuit any second," she exaggerated. She enjoyed using outdated, trite phrases, or, as she called them, vintage terms.

A little flustered at seeing Ruari suddenly materialize before him, Ormidtz gave a lopsided grin and stood up, pulling out a chair for her at his table.

"Chivalry lives," she commented laughingly, pretending not to notice his confusion, a state most men seemed to fall into when they came face-to-face with her for the first time. A volatile and passionate woman, she wallowed in the sexual tension that her presence always created.

"Not many men make these gestures anymore, you know, since for centuries women have been acknowledged to be equal to men," she added jokingly.

"I myself believe that men and women can never be wholly equal, for while they can match in intelligence and spiritual prowess, they are physically and emotionally different. I'm nonetheless more than happy to cede more power to women, but also believe that the virtue of politeness makes life more pleasant, don't you think?" Ormidtz responded.

"Amen to that, especially when I'm at the receiving end of that virtue," was Ruari's smiling rejoinder.

"It's interesting that you use words like amen, yet don't believe in the Tractate or religion in any form." Ormidtz seized the chance to quiz her.

"How do you know I'm an atheist?"

"As a special agent from the Inter Galactic Security Force, it was duty to familiarize myself with the profiles of the more important scientists working at the Polar Lab," Ormidtz replied in explanation.

Ruari seemed to find his answer plausible and green eyes dancing, she laughed out aloud. "You've got me there," she said. "It's just that some words are so appropriate for the occasion that I just keep using them even if they're obsolete and I don't believe in their connotation."

In response, Ormidtz smiled and waited for her to continue. He knew she had more to say about her beliefs.

As if on cue, Ruari postulated, "Do you know there's no such thing as the real world?"

"How is that?" asked Ormidtz curious to know how, the literal-minded scientist could come to such a metaphysical conclusion.

"It all depends on your perspective. From one perspective certain physical truths about the universe are upheld, while from another, these truths are annulled and other facts are proven true," said Ruari.

When Ormidtz raised a questioning eyebrow, she continued. "For example, you could get an overview of the universe by studying its mathematical structure. On the other hand, as an observer living within the structure, your view from the inside would be totally different."

"All this is too abstract for me," objected Ormidtz, egging her on with a smile. He was enjoying Ruari's discourse, as much as he used to enjoy Megan's.

"Well then, think of it this way," said Ruari, her attitude that of a teacher explaining a complex idea to a student. "Physical reality can be viewed in two ways. It can be three-dimensional space where things change over time, like the way you and I experience our lives currently. Or we can think of ourselves as part of a four dimensional spacetime that simply exists, unchanging, never created and never destroyed, to quote a famous mathematician. It's an either-or situation, and those who live inside the three-dimensional structure, can of course never experience the latter version, and vice versa!"

"What you just explained is one way of interpreting the Tractate, wouldn't you agree?" Ormidtz countered in a teasing voice.

She clicked her tongue in pretend annoyance and continued somewhat irreverently, "The theories I put forward to you are scientifically proven results from empirical tests, and have little in common with your frou-frou Tractate. At one end of the spectrum, quantum physics proves that particles are being constantly created, annihilated and recreated, first assuming one form then another, as energy interacts with energy at the subatomic level. On the other hand, cosmology proves that spacetime and motion are two sides of the same coin, and that there's nothing called matter, because matter is just the curvature of the spacetime continuum."

"Do you realize that you've just mathematically postulated exactly what the Tractate states about the existence of the Realities?" Ormidtz asked, unable to curb his laughter.

Ruari frowned and shrugged an elegant shoulder.

"The Tractate is obsolete and has no relevance to modern life," she said, unwilling to even consider that there might be a link between science and mysticism. She flicked a sly look under her lashes at Ormidtz to see how he would react to her provocation.

Then without waiting for a rejoinder, she continued. "On the other hand, we've just begun to uncover some pretty amazing things in the universe. We've found particles like the tachyons that travel faster than the speed of light, their existence falling within the realms of the still relevant Einstein's theory of relativity. Then there's the positron field which moves forward in time and its opposite, the electron field, which moves backward in time."

"So time travel is possible, after all." Ormidtz's teasing tone masked his sadness at her disbelief in the bond between spirituality and science.

Ruari shot him a glance, wondering if he was ridiculing her. When Ormidtz said nothing more but looked at her innocently with his strange eyes, she continued, "Do you know there're things like the zero mass photons that can escape any environment, while at the other end of the spectrum there are virtual particles that possess energy and momentum, but have no physical mass. Mind boggling findings, don't you think?" Her eyes danced, and her voice quivered with enthusiasm as she expounded on her specialty.

"Do you think that these virtual particles being all energy

and momentum but having no physical mass, could be the souls of humans?" said Ormidtz.

"I don't believe such things as souls exist," Ruari said firmly, standing up and scraping back her chair. "Religious leaders created the idea of *atmans* and the concept of heaven and hell, to scare people into doing what they want them to do." After a pause she added, "You just have to put a spiritual twist to everything, don't you?"

Her lighthearted but querulous tone sent a shock through Ormidtz causing him to spill the dregs of his tea on the table top. He dropped his gaze not wishing to let Ruari see the astonishment and longing in his eyes. She had risen to his bait, and had responded exactly the way Megan used to during their late night debates. No matter what arguments he put forward to her, like Ruari, Megan clung to her practical world, refusing to accept that the Reality she observed wasn't the only one that existed. She wouldn't believe Ormidtz when he told her that there were worlds invisible to her only because she was unwilling to develop her powers to open her third eye.

But whatever views she held, they did not stop Ormidtz from adoring Megan just the way she was, with all her beliefs and her non-beliefs. He had always clung to the hope that sharing a life together, he would be able to eventually convince her that the Tractate was true and that Realities existed. But their *karma* did not allow that, and their paths parted far too early for him to influence Megan in any way.

Bringing his thoughts back to the present, he stepped away to fetch a kitchen towel. As he turned to mop up the spill, he saw Ruari clutch the back of her chair and shake her head vigorously from side to side as if trying to clear it.

"Are you okay?" Ormidtz dropped the towel and moved closer to her.

"Yes, yes," she assured him, impatiently waving away his concern for she hated to have people think she was unwell. "Ever since my coma, I'm plagued by headaches and hallucinations."

"What do you see that you don't believe is real?" Ormidtz was anxious to know if she could recall anything she had experienced during her coma.

"Oddly enough, I see moths, dark passages, monks. None of it makes much sense to me."

"Are you interested in entomology? Or perhaps you find the study of butterflies and moths fascinating, like a lepidopterist?" Ormidtz understood why she was having these dreams, but wished to eliminate any chance of coincidence in these visions, whether accidental or meaningful as in synchronicity.

"No, no," Ruari replied emphatically. "My only hobby is riding. These are just random images created by my newly awakened brain cells. My neurologist warned me that it would take me a while to revert to full normalcy."

"Then perhaps you should rest a bit," suggested Ormidtz.

"I have to return to my work," she replied, still standing but not making any move to leave. A pause, and then she added, "Before I return to Level 3, there was something I wanted to ask you."

"Sure," said Ormidtz looking at her expectantly.

"Do you know that all three of us in the team met with strange accidents all at the same time? It's rather odd, don't you think?"

"Yes, I was told about it," was Ormidtz's brief reply as he

was a little chary about where her questions were leading.

Ruari persisted. "Why do you think these things happened?"

"I agree it's rather unusual but then the world is full of strange happenings and coincidences," he parried, trying to make light of the matter.

"We should have arrived at the Polar Lab more than a week ago. Do you think the delay will have any impact on the project?" Ruari asked.

"The Director told me that since other unforeseen snags have already shortened the time remaining for the launch, the project must now be initiated within twenty-four hours," replied Ormidtz.

"Before we came to the Polar Lab, the Inter Galactic Security Force briefed us about the Veil Lifter, informing us that there's a flaw in its mathematical model," mused Ruari. "But while they spoke very knowledgably about the project, I felt they didn't give any satisfactory explanation about how they came to the conclusion about the error."

"I received a similar briefing," said Ormidtz, "My reading is that the Inter Galactic Security Force was anxious to get everyone started on fixing the problem in the model and didn't want to spend too much time on explanations."

"I don't know," said Ruari doubtfully.

"Anyway, now that all three of you are at the Polar Lab, you can easily make the corrections in your model and the project can be launched within the timeframe."

"But there cannot be any error in the model. I don't make mistakes," Ruari replied indignantly.

"Really?" asked Ormidtz incredulously. "You've never made any mistakes in your life?"

"Not in my work, I haven't. My reputation is built on the accuracy of my calculations," she said with an arrogant toss of her head which she immediately regretted. Overtaken by vertigo she dropped in a near swoon. Ormidtz, already standing close by, caught her in his arms. She smelled deliciously clean and fresh with a faint trace of African violets wafting around her. Her scent, her closeness, overwhelmed him. Unable to control himself, he crushed her body to his and kissed her, first gently then escalating to a passion that was rough and demanding.

Initially surprised, Ruari pressed back eagerly, returning kiss for kiss for she too had been attracted to him from the time he woke up in the hummer. Coming out of her dizzy spell, Ruari fluttered open green eyes and whispered incoherently, "Your eyes are golden, they glitter, they're deeper than the ocean. I feel I know you. Why? Who are you?"

Ormidtz experiencing carnal desires after eons, savored the moment, not willing to let it go. The pleasures of the body often overtake reason even of the most rational minds, and he found he couldn't stop, didn't want to stop. He kissed her long and hard, his fingers digging deep into her silky red hair, his mouth travelling down to the sensitive spot behind her ears, then retracing a path to her eyelids, brows, to again fasten itself on her throbbing, inviting lips. He had Megan in his arms once again and didn't want to let her go.

"Who are you?" Ruari sighed again, her voice barely audible. A part of her wished to meld into him, but another part, sensing some deep danger, wanted to rein her in. She ignored the warnings and clung to Ormidtz, running her fingernails through his flowing silver hair, tracing his facial features with her fingertips, feeling the smoothness of his strange golden skin.

The eternity of the moment brought the world to a standstill.

Then suddenly aware of what he was doing, Ormidtz released his hold and gently pushed her away. He reminded himself that over his many lifetimes, he had managed to reduce his bodily wants so that he could transcend to higher and purer states of consciousness. If he wanted to return to Waara, he should not, could not regress to a lower state of existence. No matter how much he desired Ruari, (or was she Megan?), he must restrain himself.

His glittering eyes turned opaque, emotionless as he stepped away from her. Trying to play down what just happened, he said casually, "Another dizzy spell?"

Ruari, who was usually in control of any situation, was still confused. Breathing hard, her mouth seductively open, she nodded wordlessly, unable to take her eyes off Ormidtz.

Ormidtz felt drawn to her like a magnet as he felt himself succumbing to the spell of her deep green eyes. He leaned forward to pull her against himself once more when a kitchen staff walked into the cafeteria to replenish the beverages.

Ormidtz immediately stepped back and defusing the palpable sexual tension between them, crooked his elbow towards her and said in a light tone as if nothing had happened, "Come, I'll walk you to the lab. I need to be there myself."

Seeming to awaken from a dream, Ruari turned away rudely, rejecting Ormidtz's help. In total denial that she was more strongly attracted to Ormidtz than she had ever been to any man she had known, and furious with herself for not being the first to move away, she angrily straightened up. It was her second mistake. Still lightheaded, the abrupt movement made her sway on her high heels like a skyscraper hit by an earth-quake.

Forced to accept that she was yet to fully recover from the ordeal of her coma, Ruari grudgingly allowed herself to take Ormidtz's elbow. She didn't slip her arm through his, instead she placed her hand on his, creating a wide gap between their bodies which kept him at arm's length. Feeling like an eighteenth century gentleman, Ormidtz hid his amusement and imagined he was escorting his crinolined partner to a grand ballroom to dance the stately minuet.

Even as he mentally ridiculed the situation between them, Ormidtz sadly concluded that Ruari's arrogance and indifference would be major obstacles to her spiritual evolution, confining her rebirths to the Zenad Reality for any number of reincarnations. He was disappointed in her because Ruari had the potential to reach any goal she set herself and could easily evolve to high levels of pure consciousness.

At the same time, he ruefully admitted to himself that in spite of Ruari's spiritual vacuum, he was mesmerized by her beauty and sharp intelligence which once again made him compare Ruari to Megan. Ruari's over-confident and rather brusque nature couldn't be more different from Megan's soft, kind personality, yet at times, Ruari's attitude towards spiritualism was identical to Megan's. Ormidtz couldn't dispel the notion that it was possible that Ruari was Megan's reincarnation.

But if Ruari was Megan, why had Megan's character changed so radically?

CHAPTER XI

THE VEIL LIFTER

Zenad Reality
The Polar Lab

Side by side Ormidtz and Ruari walked into Level 3 to hear Raj's frantic shout, "Director, the Flinders monitor has gone dark."

Pandemonium broke loose in the relatively quiet room. Men and women manning the many stations started talking simultaneously, their voices rising in a crescendo of whats, hows, whys, and not-agains.

Over the din, Ormidtz heard the Director swear loudly, "In the name of the Tractate, what on earth is going on? There cannot be another glitch. Paul, contact Flinders Lab immediately."

"Yes, sir, I'm already on it" said Paul, moving swiftly, in spite of his girth, to the secure satellite communication console that connected the Polar Lab to Flinders Island. The sparsely populated, remote island in the South Pacific was the location of one of the partner laboratories set up in collaboration with

Australia and Tasmania. But right now, the Flinders Island screen was hazy with random, disjointed pixels dotting its surface. No images, no codes, no communication, only sharp static puncturing the air.

Raj joined Paul and both worked feverishly, pressing knobs and punching computer keys to activate the emergency radio satellite that would get the monitor dedicated to the southern hemisphere online again. The tension and stress in the lab was as viscous as molasses. Fame and reputations hung on the line, not to mention the loss of billions of dollars of investments.

The Director, no longer trying to hide his anxiety, lost his calm, and shouted, "We really don't need any more delays. Unexpected and bizarre obstacles have hit us from every direction. Flinders Island is the last straw. I'm going ahead and initiating the pre-launch procedures before anything else breaks down."

Leaving the Director to deal with the crisis, Ormidtz and Ruari hurried over to Izem and Erlang.

But the Director had followed them and now asked the little group, "How much time do you need to remove the glitch, if there's any at all?" asked the Director, shooting a sidelong glance at Ormidtz.

"Another two hours or so, would be my guess," said Ruari, settling down at her console.

"That's out of the question," the Director announced. "We're out of time and I'm launching the Veil Lifter as soon as Flinders is operational. I cannot risk any more delays."

Alarmed, Ormidtz intervened, "But Director, it's inadvisable to launch the Veil Lifter while the errors in the model remain undetected."

At that moment Paul and Raj, joined them.

"The Flinders monitor is back on track, and we are currently in communication with all our partners," Raj reported triumphantly to the Director.

"Perfect," pronounced the Director. "Now go ahead and start the launch sequences." Then turning to the three scientists, he added, "The sequence procedure will take about forty-five minutes. You have that much time to revise your model."

"But you must wait for the correction," Ormidtz protested vehemently. "Ruari, Erlang, Izem, please explain the consequences to the Director."

"If there is an error in the model," Ruari dutifully replied, "The Veil Lifter will initiate a quantum fluctuation that will plunge the Higgs Field into a lower energy state."

"If that happens, then under the principles of Chaos Theory, there's a high probability that the sudden, discrete change of state could end in catastrophic disaster," concluded Erlang.

"Furthermore," added Ormidtz, "If the fluctuation creates a breach in the Ocyyst Barrier, all evolutionary processes will grind to a stop, and all fields of thought, the core input and output of creation, will be obliterated."

"Ocyyst Barrier? What's that?" asked Paul.

"It's said to be the firewall at the edge of space that separates regions dominated by antimatter and hi-neg particles from the rest of space," explained Izem.

"You see, fractions of seconds after the explosion of space, often referred to as the Big Bang, equal parts of matter and antimatter particles were created which began to annihilate one another," Erlang took up the thread.

"As we mentioned in the hummer on our way here, for

reasons as yet unknown, the baryogenesis process allowed one out of a billion particles of matter to survive. This anomaly eventually spawned the universe with its humans, other beings, planets, stars and galaxies," Ruari added absentmindedly, her eyes on her console.

"The theory is that after the explosion of space, equilibrium was maintained simply because cosmic inflation swept the antimatter particles, pairs to the surviving matter particles, behind the Ocyyst Barrier," said Izem.

"I'm beginning to get the picture," mused Raj. "So, if the Ocyyst Barrier were breached, the influx of anti-matter interacting with ordinary matter would annihilate both, releasing high energy gamma rays. The asymmetry of the universe, which paradoxically keeps the universe stable, would be destroyed."

"But if that happened, a phenomenal amount of energy would be released, causing the universe to implode into a black hole. We and the world would be destroyed," added Paul blanching, his pale blue eyes nearly white with horror.

The Director clicked his tongue impatiently. "All this is surmise. You can't scientifically prove the existence of the Ocyyst Barrier, or any of your other hypotheses," he said, summarily dismissing all pleas to delay the launch.

"Even if it's just an hypothesis, I'm still curious," said Raj. "What do you mean when you say 'all fields of thought', and 'core input and output of creation' Ormidtz?"

"You've asked a very basic, but very important question, Raj," replied Ormidtz. Then turning to the others, he asked, "Do any of you recall the Tractate on Enlightened Consciousness?"

"Of course we don't," said Ruari irritably. "It's something we commit to memory as children. We have no use of it later on in life, and I'm sure that like me, many here can recall little, if any, of it."

There was a general murmur of assent.

"Then let me remind you that in a nutshell, the Tractate states there is but one universe with no beginning and no end."

Erlang interrupted, "Ormidtz, do you really think this a good time to discuss abstract ideas?"

"It may seem to you that the Tractate has no bearing on your project, but everything is connected, and you must understand one to resolve the other," countered Ormidtz.

Erlang shrugged and turned back to the Director. "Director, I'd like to backtrack to your argument that a hypothesis remains just a hypothesis until it's scientifically proven to be true."

"Yes, historically that statement has withstood the test of time," answered the Director.

"Very well, Director, but as a scientist you must acknowledge that time-translational invariance can give same results from experiments performed at different points in time," said Erlang. "If that is so, it then follows that mass can neither be created nor destroyed, instead it either takes another form or is rearranged in space. This argument has led us to conclude that new galaxies, supernovae, comets and other bodies are constantly being created and destroyed even when we cannot observe them from earth."

"The Tractate refers to this exact phenomenon when it says that there is no beginning and no end," interjected Ormidtz.

"Leave the Tractate out of this. It has nothing to do with our discussion," said the Director unconsciously echoing what Ruari had said earlier in the cafeteria. "We have experiments and readings that confirm time-translational invariance and its effect on matter, but the existence of the Ocyyst Barrier has never been proved."

Izem interposed, "But Director, it's from such assumptions that we scientists have hypothesized the existence of clouds in space which hide comets and stars. We have yet to find direct physical proof of such clouds, but we know they exist or must exist, because of other observed phenomena and results from our theoretical assumptions and conclusions."

"So how does the Tractate connect to any of these theories, Ormidtz?" asked Raj curious to understand Ormidtz's claims to the spiritual underpinnings of the Veil Lifter.

"The Tractate is a reminder of the seven planes of existence, or the seven Realities," said Ormidtz. "It doesn't matter if you believe in their existence or not. They exist. Like the cloud at the edge of the universe behind which comets hide. Or like the Higgs boson which you cannot 'see' but know it exists because of its impact on matter."

"True," agreed Izem, "Cosmologists, particle physicists and astrophysicists, all accept that the explosion of space created matter by bonding subparticles around the Higgs boson. Galaxies and planets were formed, and later as stars began to explode, they ejected elements which eventually brought humans into existence." He paused, then added, "But I still don't see the connection with the Tractate, Ormidtz."

"Don't you see," said Ormidtz, "Curiosity about the meaning of life has led humans to partially uncover the mystery behind the creation of the universe. But this discovery is only a fragment of the whole, for it's just a piece of shard that humans perceive through warped lenses of the Zenad Reality. The universe that you claim to see around you exists in every Reality, but because it came into being through a different process, most humans in Zenad, because of their low level of spiritual evolution, are unable to recognize or experience these other universes."

"Assuming you are correct, which I seriously doubt, why should it matter to us if there are other Realities? We live and die here in Zenad and that's that," said Ruari in her matter-of-fact voice.

Disappointed by Ruari's continual rejection of the Tractate, Ormidtz chose to ignore the interruption and said, "It's important to understand the Tractate and the role of the Realities to fully appreciate what is at stake today in the context of the Veil Lifter. Most humans and all of you here, believe life begins at birth and ends at death. But that is not the case."

"Are you talking about reincarnation?" asked Raj.

"Well," said Ormidtz, "Consider elementary particles that appear to pop in and out of existence. You don't understand the phenomenon yet you accept it because you observe it in the laboratory. So why can't you think about this now-you-see-it-now-you-don't phenomenon as a particle completing a life cycle in Zenad Reality, say, then dying and moving on to a new Reality. Then, after a while, the particle returns to or is reborn in the Zenad Reality in the form of a wave. What appears to be a nanosecond to the observers of this quantum occurrence, could mean a full lifetime to the particle, whether in Zenad or in any other Reality."

"So you're implying that the phenomenon we observe in particles is a kind of reincarnation?" asked Paul, echoing Raj.

"There are people and cultures who do refer to it by that

name," conceded Ormidtz. "But whatever term you use, the behavior applies to humans as well as to subparticles. Think about it this way. When a human dies in Zenad, only his physical body ceases to exist. His essential being is transported from Zenad into another Reality where he is reborn in some form of matter. In most cases he will not remember his past life, and will believe the current one to be his first and only existence. That's why it is important to repeat the Tractate often and remind ourselves that life or existence in any Reality is but a passing phase, a *maya*."

"And the Veil Lifter is connected to the Tractate, how?" Raj asked, still trying to get a handle on the metaphysical concepts raised by Ormidtz.

"I think Erlang can better explain the fundamentals of asymmetry between matter and antimatter," said Ormidtz, drawing the scientist into the discussion in the hope that a respected colleague may be better at convincing the others of the dangers ahead.

"Well," said Erlang, "We all know that fundamental particles, the building blocks of matter, are governed by four basic forces – the strong force, the weak force, the electromagnetic force and the gravitational force. When space exploded, these forces ejected some of the antimatter into a spatial region behind the Ocyyst Barrier."

"This isolation could explain why more matter than antimatter lingered in the primordial universe, creating conditions for life as we know it," said Ruari. Then annoyed that she still felt his kiss burning on her lips, she added sarcastically, "That is, life in the Zenad Reality, if you choose to believe Ormidtz and the Tractate."

Ormidtz ignored her barb and continued to elaborate on the scenario. "The Ocyyst Barrier forms a neutral boundary between the region of the universe with higher negativity, and the region with the higher positivity. The Barrier ensures balance and harmony in the Zenad Reality, and since all Realities are interconnected, the Barrier also ensures stability of all seven planes of existence. And as Commander of the Inter Galactic Security Force, it's my job to protect and maintain this stability."

"Look," said the Director curtly, "I've given a very patient hearing to your arguments, but I'm still not convinced that we face any real danger here. We've already wasted too much precious time on your hypothetical Barrier, and I cannot risk any further delay. Raj, Paul, please initiate the coordinates to launch the project."

"Before you launch the Veil Lifter," Ormidtz spoke quietly but urgently. "Let me remind all of you one last time. If the Ocyyst Barrier is breached, hi-neg ions will be released, and the entire universe and all Realities will be destabilized. Harmony at all levels will be lost, and the human transcendental mechanism will be destroyed. Hi-neg beings propagate evil. Malevolence and villainy will dominate Zenad and will spill into all the other Realities."

"Let's put aside hi-neg beings and Realities for the moment, and focus on the model," Izem broke in, taking a conciliatory approach to dissipate the tension. "I have a suspicion that the algorithm may have failed to take into account the asynchronous stresses that the magnets in the collider will have to bear. Consequently, if unmodified, the process could generate magnetic monopoles which will pull apart matter, disintegrating the collider."

"Yes, monopoles can cause disaster because they are particles with single magnetic charges at either the north or the south end, in contrast to normal particles which have magnetic charges at both poles," nodded Erlang.

"I think all of you are over dramatizing the situation, creating a doomsday scenario where none exists," said the Director.

He turned to the two young astrobiochemists and barked, "Paul, Raj, start the initiations right now. That's an order."

The Director strode off, while Ruari, Erlang and Izem turned to their tasks to uncover the glitch. They had less than forty minutes to resolve the anomaly in the model.

As the two young men turned to walk away from the group, Ormidtz called to them, "Paul, Raj, a minute of your time please."

They slowed down and Ormidtz ran up to them, speaking in a low voice, "You must understand that the Director is taking a huge risk. But since he's adamant to launch the Veil Lifter without any heed to the consequences, I'm reassessing the situation and the possible options for averting the danger. If I judge that the safety and security of the project personnel are being threatened in any way, I'll be forced to intervene. In that case, I'll need your help."

"I'm not sure how we can be of help, but we'll do what we can, won't we?" said Raj turning to Paul for support.

"Of course," said Paul a little doubtfully, still convinced that Ormidtz was a being from another world.

"But now, Ormidtz," said Raj with regret in his dark eyes, "I'm afraid we have to follow the Director's orders and initiate the launch. He could be right, you know, and there will be no disaster."

δ

Nervous and edgy, Ormidtz let the young men go and sat down at an unoccupied computer station close to the three scientists he had rescued. Trying to still the fear that was threatening to engulf him, he looked towards Erlang and said, "Good luck with your work."

Erlang nodded, then turned to his colleagues, "We have to start working on the problem right away. We have just forty minutes to find the error and stabilize the model."

"Let's not waste any more time. Let's partition the model into three parts, and each of us can conduct in-depth review of one section. I'll look into the matrices," volunteered Izem.

"I'll re-examine the geodesics," said Ruari.

"And I'll take the rest," said Erlang.

As the three scientists turned to stare intently at their monitors, Ormidtz explored his possible choice of actions if the situation turned into a disaster.

It perturbed him deeply that Ruari insisted she never made mistakes in her calculations. At the same time, her unshaking confidence in the model created doubts in his mind about the model being at all defective. Perhaps there was no error and there would be no disaster. But then Thebitz had interrupted his evolutionary transcendence to call him back from Waara. Unless he was absolutely sure, Thebitz would never commit an act that would damage Ormidtz's imminent merger with the Singularity to uncover the Seventh Reality. Having greater faith in Thebitz's message than Ruari's self confidence, Ormidtz concluded that the model had a flaw and would create chaos when the Veil Lifter was launched.

Would Izem and Erlang be able to override Ruari's arrogance and self denial to isolate the glitch in the model?

A shout from Izem interrupted his contemplation.

"Erlang, Ruari, I may have pinpointed the error. I'm at the second tier of the model and there seems to be something odd about the matrix inversions. Would you check them out as well?" Izem exclaimed excitedly.

Erlang replied "Yes, I'll look into it."

In spite of the lack of response from Ruari, Ormidtz became hopeful, watching Erlang closely as he worked. But something wasn't right.

Erlang's eyes were directed towards his monitor but they seemed out of focus. He appeared to be in a trance-like state, his mind clearly engaged elsewhere. Ormidtz was sure that Erlang was mentally absent from the Zenad Reality, but where was he and what had drawn him there?

Watching a tableau over which he had no control, Ormidtz saw Ruari place herself on the same page as Izem and Erlang with a few strokes of the keyboard.

She stared at the screen for a few moments then asked, "Izem, do you mean the inversion of the geodesics matrix?"

"Yes," said Izem. "I think the unit conversions are the culprits. Do you notice anything?"

She shook her head and said, "I developed that section and I don't see anything wrong."

"Neither do I," said Erlang in an absent-minded voice, his eyes still locked in a hypnotic trance.

Ruari gave Erlang a quick look, the sidelong glance not escaping Ormidtz watching them like a hawk.

"I'm convinced the matrix isn't the problem here," she repeated, "but I'll double check the geodesics anyway. In the meantime, Izem, why don't you explore other areas? That'll be faster."

"Let's do that," Erlang agreed readily.

Ruari frowned as she gave Erlang another penetrating look. It was unusual for Erlang to fall in so easily with her suggestions. Always fixated on details, he would normally argue and explore several options before coming to any conclusion. What game was he playing?

With an imperceptible shrug, she returned to her work. As far as she was concerned, she didn't care if Izem had found a glitch but she refused to accept the fact that she could have made such a basic, but critical error, as unit conversions when computing her estimates. Admitting to so fundamental an oversight would ruin her career and reputation. She would never be able to secure funding for all the projects she had in the pipeline.

She therefore chose to ignore Izem's finding, willing to face whatever consequences that might ensue from the faulty model. Maybe, as Ormidtz predicted, the Ocyyst Barrier would be breached. On the other hand, there was always the off chance that there wouldn't be any disaster. The Veil Lifter was a pioneer in its field and no one could accurately predict what would happen when the project was launched.

She felt eyes on her and looked up to catch Izem staring at her, a puzzled frown furrowing his brow. Since he said nothing, she continued to scroll down the computer screen.

Izem swung his gaze from Ruari to Erlang and back again. He was perplexed why both his colleagues, very uncharacteristically, rejected his findings outright without giving him a chance to explain his conclusions.

He was, nonetheless, about to forcefully argue his case, when a voice spoke to him, "Izem, don't interfere. It's all for the best."

"Who said that?" demanded Izem as he whipped around.

Erlang and Ruari gave him an odd look.

"What do you mean? Neither of us said a word," said Erlang.

"It is I, Zepar," the voice in his ear continued. "I took up abode inside you during your *zikr* experience and never quite left."

Izem hurriedly moved away from his colleagues so that they didn't think he had lost his mind and was talking to himself. He found a secluded corner, pulled out a slim, portable communication device and pretended to talk into it.

"Who are you?" asked Izem.

"Didn't you hear me the first time?" said Zepar. "I'm Zepar, the djinn associated with sound, your special area of expertise."

"I don't know any Zepar," said Izem.

"You know me, and you don't know me," came the enigmatic reply.

"Show yourself," said Izem in as commanding a voice as he could muster.

"You're joking of course," said Zepar. "I cannot be seen, only felt and experienced."

"What do you mean?" asked Izem, a tremor in his voice.

A sequence of atonal chords jangled Izem's nerves. "You're an expert in the field of sound. If you search hard enough, you'll recognize my presence in the complex, acoustical equation hidden in your mind."

"I don't understand you. What do you want from me?" Izem asked nervously.

"My advice is don't make any corrections to the model. Let fate take its course," said Zepar.

"How do you know anything about corrections?" asked Izem.

"I know everything you know, and more," said Zepar.

"How?"

"Because I'm in your mind, and I also have my own vast experience," said Zepar. "So, I'm telling you again, don't interfere with fate."

"What fate are you talking about?" asked Izem.

"If the error is left in the model, a cosmic change will occur that will transform the universe," replied Zepar.

"But the Ocyyst Barrier will be breached and our universe will be destroyed," protested Izem.

"Not so, human," replied Zepar in a deprecating tone. "The universe will not be destroyed, only its characteristics will change."

"What do you mean?"

"You sound like a needle stuck on an old vinyl record," said Zepar. "I'll nonetheless answer your question for you really are an ignoramus in these matters."

Ignoring Zepar's rudeness, Izem barked, "Just answer my question, will you?"

"Now, now," said Zepar, "Calm yourself otherwise I may be forced to drive you insane with my sound frequencies."

When Izem was frightened into silence, Zepar continued,

"Ah, that's better. Now, if the composition of the universe changes from being hi-positive to hi-negative, it'll give beings made of fire, like myself, an opportunity to lead the life that humans have led all these eons."

"But excess negativity will preclude the creation of light and all the universe will be in darkness. Surely that cannot be good for beings of fire like yourself?" asked Izem.

"But that's where you're wrong," laughed Zepar, sending unpleasant twinges through Izem's nerves. "Fire is visible in light, but that doesn't mean it doesn't exist in the dark. In the hi-neg environment we'll merge with the gloom and relish life in a dark universe. Unlike you humans who are always searching for light, we hi-neg beings can exist in both darkness and light."

"And I must chose to ignore the mathematical error for your benefit," said Izem. "Why should I agree to that?"

"Because you have no other option," said Zepar with a fiendish laugh audible only to Izem. It suffused the scientist's auditory senses, driving him to the edge of insanity.

Eyes bulging in terror, Izem looked around wildly for someone he could alert about the dangers. He caught sight of the Director striding towards the elevator, and called out, "Director, Director, I must talk to you at once!"

"I can't stop now, Dr Izem," said the Director, "I'm going down to Level 4, but you can join me and we can talk in the elevator."

As Izem and the Director stepped into the elevator, a pale, mist like cobweb flew over their heads and settled on the cab ceiling, invisible against the grey paint.

δ

But for the hum of a score of computers, the soundproofed Level 3 was unusually quiet.

The prolonged silence uninterrupted by human voices prompted Erlang to lift his head and ask, "Where's Ormidtz? I thought he would hang around to make sure that we revised the model before the project was launched."

At the adjacent station, Ruari looked up and craning her neck to scan the room said, "I don't see the Director or Izem either. All three of them are absent. I wonder where they are. At this critical moment they can't possibly have gone for coffee."

"Very odd," commented Erlang. Then turning to Ruari, he asked, "Have you found the glitch?"

"What glitch? I told you there's no error," replied Ruari.

"So you haven't been looking?" said Erlang more a statement, than a question.

"Well, I didn't exactly see you absorbed in the model, either," she retorted.

Erlang focused his deep, dark eyes on Ruari and said, "What's going on with you, Ruari?"

"Nothing," she said evasively, her long lashes concealing her eyes from Erlang's penetrating look.

"Ah", he replied, "So there *is* something bothering you."
Silence.

"We've known each other for many years now, Ruari" said Erlang, filling the void. "You know you can trust me."

Ruari still remained silent.

"Well, since *you* won't talk, can I share something with you?" said Erlang.

Visibly more at ease since the pressure was off her, Ruari lifted her eyes and gave him her full attention. "Sure."

"But whatever I'm telling you is in strict confidence. You must keep it to yourself," said Erlang.

It was Ruari's turn to stare at Erlang. "You're scaring me. Why are you behaving so strangely?"

By now both had abandoned any pretense of working.

"You see," began Erlang, "Ever since I was brought out of my catatonic state, I've been having dreams in which I'm somewhere else, living a very different life. It's a life without stress and filled with peace and harmony. I have these dreams almost every night and they seem so very real. When I wake up, I want to go back to sleep just to return to that idyllic place. I've lost interest in my work and in the life that I experience during my waking hours."

"Where do you think you go?" asked Ruari.

"I feel like I'm in a little village in China. I see green hills. I smell clean, fresh air. I hear the sound of children playing."

"I, of course, don't believe that the soul travels out of the body when we sleep, because I don't believe in the existence of souls," said Ruari. "So I think your catatonia released memories of your own childhood which had been buried deep within your grey cells. The trauma somehow interfered with the layers of working memory, messing up the file retrieval systems of your brain."

"Why on earth do you know all this?" asked Erlang.

"Well, when I came out of my coma, I did some serious research to find out what actually happened to my brain," explained Ruari. "That's how I know."

"Well, to return to your theory, I was born and raised in San

Francisco," said Erlang with a laugh. "Which makes your childhood thesis null and void."

Ruari opened her mouth to answer but Erlang held up a long finger to silence her and continued, "But I did spend a few years of my youth as an acolyte monk at a Shaolin temple in China."

"So my theory does hold water," Ruari said triumphantly. "Those memories are now resurfacing after your ordeal."

Erlang shrugged and said, "Whatever maybe the explanation, the end result is the same. I'm tired of living and look forward to my next reincarnation."

"I can't say that I don't want to live anymore. In fact it's quite the opposite. I want to enjoy life and experience all that it has to offer," said Ruari, a slight blush creeping up her cheeks as she remembered the warmth and urgency of Ormidtz's body against hers.

After a brief pause, and once more in control of her emotions, she confided, "I too have hallucinations and dreams, you know, but my neurologist says it's normal after awakening from a coma."

"What do you see?"

"Oddly enough, moths, Franciscan monks, ancient burial grounds," said Ruari musingly.

"But do the hallucinations feel tangible? Do you *want* the dreams to be real?" Erlang asked.

"No, indeed I don't," said Ruari emphatically. "They're too weird and meaningless."

"That's where we differ," said Erlang. "You want to forget your dreams, but I want my dreams to come true. I want to wake up one day soon and find myself in that Elysium."

"True, you and I are very different," agreed Ruari. "You believe in the powers of meditation whereas I'm grounded in facts and figures. Perhaps you dabbled too deeply, and now can't distinguish between your real world and the imaginary one."

"Maybe," Erlang said noncommittedly and lapsed into silence.

After a moment Ruari prompted, "So now you're no longer interested in the Veil Lifter?"

"Something like that," said Erlang dismissively. Then rousing himself from his contemplative mood he said, "But tell me, Ruari, how do you explain your own lack of interest in fixing the problem in the model? I've been watching you and you've made no effort to review the algorithms."

Ruari hesitated, wondering how much she could confide in Erlang.

Then deciding that she needed an ally, she looked directly at him and said, "I'll never admit that I may have made a mistake in my calculations. I have huge funding waiting in the pipeline for several long-term projects. If any hint of carelessness on my part in a project like the Veil Lifter leaks out, the donors will immediately withdraw their support. My reputation will be ruined and my career destroyed forever. I cannot let that happen."

"What about Ormidtz's prophecy that the error will destroy the universe?" Erlang asked. "Are you willing to risk the end of humankind to satisfy your vanity?"

She stuck out her delicate chin in a challenge and said, "If you think Ormidtz is right, why are you chasing unsubstantial dreams of Elysium instead of locating the error and saving the world? I too have been observing you. You appear to be here only physically. Mentally you're in your Chinese village."

Erlang hung his head, avoiding her eyes. After a moment he said dejectedly, "I don't want to live anymore. I cannot kill myself for that is against my beliefs, but if the Veil Lifter destroys the universe then there's a chance that I might be reborn in my Shangri La."

Ruari stopped herself from giving a disbelieving laugh for she sensed that Erlang was really serious.

"But," continued Erlang, straightening up, "In your case, you'd rather die than admit your mistake?"

"Yes," she replied without hesitation. "Say, I don't admit my mistake and Ormidtz turns out to be wrong. The universe will continue as always after the Veil Lifter is launched and my career will soar."

"And if Ormidtz is right and the universe is destroyed?" asked Erlang.

Ruari shrugged. "In that case, admitting to the mistake will not change anything for we'll all be dead."

"But what if you locate the error, fix the model and ensure the stability of the universe?" argued Erlang.

"In that case," said Ruari, "The universe may be saved but there'll be disastrous consequences for my career. So, as far as I'm concerned, it's better not to admit my mistake and if the universe explodes, then let my life terminate with it."

Erlang sat quietly for a few moments, absorbing Ruari's self-centered but logical, decision-making process. He knew that she could be cold-blooded when her own interests were threatened, but her total disregard for human life couldn't help but shock him. But then, he, himself was no better. He too, wished the Veil

Lifter to fail for selfish reasons, because if the world was destroyed, his own death would come faster and his new life would begin sooner.

"Yes, we each have our own motives for not fixing the problem," nodded Erlang. "So now what should we do?"

Ruari thought for a moment, then said, "I think we should make our way to the Emergency Shelter. If the launch is successful, we can bask in its glory. If it fizzles out and fails for whatever reason, it'll be hard to pinpoint blame on anyone and we'll live to fight another day."

"And if the universe is destroyed?" asked Erlang.

"Well, we're both content to be annihilated with it, aren't we?" said Ruari, with a ruthless look, the iris in her green eyes collapsing into narrow slits. He recognized the look. He had seen that look many times before just after Ruari had solved a mathematical conundrum.

"But I don't want to live another day, and I don't care if the Veil Lifter is successful or not," Erlang said in a faraway voice. "You go to the Shelter. I'll remain here for I don't want to be saved."

δ

From his vantage point at the nearby computer station, Ormidtz watched Erlang and Ruari and hoped they were making good progress in locating the glitch.

Then his peripheral vision caught Izem abruptly speeding towards an unoccupied part of the lab, his portable communication device held to his ear. He appeared distraught as he ran his fingers through his thick brown curls, leaving hair ends sticking out like straw in a scarecrow's head. Why was Izem so agitated? With whom was he communicating? What did he hear to drain the blood from his face, turning him pale and ashen?

Something was very wrong.

Ormidtz hurriedly left his station making for Izem, but changed direction when he saw him wave frantically at the Director. What did Izem learn that he must share so urgently with the Director?

He must find out.

Ormidtz raced after Izem, following him into the elevator where the Director had just hit the button for Level 4. Ormidtz recalled from the site map in the cafeteria that the core computer systems were housed at that level. Always alert to her treachery, Ormidtz wondered if Umani had influenced Izem and the Director to freeze Ruari and Erlang's computers from the main controls to stop them from making the corrections.

"What are you doing here, Ormidtz?" the Director asked roughly, his gruff and impatient demeanor in contrast to his earlier affability, making Ormidtz fear that he could be right about Umani being in control of the Director's mind and body.

Ormidtz improvised quickly. "I have yet to check out the other levels of this vast complex. I'd like to do so now. May I join you?"

"Looks like you already have," said the Director, shrugging indifferently.

As the elevator purred into action, Ormidtz braced himself for the slight gravitational jerk that usually occurs when the machine accelerates for ascent or descent. But he felt no jerk. The car swayed imperceptibly, then came to a halt. No emergency protocols kicked into action and the elevator door remained shut.

Uncertain if this was a genuine mechanical failure or a prelude to an attack by Umani, Ormidtz scoped out the elevator car for an alternative exit. Claustrophobic fear in the confined space was already threatening to overpower him, as he noticed that the Director and Izem had changed their positions to flank him on either side.

His uncertainty didn't last long. Stinging electric impulses from the Director seared through him. "Ormidtz, will you never learn? Will you not heed my words? There is still time. Turn back and let the Veil Lifter do what it must do."

"Yes, let the inevitable take its course."

Who said that? Ormidtz swung his head in the direction of the audio waves. They were emanating from Izem. So Umani had taken control of both the Director and Izem. In the confined elevator cab, Ormidtz now faced a formidable double challenge.

Nerves at his temples twitching with tension, Ormidtz sensed rather than saw, Izem's faint movement as he raised his arm, aiming the edge of his hand at Ormidtz's neck. Ormidtz dodged, dropping to his knees. Izem's hand hit the wall of the elevator cage, the force of the blow puncturing the wood paneling and exposing the steel frame of car.

The Director, while not as agile as Izem, was brutally strong. He moved in and caught Ormidtz in a vicious, old fashioned head crunch that nearly blinded Ormidtz. As Izem pirouetted swiftly into position to deliver another karate chop, Ormidtz dug his elbow into the Director's solar plexus, forcing him to slightly reduce the pressure on his temples.

The momentary release was enough for Ormidtz to half rise and hook his foot around the Director's ankle and send him spinning towards Izem. Izem was thrown off balance, and his second chop also missed Ormidtz. It glanced off the side of the Director's forehead but the deflected force was still powerful enough to knock the Director unconscious. Ormidtz drew in a shaky breath, glad that for the moment, the Director was no longer of any use to Umani as a weapon.

Hoping to nullify Umani's control over Izem as well, Ormidtz took advantage of the brief respite and cried out, "Izem, you're possessed by an evil being. She's holding your mind and body hostage. Concentrate on your inner self, and you'll be able to disengage yourself from her influence. You don't have to be party to her destructive actions."

"I'm no evil being," came the reply from Izem's mouth. "I'm Zepar, the djinn of sound."

Gold-flecked eyes paling in shock, Ormidtz stuttered, "But... but... you released Izem in Ajmer."

"Just because I said I did, doesn't mean I actually did so," replied Zepar. "You used Izem's physical brain to transition into the Reality where his *atman* had fled, whereas I hid in his mind. It was impossible for you to detect my presence."

"Why didn't you vacate his mind and body as you promised?" asked Ormidtz.

"Well, the old blind beggar warned you that djinns sometimes tell the truth and sometimes don't, so a promise from one of us is not binding," came the careless reply.

"Then vacate it now, Zepar," Ormidtz commanded.

"I cannot do that. Like Umani, I want the universe to become transformed so that beings like myself become endowed with free will which we lack. Why should only humans enjoy that privilege?"

"But you're already privileged as a being of fire and light. You have special powers that most humans don't, such as moving through Realities, flying to any part of the universe you fancy. What additional benefit will you get from a hi-neg universe?" Ormidtz asked.

"In a hi-neg universe all roles will be reversed. Now humans aspire to merge with the Singularity which is of course completely denied to us. In a hi-neg universe we, the beings of fire, can aspire to merge with the Negative Singularity," said Zepar.

"Aren't you able to reach the Seventh Reality now?" asked Ormidtz.

"No, that privilege lies only with you weakling humans."

With that disparaging reply, Izem brought the dialogue to an abrupt end. Kicking one leg up from the hip, he aimed his rigid foot at Ormidtz's face. Experience having made him chary of beings of fire, Ormidtz snapped back his head at lightning speed, just managing to evade the lethal blow. Missing its mark, the kick lost momentum, crashed against the elevator wall to land harmlessly on the Director's inert body.

In that split second, using the prone body as a spring board, and Izem's shoulder as a launching pad, Ormidtz leapt up to grab the ventilator grid on the ceiling of the elevator car which he had earlier marked as an emergency exit.

The tips of his fingers white with the effort, Ormidtz curled his knees to his chest and thrust powerfully against the grid, dislodging it sufficiently to slide feet first into the hoistway. He grabbed the governor rope to steady himself, searching for a way to the elevator door at the upper level which he could see a couple of feet above his head.

Just as he was about to take a step, the traction sheave kicked into action and the elevator lurched upward, whining in protest as the machine began to move at an ascent speed that exceeded its safety limit. The hurtling car burst through the ceiling of the machine room and shot out in an arc to the edge of the snow-coated forest. It hit a rocky promontory hidden under a snow drift, the car buckling and crumpling like aluminum foil as it finally came to a stop.

Ejected from the shaft, Ormidtz flew out in a projectile. His martial arts training taking over instinctively, he twisted his torso in midair, landed on all fours and rolled to a stop on top of a small pile of snow. The little mound of soft snow was however, concealing a tree well, and he slid feet first into a deep hole at the foot of a young fir. The last thing he saw before he was swallowed by the tree well was Izem lying in a heap a short distance away.

"Izem will not survive this. Help him, Thebitz," pleaded Ormidtz and lost consciousness.

CHAPTER XII

THE BETRAYAL

Zenad Reality

The Polar Lab

In the quiet darkness, Ormidtz felt himself drifting, light and airy, towards Waara. He felt elated. He was returning to the place where he had found near-perfect peace. He didn't need to face Umani anymore.

But like a balloon tied with string to the back of heavy chair, an unknown force was pulling him back. Snatches of memory tugged him away from Waara, punctured his euphoria. Disconnected words washed over him: Ruari, Megan, tainted souls, entwined fates, chaos, disaster. More disjointed thoughts floated through his mind: The Ocyyst Barrier must not be breached, Ruari's soul must be saved.

The words, the thoughts, shattered his complacency, scraping away the patina of deceptive serenity that was shrouding his rational thinking. Leaving behind the debris of his false sense of euphoria, Ormidtz surfaced from the comforting darkness. Intense pain at once coursed through his body as he returned to wakefulness and the harsh reality of Zenad.

Through the mist of agony, Ormidtz realized that he was buried in a hole. Cold, wet snow blanketed his face but he could breathe, so he must be in some kind of air pocket. This would sustain him while he assessed his situation. One by one he checked the different parts of his body. His thighs and lower legs were trapped inside closely packed snow but he discovered that a gap at his lower extremities allowed him to twirl his ankles. One arm seemed to be functioning, but when he tried to move the other one, streaks of pain shot up all the way to his head, giving rise to a nerve-jangling headache.

The spasm pierced the haze surrounding his memory databank and recent events came flooding back. Judging by his predicament, Ormidtz concluded that when he was ejected out of the elevator cab, he had been propelled, feet first, into a tree hole in the snow-covered terrain outside the Center. Ormidtz recalled that the Director and Izem had also been in the elevator with him and both of them might have been seriously injured from the explosion. It also meant that if the Director was still here, there was a good chance that the Veil Lifter hadn't yet been launched. There was still time to avert the destruction of the universe.

But to take any action he must get out of the tree hole and return to the Polar Lab immediately. He felt around with his foot and hit a root of the fir tree. Using the length of wood as a lever, he pushed himself upward, digging a tunnel to the surface with his good arm. It was slow and painful, but he didn't stop until he had made a gap large enough for him to see a patch of brilliant blue sky. The snow storm had passed, the sun was ablaze and reflections from ice crystals and steel shards caromed into his tunnel, momentarily blinding him. He blinked rapidly as he crawled out of the aperture onto the snow, only to lie back and wait for the agony from his broken arm to subside.

A foot nudged his damaged arm and a moan rose from deep inside his throat. He opened his eyes a slit to see the Director hovering over him.

"You don't die easily, do you?" Ormidtz heard the Director ask.

"Not in Zenad, I cannot die here," replied Ormidtz, communicating in electric waves for he was certain that Umani was once again in possession of the Director's body which had obviously been revived by the intense cold.

"Well," said the Director, "Then I just have to ensure that you are in too much pain to interfere with the launch of the Veil Lifter."

And making good his threat, the Director twisted his torso in a powerful torque, releasing the resulting force in a kick aimed at Ormidtz's head. Ormidtz shot out his good left arm and grabbed the snow-covered, lower branches of a nearby fir. He released his hold on the branches in such a way as to be catapulted down a slope in the terrain. He groaned as the broken edge of his right ulna rubbed against its partner bone, the radius.

Trying to put as much distance as he could between the Director and himself, Ormidtz slid helter-skelter down the incline towards the gaping hole in the roof of the elevator machine room. He steered with his legs trying to slow his descent until reaching the edge of the opening, he jumped in, trusting to luck that a piece of the wreckage would break his fall.

He landed on a shattered elevator door resting precariously against a maintenance ladder embedded in the shaft wall.

Moving as little as possible to maintain the delicate equilibrium in the shaft debris, Ormidtz removed his trouser belt and crafted a rough sling for his broken right arm which was now dangling from his elbow. The precaution didn't help. Slight though it was, his shifting weight dislodged the broken door which hurtled downwards like a whitewater raft tipping over a steep cataract.

Lightheaded from the pain but seeing no other option, Ormidtz lunged forward and hooked his good arm around the handrail of the maintenance ladder. He slithered down the metal and jerked himself to a painful stop at the first opening that offered entry into the building. As he crawled through the gap into the lobby of the Polar Lab, the shattered elevator door which had helped break Ormidtz's fall, crashed to the bottom of the shaft ending up in a twisted heap of buckled wood and metal.

Shivering from the shock of the close save, he crawled forward on hands and knees only to stop abruptly at the sight of a pair of red patent leather high heels. They looked familiar.

"What on earth happened here? Are you alright?"

"No, I'm not," Ormidtz replied, irritated at the inane question.

"I'm sorry, that was a silly question," Ruari apologized. "It's obvious you met with an accident. The elevator seems to have exploded. What happened?"

"I'll explain later," said Ormidtz, stifling a groan as he stood up. "There's no time to lose. Could you just help me get to the lab, please?"

"Can you walk?" asked Ruari.

"Just barely," he replied, leaning against the wall as dizziness overtook him.

"Here, take my arm," she said.

Ormidtz grabbed her forearm and steadied himself against her strong, athletic body. He took a tentative step and finding that he could walk, let go of her arm. For some reason, when Ruari was close, he had little control over his emotions. Pain or no pain, he wasn't going to put himself in a similar position as he had earlier in the cafeteria. In agony, but adamant, he limped down the corridor on his own.

His stubborn show of independence aggravated his throbbing arm, suffusing him with a blinding headache. He failed to hear Ruari walk away from him in the opposite direction.

δ

Leaving Ormidtz behind, Ruari quietly tiptoed to the elevator to reconfirm that it was totally out of commission. She had no choice now and must walk up three flights of stairs in her high heels to the Shelter. She turned back into the corridor and ran swiftly on tiptoes, following red arrows that clearly marked the Emergency Evacuation Route. She reached a fork in the corridor, one path leading to Level 2, and the other to the Shelter.

She started running towards the Shelter when a scraping, dragging sound made her pause. She flattened herself against the wall as she didn't want anyone asking her questions about her odd behavior. She held her breath as the sound grew louder, then let it out in relief when she saw Izem turn the corner.

Both gasped. Ruari because Izem was bleeding profusely

from scrapes and cuts, and Izem because he didn't expect to see Ruari so far away from the Level 3 where she should have been working with Erlang on the model.

"What happened to you?" Ruari began.

At the same time Izem asked, "What's going on?"

Both stopped and waited for the other to answer.

When Ruari didn't reply, Izem asked again, "What's going on here? Have you solved the problem? Where are the others?"

Ruari thought fast. "It's a long story," she parried. "I'll explain it all but first tell me what happened to you?"

"It was all very strange," Izem said. "I remember joining the Director in the elevator because there was some important information I needed to share with him very urgently. Now I don't even remember what it was. Anyway, just before the elevator doors closed, Ormidtz slipped in to join us. I remember nothing after that until I woke up to find myself lying in the grounds of the Polar Lab, badly bruised but fortunately with no bones broken. As I walked to the entrance of the Polar Lab, I saw a lot of debris strewn around, so my guess is that the elevator must have malfunctioned, exploded and ejected all three of us into the snow. I hope the Director and Ormidtz are alright."

"So where are Ormidtz and the Director?" asked Ruari, slyly trying to gauge how much Izem really knew about what was going on.

"I really don't know. When I regained consciousness, I saw no one around. So I entered the Polar Lab through the cafeteria to make my way back to Level 3," Izem replied, wincing as he shrugged his shoulders.

"The forty minutes the Director had given us to revise the model has long since expired, and we've not been able to make any corrections. I think he'll launch the Veil Lifter without our input," said Ruari.

Izem shot her a searching glance. "I remember telling you and Erlang that I had found the error but both of you denied that there was any problem in that section," he said.

"That's because I found that the section I had written was error-free. Erlang however, was continuing to review the part you pointed out to us," said Ruari, improvising unashamedly.

Disoriented by his fall and injuries, Izem was still slightly confused and accepted Ruari's explanation. "I see," he said. "Then where are you going now?"

"I was heading for the cafeteria. When I saw the elevator was broken, I started walking down the corridor," she lied.

"But the cafeteria arrow is pointing in the direction you just came from," Izem replied, beginning to doubt Ruari's actions.

Ruari couldn't be cornered that easily. "I heard noises down this part of the corridor. It sounded as if someone was badly hurt so I rushed down here to offer help," she explained glibly. "I'm glad I did for it turned out to be you. Come, let me help you return to Level 3. You can lean on me if you're feeling weak."

"Thank you," said Izem, "But I can manage on my own."

They both headed back towards Level 3, but at the fork, Ruari parted company from Izem, and walked down the corridor towards Level 1 and the cafeteria.

"I'll see you soon," she waved to Izem as he turned the corner.

Ruari waited out of sight until she could no longer hear Izem's footsteps. Then she retraced her steps and sped towards the Shelter.

CHAPTER XIII

THE OCYYST BARRIER

Zenad Reality
The Polar Lab

Level 3 was quiet, and all that could be heard was the deep rumbling and humming from the bowels of the complex as the Collider was readied for operation and the usual sounds of low voices discussing results. Built to absorb shocks from earthquakes of over eight on the Richter scale, no one in Level 3 was aware of the explosion in the elevator.

The low decibel acoustical rhythm was suddenly disrupted by a shout from Paul. "Where's the Director? We're just minutes away from launching the Veil Lifter."

The words were hardly out of his mouth when the Director marched into the lab and barked, "Why is the Collider still idle?"

"We're waiting for your final go-ahead," replied Raj.

"Well, you have it now. Start the process immediately."

Both Paul and Raj turned their attention to initiating the

launching procedures as the other scientists also got engrossed in following the launch routines. No one noticed Ormidtz hobble into the lab, his useless arm in its improvised sling, pressed against his chest. Since Izem could be hurt and still lying in the snow and Ruari was behind him in the corridor, Ormidtz thought it best to look to Erlang for some information.

Catching sight of the scientist at his station, Ormidtz limped awkwardly towards him. "Erlang, what's going on? Have you made any progress?"

Erlang looked at Ormidtz with dead eyes and replied in a monotone, "The launch has been initiated."

"So you and Ruari made the correction?" asked Ormidtz hopefully.

Erlang seemed to drag himself back from somewhere far away. He lowered his eyes and slowly shook his head. "No, we didn't."

"I met Ruari in the corridor," Ormidtz said. "She should be returning to the lab soon."

With great effort, Erlang looked into Ormidtz's eyes and confessed, "Ormidtz, neither Ruari nor I am interested in fixing the model."

"But why?" asked Ormidtz in consternation. "The Inter Galactic Security Force warned us about the consequences. Don't you want to prevent the catastrophe?"

"Not really," Erlang replied. "I want to die soon so that my reincarnation and evolution into a higher level of consciousness can begin as quickly as possible."

Ormidtz stared at Erlang, a premonition of disaster filling him with dread. It hadn't occurred to him that the experience of body-soul separation arising from mental and spiritual trauma could have psychological consequences on the scientists. He recalled that Erlang had been reluctant to transition away from his life as a Shifu in the little Hunan village manifested in the Machim Reality.

"But what about Ruari? She doesn't believe in reincarnation. Isn't she afraid to die?" said Ormidtz.

Erlang sighed deeply and looking away, said, "We both know that Ruari is very egotistical and arrogant. She refuses to admit that she has made an error in her calculations. She would rather die than have her reputation sullied."

"But where *is* she?" said Ormidtz looking to his right and left. "She was right behind me in the corridor and should have been here by now."

"She told me she was heading for the Shelter and argued that if, in spite of the error there's no catastrophe, then all would be fine. If, on the other hand, the error annihilates the lab, the Shelter will keep her safe during the explosion. No evidence will survive to pinpoint the source of the error and her career will be protected," Erlang said in a tired and resigned manner.

Horrified that Ruari was willing to risk the destruction of the universe for purely selfish reasons, Ormidtz pinned his waning hopes on Izem who had, after all, located the problem in the model.

"Where's Izem?" said Ormidtz, shivering from exhaustion.

"Right behind you," said Erlang looking over Ormidtz's shoulder.

Izem, face bruised and clothes torn, had just dragged himself into the lab.

Ormidtz turned around and said, "Izem, were you able to make the correction?"

"Who is Izem? I am Zepar," came the reply.

"Zepar, why are you still here?" asked Ormidtz. "Can't you leave Izem alone? Wasn't it enough that you made such a savage attack on me in the elevator?"

"Well," said Zepar, "The time is at hand for hi-neg beings to dominate the Realities. I have no intention of vacating Izem's body or even leaving Zenad. I'm enjoying myself too much."

"Erlang, Izem, please help me stop the catastrophe," pleaded Ormidtz, a sense of hopelessness seeping into his voice.

Just then, the Director strode to the main console and raised his hand to punch in the final codes. Abandoning any hope of getting help from Erlang or Izem, Ormidtz gritted his teeth and hurled himself at the Director in an attempt to disrupt the launch. But he was too far away from the console and too weak from loss of blood to generate enough momentum to dislodge the Director from his seat. He landed a few feet behind the Director who, oblivious of any disturbance, continued to tap away on the keyboard.

In a last desperate attempt, Ormidtz yelled to the two young astrobiochemists, "Raj, Paul, abort the launch! We'll be annihilated if the Collider is activated."

The urgency of Ormidtz's command compelled Raj to lean forward and hit the pause button in the launch sequence. Always loyal to Raj, Paul followed suit. The two controlled the connectivity with the international partners and without their green signal, neither Australia, Chile, China nor Switzerland would activate their end of the program. The Director could, and would, override the pause command, but the time needed to make the adjustments to the system bought Ormidtz a few crucial moments.

He combed his formidable databank and came across two pieces of information that offered him some hope. Erlang had said that if the Veil Lifter was launched without modifying the model, magnetic monopoles would be generated that would tear apart matter. The Collider would disintegrate and the toxic subparticles that would be released would shatter the Ocyyst Barrier. Izem, on the other hand, had concluded that the activation of the defective Veil Lifter would release strangelets embedded in the powerful gravitational field within the Collider.

Thinking furiously on how to best utilize these facts, Ormidtz chalked out a strategy. If he harvested high energy cosmic rays from the earth's atmosphere to convert his essential being into a particle consisting of strange quarks that closely resemble strangelets, he should be able to meld with those strangelets already embedded in the Collider. Then, as the magnetic monopoles tore apart the Collider and he was ejected into space, he could harness the powerful gravitational field of the embedded strangelets to reinforce the Ocyyst Barrier and repel the toxic subparticles, thus preventing any breach.

The plan was foolhardy and dangerous with a minimal probability of success. His *atman* may not be able to survive the rapid shifts that his structural existence would have to undergo and it could fracture beyond redemption. As a result, he may not be reborn in any of the Realities and could become a lost and homeless soul existing in vacuum.

He didn't know if his strategy would work, but it was the best that he could device. This was his last chance and he had to take the risk.

δ

A nanosecond later Ormidtz realized, that to put his plan into action, he would first have to release his *atman*. He would have to raise his consciousness to a level that would override his physical pain and sever his essential being from the *maya* of his corporeal body. In preparation, he emptied his mind and focused on his third eye, but surges of recurrent pain interfered with his concentration, preventing him from passing into the necessary stage of deep meditation. Exasperated at his own weakness and impotency, he moaned and thrashed his head from side to side.

A relieved sigh greeted his ears. He opened his eyes to see Paul and Raj hovering over him, trying to ascertain if he was still alive.

"Ormidtz?" said Raj giving him a gentle shake.

He smiled up at them. "I'm still here," he said. Then, as the sight of the two men gave him an idea, he added, "But I do desperately need your help."

The two nodded, unsure of what Ormidtz had in mind, but for some reason, ready to trust him all the way.

"To prevent the disaster that the Inter Galactic Security Force has predicted," Ormidtz continued, "I must descend to my deepest meditational level, but the pain I'm experiencing from my injuries is sapping my life force and interfering with my concentration. Your physical and mental strength can help me overcome this obstacle."

"What do you need from us?" whispered Raj, still afraid of the Director's reaction if he caught them helping Ormidtz.

"I need your spiritual energy. We must all join hands and

each of us must focus on reaching the highest level of consciousness possible."

"How do we do that?" asked Raj.

"Just relax, empty your minds, and lay bare your senses. That will allow me to draw on your spiritual energies." Ormidtz winced as tried to move into a more comfortable position.

"But the Director...," Paul began hesitatingly.

"The Director's mind has become possessed by a powerful negative being who is forcing him to launch the defective program, but we're safe for the moment because the evil being is so confident of success that she doesn't care what we do," said Ormidtz.

The two men looked at him with terrified, incredulous eyes, but not pursuing his bizarre explanation any further, Raj ventured to ask, "What do we do when you've reached your desired level of consciousness?"

"As soon as the process is complete, let go of my hands and instantly disengage yourselves from me, both physically and mentally, as otherwise you too will become vulnerable to the negative being's evil power. After that, immediately initiate the evacuation protocols, making sure that everyone reaches the safety of the Shelter," said Ormidtz.

"Why is the evacuation necessary?" asked Raj.

"Because I'm transporting my essence into the Collider to offset the error in the Veil Lifter. I don't know how that will impact the system, but I'm afraid there's a high probability it might terminate in an explosion," said Ormidtz.

"How will we know when your process is complete?" Paul's whispered shakily, his voice hoarse with tension and fear at Ormidtz's predictions.

Ormidtz gave a lopsided smile. "Don't worry, my friends, you'll easily recognize the moment. Now, please join hands with me and concentrate hard. Time has run out."

As Paul and Raj clasped his hands, a surge of their combined vital energy swept over Ormidtz, momentarily disorienting him with their deeply knotted thoughts and emotions. They had obviously received little training in creating spiritual and mental accord within themselves so that Ormidtz had to surf their discordant waves to seek the underlying harmony that all humans possess but few are able to harness effectively.

He located Raj's element first because the young man's mental waves were better synchronized than Paul's. It was likely that Raj practiced yoga. Ormidtz continued his search until he located Paul's theta wave, the state when the mind is at its most creative. Ormidtz merged both elements into his own stream of consciousness, creating a wave with a crest high and powerful enough to overcome his physical sufferings and release his *atman.*

With a sigh he floated away, free of the body that he loved so much.

Several moments later Raj and Paul surfaced from their meditative trance to find Ormidtz lying limp and lifeless, his hands still clasped in their own. As both of them quickly severed contact with Ormidtz, Paul said in an awed voice, "I told you Ormidtz is not of this planet."

"Whatever he is," said Raj, "I trust him and I think we should follow his instructions. Let's evacuate the Polar Lab."

CHAPTER XIV

THE RUPTURE

Zenad Reality
The Polar Lab

Liberated from the burden of his human body and reduced to only his essential being, Ormidtz moved with the speed of Mercury, the messenger god. His particle-like *atman* flew into the Proton Booster Accelerator, also called the Collider, where beams of protons and ions were being hurled at a velocity approaching the speed of light to enhance the probability of subparticle collisions.

He was immediately sucked into the electric field of radio frequency cavities which flung him into extreme high speed propulsion. The powerful centrifugal force inside the Accelerator was counterbalanced by the magnetic field created by the giant magnets which held him securely within its beam. His essential being shadowing the other subparticles, penetrated another accelerator and as his velocity increased, Ormidtz was launched into a lengthy, unpredictable ride.

He hurtled through the Accelerator in anticipation of a possible collision with a proton for only then could he hope to successfully carry out his plan. He didn't know which would be worse – a successful collision which could break him down into quarks and gluons, or not colliding and being siphoned off to the beam dumping section where he would be absorbed into graphite. If it was the latter and he was drained off, then not only would his mission have failed, but there was also a distinct possibility that he could be expelled from all Realities into eternal extinction.

Unshackling himself from a train of thought that sapped his energy, Ormidtz succumbed to the revolutions which spun him with increasing speed through the hundred-mile circumference of the Accelerator. The intense cold inside the Accelerator pipes allowed the electromagnets to operate without any electrical resistance, but the low temperatures also neutralized his *atman*'s positive charges, making him weak and vulnerable.

As he swirled through the pipes, he ruefully reminded himself that the favorable outcome of his plan depended entirely on the slender chance that Izem was right in his assessment that the flawed Veil Lifter would generate strangelets inside the Collider. Also imperative for the plan to succeed was that the strangelets were created before the magnetic monopole particles were produced, for only under such stringent conditions could he expect to pair up with strangelets and be ejected into spacetime before the magnetic monopole particles tore apart the Collider in a colossal explosion.

In suspended animation, Ormidtz swept through the Collider in ever increasing laps, waiting for an outcome with a million-to-one chance of success. He was trapped in a set of complex simultaneous equations with countless variables and no known solution.

As the orbiting speed inside the accelerator approached c, the speed of light in vacuum, Ormidtz waited for the opportunity to pair up with strangelets embedded in the gravitational field inside the Collider. He was hoping that the explosion triggered by the magnetic monopole particles would eject him and the strangelets along a stable trajectory towards the Ocyyst Barrier. The waves of the powerful gravitational field of the strangelets would then ripple out to envelope the region, boosting the strength and resistance of the Barrier to a superlative degree. This would ensure that the surplus hi-neg elements would remain trapped behind the Barrier and cosmic balance would be maintained.

Confidence in his ability to save the universe on such a farfetched and unreliable strategy began to dwindle as Ormidtz covered lap after lap without interacting with other particles. At the very moment when his faith in himself had dropped to near zero, he felt the velocity inside the Accelerator escalate to just under the speed of light. In reaction to the increased velocity, a stream of protons careered towards him from the opposite direction, random collisions shooting out neutrinos, positrons, photons, muons, quarks. Miniscule black holes were created to instantaneously collapse within themselves, the minute amounts of precious dark energy released by the degeneration of the particles being siphoned off into special vats to be examined at leisure.

In the near-c speed of the process, not every proton collided with another, but when it did, subparticles spilled out in every direction. Photons, positrons and muons sparked in tiny displays of firework, and like firework died and disappeared from sight. Each subparticle had a very brief halflife in Zenad and decayed within seconds of being created, some passing into another Reality to become invisible to any observer in Zenad. Other particles remained in Zenad, but because they had reached a velocity faster than the speed of light, they evaded detection by both the human eye as well as machines.

Inside this cauldron of hyperactivity, Ormidtz's *atman* sped along with millions of protons which were being stripped from hydrogen atoms and fed into the Collider in a steady stream. These particles which were travelling in the same magnetic beam at nearly the speed of light, remained however, stationary relative to one another. Ormidtz's *atman* was one such 'stationary' particle, and if the physical and chemical transformations within that magnetic beam generated strangelets as Izem had predicted, then Ormidtz stood a fairly good chance of bonding with them.

But he still faced another formidable challenge.

Since strangelets decayed almost the instant they were created, Ormidtz would have only a picosecond – one-trillionth of a second – to attach himself to these exotic elements. In the event that he failed to avail of the extremely narrow window of opportunity, his initial fallback plan was to pursue the strangelets into their new Realities and transport them back to Zenad to complete the bonding maneuver. But he rejected the measure of safeguard immediately for that would require time and he had none to spare.

His options were reduced to Hobson's choice. There were no other options. His plan couldn't fail. He must link up with the strangelets before the magnetic monopoles particles were created so that he and the strangelets could be spewed out into spacetime by the immense force that the explosion of the Accelerator would generate.

Fear and uncertainty mounting steadily within him, Ormidtz continued to swim through the flood of protons until in his trillionth lap a simultaneous collision between several thousand protons produced the hoped for strangelets. The intensely cold environment inside the pipes made the gravitational field of the strangelets ineffective, allowing Ormidtz to be immediately sucked into its orbit. A picosecond later, the flawed Veil Lifter generated magnetic monopoles particles which instantaneously reached critical mass and tore apart all matter. The Collider shattered and the Polar Lab erupted like a volcano, spewing debris far and wide over the snow covered tundra.

The explosion ejected the strangelets towards the Ocyyst Barrier and in sync with the motion of the strangelets, Ormidtz flew into spacetime. His *atman,* now free from the neutralizing effect inside the Collider, regained its positive charge so that Ormidtz remained unaffected by the gravitational force of the strangelets which repelled all negative subparticles in the vicinity to the extreme edge of the universe.

At the same time, the powerful gravitational field of the strangelets enveloped the Barrier in a protective shield which prevented it from rupturing. Exponentially strengthened by the additional buffer, the Ocyyst Barrier erected a series of firewalls, corralling the dangerous and disruptive hi-neg antiparticles into a contained area at the extreme end of spacetime.

If the Ocyyst Barrier had been breached and these hi-neg antiparticles had been released into Zenad Reality, the entropy of the Reality would have been reduced to zero, the lowest energy state that a quantum mechanical physical system can sustain. At zero entropy, Zenad would have been stripped of all its life-giving energy which in turn would have doomed all the Realities into a state of impotence and stagnation.

But disaster had been averted, and the disorder and randomness that generate the energy essential to the very existence of the universe and humankind, continued uninterrupted in all the Realities. Cosmic harmony and tranquility reigned in Zenad and all Realities.

His mission complete, and no longer attached to strangelets, Ormidtz's essential being peacefully floated in the spacetime continuum, riding the waves of the expanding space for minutes, for eons, who knew? Who was counting? For the timespan for evolution, like so many other things in the universe, is relative. The evolution of humans took millions of years in the Zenad Reality. In another Reality, it may have taken just a moment, or perhaps millions of years longer than it did in Zenad. But then, in other Realities humans evolved differently. They were still humans but had physiological characteristics and skeletal structures as yet unknown and unrecognized in Zenad.

Only the essential being of a human remains unchanged in every Reality. Beyond physical grasp, and no matter in which Reality it abides, the *atman* is always the same, an undefinable entity of pure consciousness, of unadulterated energy.

CHAPTER XV

THE ABYSS

Vakin Reality

I'm exhausted.

I know that the universe, Zenad and all the Realities are now stable, safe, yet I feel no sense of euphoria, no elation. I know I have prevented extreme negativity from suffusing all Realities, yet all my consciousness acknowledges is that there's nothing to look forward to, nothing to aspire to.

I'm exhausted.

I'm aware that, unlike most humans, I can convey my atman to any Reality. Even up to the penultimate Waara which is the purest level of consciousness that a human can achieve before he merges with the Singularity. But I cannot and do not wish to summon the spiritual strength to make a choice. I do not care where I go.

I'm aware that my essential being has been transported into the murky, viscous Vakin Reality. I have descended into the Reality where creation began, and I now wallow in the fundamental swirling mixture where matter is yet to be created. There are no planets, no stars, only primordial, undulating, pulsating space, the uterus of life, the womb of the universe.

My spiritual consciousness is at its lowest ebb and I spiral down into a quagmire of lost hope. I have abandoned any desire to return to Waara or to be anywhere else but in this comforting abyss.

Deep in this primeval haze, a faint electrical impulse jars my introspection, disturbs my deep melancholy. "Ormidtz, why are you here?"

"Because I have lost my way and must return to the beginning." My disjointed, warped response echoes and resonates like sound waves flowing in slow motion through a dense medium with high resistance and viscosity.

"Do you know how you got here?" The electrical impulse again interrupts my introspection.

"I really don't care how I got here, why I'm here, and where I go from here," is my callous reply.

"Ormidtz, you are here because Umani sent you here. The bonding with the strangelets and ejection into spacetime by the exploding magnetic monopole particles has pushed your essential being to the brink of irrevocable fragmentation."

I do not answer, for I do not care.

But the vibrations continue relentlessly.

"Ormidtz, the ejection from the collider sapped your very life force. You became very weak and so offered no resistance when Umani took control of your evolutionary process. You don't belong here. Your spiritual evolution is of the highest order and you must find your way out of this quagmire."

The vibrations accelerate, agitating my placid state of mind.

264

"I don't belong anywhere, Thebitz," I say, for I can recognize his telepathic wavelength anywhere. "Let me be. Why must I aspire to be one with the Singularity? Like so many humans, I'm content to oscillate within the Vakin-Zenad arc for eternity. I accept that it's not for me to seek transcendence into Realities of higher consciousness. Such is my karma and I embrace it."

"It isn't so. It isn't so." The electrical impulse transforms itself into high voltage current, and pierces my tranquility, irritating me, annoying me. "You are different. You move between Realities and you retain your memories and the knowledge that you gain in every reincarnation. There's a reason for your special powers."

"You can take away the powers, Thebitz. I neither need them, nor want them. I'm neither a prophet nor a mystical messenger. Nor am I of the ancient hermit sect who use pain to achieve a shift in consciousness. I'm afraid of pain. I don't want to suffer physical trauma nor moral dilemmas."

"You're right. You are neither a messenger nor a prophet. You are the Protector of positive forces: the Gatekeeper against extreme negativity; the Guardian of balance and harmony in the universe; the Preventer of cosmic wars. You cannot escape your destiny, Ormidtz."

"Just leave me alone, Thebitz. I'm happier now than I've been in a very long time. What does it matter if negativity reigns the realities? What does it matter if hi-neg is the acceptable norm. Evil will become good, and good evil. Black will be white and white black. Darkness will be sought and light shunned. A photograph's positive print will be discarded and the negative, with its deep shadows will be preserved and admired. So what difference does it make whether the universe and the Realities are ruled by positiveness or hi-negativity?"

"Ormidtz, you already know the answers to your questions. You know that in a hi-neg universe, Love and other Virtues will be spurned, while Hate and other Vices will be cultivated and embraced, jeopardizing the ethical balance of the Realities. You cannot let that happen."

"I can do as I please for I've been endowed with free will, Thebitz. And I choose to remain in the obscurity of the Vakin, in the chaos of pre-birth, where I'm not burdened with responsibilities, not even for myself."

"Ormidtz, you must resist the lure of the broad and easy path trodden by most. That road will lead you astray." I'm surprised to detect a pleading undertone in Thebitz's vibrations. "You know well that I cannot force you to do anything against your will. The choice will always be yours. But choose wisely, Ormidtz. The Universe and the Realities will always need a human to protect them against onslaughts of extreme negativity, for cosmic ethics does not tolerate intervention from any other source."

I do not answer. The electrical impulses fade away and I return with relief to my reveries.

But it was only a brief respite. Once again a thought wave intersects my own.

"You're right, Ormidtz." In spite of my mental haze, I recognize Umani's wave patterns. "You can choose to eschew the usual path of physical and spiritual evolution to higher levels of consciousness, and remain here in the primordial Reality of Vakin, where you'll remain undisturbed for all time. You can also choose to transcend to Zenad Reality and follow the path that leads to physical fulfillment and self glory, the path to pleasures and delights of human life in Zenad. You have the power to make these choices, Ormidtz, remember that."

"Yes, Umani," I readily assent. "In Vakin, where matter is yet to form, there's no personal conflict between right and wrong; between spirituality and the need to fulfill physical desires; between duty and carefree existence. I can drift for as long as I like, without any obligation to protect the universe and the Realities. In Vakin I'm free from physical pain or ethical conundrums."

"This is the perfect place for you, Ormidtz, make this your eternal abode."

Umani's persuasive tones lull me into a sense of peace and security that I've never experienced in any of my lifetimes. I savor the feeling, wallow in it, drown in it.

δ

Suspended in supreme detachment, in total negation, in non-creation, Ormidtz floated in the Vakin Reality with no comprehension of the passage of time, for neither Time nor Matter had any meaning in Vakin. Here, only the noumenon existed, accumulating knowledge and awareness in preparation for metamorphosing into a human.

Bobbing in the gentle swells of the spacetime continuum and content in his slumberous state, Ormidtz felt mildly disturbed as a finger of light which, like the sun's ray piercing the ocean depths, caressed his essential being; softly probed his soporific mind.

"Arise Ormidtz, you've been touched by Enlightenment."

"I'm content in my state of despondency, Thebitz, let me be."

"Awake Ormidtz, for the Light has touched you. You must

tear apart the hi-neg aura that holds you captive. You must will yourself out of the shroud that envelops your consciousness and hampers your spiritual and physical evolution."

Ormidtz ignored his mentor and Thebitz's vibrations faded away, powerless, impotent against Ormidtz's supreme disinterest.

δ

I hear the peal of church bells, now close and loud, now faint and far, far away. I hear chanting of verses from holy books of the many religions in the Zenad Reality. The chantings ebb, and I hear a muezzin's melodious call to prayer, now rising in cadence, now overtaken by a blast from a ceremonial horn, now dying down. I smell incense and hear the clink of chains, the deep humming of intoned prayers.

I hear my name, "Ormidtz."

"Who calls?" I ask for I do not recognize the pattern.

"It is We." The answer echoes back at me.

"Who is We?"

"We are the granules of rocks from the top of the mount; We are the grains of sand from the desert; We are the dust from the windswept plains; We are the droplets from the seas. We are You. We are They. We are the Universe. We are the Realities." The soft whispers swaddle my essence as if it were a newborn baby.

"Why do you call me?"

"We speak for the Zenad Reality, from the Zenad Reality. We are indebted to you for you have saved Us and the Universe from chaos."

"Why do you call me?" I repeat.

"*Because you must wake up and realize that you are in Vakin not of your own free will. You are there because another being wishes to keep you entrapped in Vakin, away from Zenad, away from other Realities where duty awaits you. You are forfeiting your right to choose.*"

"*I know to whom you refer. Umani is not keeping me here. I want to be here,*" I insist.

"*When your power to control your consciousness in usurped, choices made by others appear to be your own.*"

"*I don't wish to struggle with myself anymore. My many lifetimes, in as many Realities, have shown me that to be a human with an atman means constantly making choices and suffering the consequences that result from those choices.*"

"*On the other hand, you also enjoy the joys and pleasures that arise from the choices you make. With night comes day. With joy comes pain. One cannot be experienced without the other. Tell Us, why are you so afraid?*"

"*I'm blessed or cursed with eternal memory. I can recall every lifetime, but those with whom I spend each lifetime pass away, transition to another Reality with no memory of what they meant to me or what I meant to them. I sometimes meet them in another lifetime, in another Reality. I recognize them, but they don't know who I am. I try to reignite our earlier relationships. I sometimes succeed, but more often fail miserably. In either case, we once again separate and go through throes of pain which they eventually forget, but I carry with me through all lifetimes.*"

"*So you are afraid to love because it causes pain?*"

"*Yes.*"

"*But love is the straight and narrow path to finding the Seventh Reality. It is only when you learn to love ardently,*" *without expectation of any return, that you can be reconciled with your beloved."*

"Are you telling me that unrequited love will prepare me for merging with the Singularity?"

"That is one way of putting it," comes the equivocal reply.

"No, I cannot do it. I do not have the strength to bear such pain over and over again."

"You do not know what you can or cannot do until you try to do it."

"I know myself well and know what is within my powers to achieve."

A breeze ripples over my atman as if the Speaker were laughing in amusement.

"Ormidtz, Ormidtz, have you learned nothing through living so many lifetimes? If you truly knew yourself, you would not be still striving for the Seventh Reality."

"But that's the fate of all humans," is my careless reply.

"Humans make their own fates by the choices they make in their lifetimes. But remember, not all humans are able to realize their full potential."

"Why is that?" I ask, curious in spite of myself.

"Because, Ormidtz, only a few choose to embark on the journey of self annihilation, and of them only a handful succeed in stripping themselves of their egos. And of these, even fewer are able to divest themselves of their physical selves and transcend to a state of pure consciousness. This discontinuity of self and consciousness releases the noumenon which implodes into infinity as it becomes wholly engulfed by the Singularity. The enigma of the Singularity is that it cannot be defined, yet it is the essence of the Universe."

"*Well, I am among the masses and not amongst the few,*" *I persist, aware of how petulant and childish I sound.*

"*That's where you are wrong, Ormidtz. Your judgement is being intentionally clouded by a powerful hi-neg being. Your desire for annihilation of your ego is being suppressed by a shroud of negative particles. You're the only one who can extricate yourself from this web. The choice, as always, is yours.*"

The whispers fade away, as a narrow beam of light cuts a swathe around me, disturbs my complacence, nudges me out of my somnolence.

I resist. I don't want to evolve out of Vakin. I don't want to transcend to Zenad or to any other Reality. I don't want to be the Gatekeeper, the Guardian, the Protector. I don't want glory. I don't want pain. I don't want to choose.

The dense fog of Vakin swirls around me, cocooning me. The murky darkness comforts me.

δ

The sliver of light, too weak, too fragile to wholly dispel the seething darkness of Vakin, undulated over Ormidtz in a faint glow, prodding him out of his lethargic, opiate state, nudging his self awareness and guiding him towards responsible choices.

Feeble though it was, the fragile ray slit open the stifling cocoon of the primordial Reality, loosening the bonds that confined his dormant *atman* to this state of non-being. Ormidtz was at last awake but not as yet free. Like a butterfly trapped in a spider's web, his *atman* fluttered in the gloom, searching for an escape route, searching for release, searching for a glimpse of the light that had awakened him. It struggled to escape but a great weight anchored it securely within the abyss.

"You're a coward who is unable to face his fears," Umani's vibrations, painful, disturbing, coursed through Ormidtz. "I will always dominate you, Ormidtz."

"Only if I allow you to," Ormidtz murmured unconvincingly, his pulsations weak and faint.

"I'm your nemesis and your worst nightmare. You'll never be free of me. You'll never be worthy of the mantle of the Protector." Umani's wrathful outburst seared through Ormidtz like an electroshock weapon.

"I may be weak, but I still have the right to make my own choice." Ormidtz feebly defied Umani. "Yes, I'm tempted to float in primordial Vakin for all my lifetimes for that's the easy path. But good and evil, love and hate, weakness and strength are the myriad reflections of the Universe and the Realities. These facets must always remain in harmony, in balance."

"I abhor harmony. I believe chaos must reign supreme and negativity must dominate the Universe." Umani's vibrations dissonated disturbingly through Ormidtz. "You're trapped in Vakin, too weak to escape and impotent to protect Zenad and the other Realities."

Umani's anger, rage and hatred caused her hi-neg wave function to peak, initiating a ripple effect which intensified Ormidtz's sense of fear and powerlessness. Sapped of his already low energy reserves, Ormidtz was awash in self pity, despair, grief and inferiority. Yet his overwhelming emotion was that of resentfulness at being designated the Guardian, the Protector, the Gatekeeper. He was aggrieved that the onus of making a responsible choice had been passed on to him.

The faint glow cast upon Ormidtz by the finger of light grew even fainter as frustration and despondency drained the last dregs of his energy. As he writhed in spiritual agony between his powerlessness to escape his imprisonment and his fear and repugnance at taking over the mantle of Gatekeeper, the sound of distant church bells, a muezzin's call to prayer, intonation of sacred texts once again pervaded his senses.

Faint whispers cascaded around him like waterfall.

"Ormidtz, why have you abandoned faith? Believe in yourself and you will find strength. Find love and you will forever vanquish your enemies."

δ

I know what love is. It can make you strong but it can also destroy you. It can make you joyous, but it can also tear apart your heart in suffering. It's a two-edged sword that must be wielded by a master to avoid permanently damaging yourself.

I also know what it is to be shunned because you are different. But I know best what is love, for I remember it all.

δ

I met her in one of my lifetimes in Zenad Reality, many eons ago.

No two people could be more different that we were. Megan MacCraith was a raven-haired beauty with impossibly violet eyes, and I was an ordinary looking man with strange golden-hazel eyes which seem to scare people. Bright and vivacious, Megan was the center of attention wherever she went. On the other hand, I was a loner, my books and my computer, my only friends. She

273

came from a wealthy family and I depended on scholarships and part-time work to pay my way through university.

Our characters couldn't be more different yet we were drawn to each other right from the moment we met. By the time we were sophomores, we had moved in together and got married soon after we had graduated, she as a mathematician and I as a cosmologist and astrophysicist. We both had absorbing and demanding jobs but we found time to be together, to take brief holidays and quick breaks whenever we could, sometimes driving to quaint towns in Maine, sometimes spending a long weekend at the Niagara Falls.

Life was perfect. Until that fateful day. That hateful, dark day, when time stood still and our happy little world imploded.

I had come home late from a conference to find Megan ashen faced, staring blankly at the wall. I had never seen her in such a state for no matter what the situation, she always had a positive attitude and was ready to tackle any challenge. At first she wouldn't say what was wrong, but I eventually prised it out of her. She had been diagnosed with terminal stage cancer and had been given three months to live.

It took me several days to recover from the shock, but once I was able to think clearly again, I resigned from my job and we set out to travel the world, going wherever she wanted to go, doing whatever she wanted to do.

As it became more difficult for her to move about, we ended our journey in a stone-walled shepherd's cottage overlooking Galway Bay in her beloved Ireland. Sheep tracks led down to the water, the path edged with wild flowers tucked between rocks and boulders green with lichen. The weather was always fickle. From dawn to dusk the bay flirted with us, now a steely grey, now a translucent turquoise, now swallowing the dying sun in a blaze of red, orange and purple.

We were blissfully isolated in our little cottage, taking long walks along the cliffs and the beach, reminiscing, remembering, and trying to stretch time into infinity.

Once she asked me how could I remember every moment we spent together, every word spoken between us.

I had never revealed to Megan my special ability of remembering all my lifetimes in every Reality. I had never disclosed my spiritual bond with the Tractate and my conversations with Thebitz. How my deep-set desire to understand the Tractate and live by its codes, in spite of doubts and unanswered questions, equipped me with powers to transition to Realities where the essential being evolved into purer levels of consciousness. How my search for my inner self, my desire to reach the Seventh Reality, endowed me with abilities few humans were privileged to have, for I remember all my transitions and all my deeds in all my existences. It's both a privilege and a curse.

I had never told Megan any of this because she wouldn't understand. She didn't believe in the Tractate, the Realities and transcendence into purer forms of existence. She wasn't besieged by doubts and had no qualms about abandoning the Tractate which she frankly declared had no part in her life. Science had repeatedly proven that humans die, turn into dust and become part of planet earth. She believed only what could be scientifically proven to be true.

Although she always had and always would be blessed with a keen mind, I knew that her no-nonsense attitude and lack of desire for spiritual self-searching were obstacles that prevented her from transcending into Realities of higher consciousness. For this reason, over the eons, Megan's reincarnations had been confined to the cycle between the primordial Vakin and the low energy Zenad. She of course, like most humans, didn't remember her experiences in her past lifetimes, living her life anew at each rebirth.

I didn't agree with Megan's philosophy, but like every human, she had the gift of free will and the right to choose how to live her life. The path Megan had chosen was spiritually far removed from my own but that didn't stop me from loving her for eternity.

But it did sadden me because I knew she would always return to Zenad or Vakin, while I, because of my life choices would reach Realities of purer and higher consciousness. So the probability of my meeting her atman in another Reality was ten to the power negative one million. That is, almost negligible.

I didn't reply to her question and she wisely didn't pursue it, for she had always sensed that I was a little different from anyone else she knew. But we lived with our differences and they never fractured our love.

Those last days we lived intensely and passionately. They were the worst and the most glorious days of my life. As she became weaker and drained of energy, I watched my beautiful, vibrant Megan waste away before my eyes. We bided our time, she waiting for her system to stop functioning, and I waiting for Thebitz to claim her soul and guide it into another Reality.

The fateful day eventually arrived. It was a beautiful clear morning heralded by a spectacular sunrise over Galway Bay. I held her close as I sensed her slipping into a Reality where I couldn't follow for my time to transition was yet to come. When my time does come, I may or may not emerge in the same plane of existence as Megan. Would our paths ever cross again? Would I ever see her again?

δ

The voices echoed and re-echoed around Ormidtz as he lay trapped in the abyss.

"Why have you abandoned your faith?"

"Believe in yourself and you will find strength."

"Find love and you will forever vanquish your enemies."

Even though the agony of lost love was still fresh after so many lifetimes, the inspiring words dissipated his state of lethargy, galvanizing his mind into action. Disjointed words impinged on his consciousness – tachyons that move faster than the speed of light, virtual particles, evolution, annihilation, rebirth.

The words took him back to the discourse he had with Ruari in the Polar Lab cafeteria. He recalled she had expounded on the odd behavior of subparticles which, within a very brief moment of time could either bond together or annihilate one another, each time being reborn as another entity. Could he use this phenomenon to accelerate his evolutionary transition out of Vakin and into Zenad? Could the properties of virtual particles eject him into another Reality freeing him from Umani's numbing subjugation?

As his mind reached higher levels of lucidity, Ormidtz searched for ways to extricate himself from Vakin. He reasoned that a successful merger between a tachyon and his *atman*, which was an entity of pure energy, should initiate a synchronicity or a significant coincidence. The synchronicity would untether his soul from the seething entropy of Vakin and allow it to escape to the Zenad Reality.

His other option was to maneuver a collision between a particle and an antiparticle. The process of annihilation would generate levels of radiation that would transform the entropy around his immediate vicinity into a state of orderliness. The slowing down of subparticle interactions would imbue him with enough energy to fast-forward his own evolutionary process to propel him out of primordial Vakin.

But Umani, acutely aware of any variation in the pattern of his thought waves, sensed Ormidtz's growing determination to evolve out of Vakin. She immediately encased Ormidtz's *atman* in a shroud of deep despondency and announced ominously, "Ormidtz, transcendence into Zenad isn't going to free you of my presence. I will always own part of you, as I own part of Ruari's soul."

"What do you mean? Why does Ruari come into the conflict between you and me?" asked Ormidtz.

"Do you recall the Etruscan passages below the *Bascilica San Pietro* ?" said Umani.

"Yes, of course I do. That's where I found Ruari's essential being."

"Then you'll remember that her *atman* had taken shelter in the lunar moth," Umani reminded Ormidtz.

"Yes, that's true," said Ormidtz.

"Well, then you will also recall that when I was in possession of the Franciscan monk's body, the moth had settled briefly on my hand. At that moment of contact her soul touched my own essence, entwining her fate with mine for eternity."

Suffused with horror at Umani's words, Ormidtz summoned up his meagre supply of courage and cried defiantly, "Umani, you have helped me make my choice."

"So you will join me?" asked Umani.

"You underestimate a human's power to overcome adversity," said Ormidtz, annoyed that Umani considered him such a spiritual weakling. "I cannot abandon the human race and I cannot abandon my Megan. I know Ruari is Megan's incarnation and that Megan's soul resides within Ruari. So no matter how much you have tainted Megan's soul, I will release her from your bondage even if it takes all my lifetimes to do so."

Overcome by wrath, Umani thundered, "Think again, Ormidtz, you still have time. The path you are choosing will put your own soul, as well as Megan's on a perilous trajectory. I can, and will, make sure that Megan never evolves out of Vakin. She will forever remain bonded to me as my slave."

His love for Megan overriding his terror of Umani, Ormidtz reiterated, "I have chosen, Umani. I choose to take on the mantel of the Gatekeeper. I choose to reject your temptations and offers. I will face my fears. I will face you. I will protect the Universe and the Realities from destructive hi-neg beings like you."

His show of courage and defiance heavily depleted Ormidtz's spiritual energy, weakening his vibrations and damping their frequency into low amplitude.

Umani's response was cataclysmic. She roiled up the dense composition of Vakin and generated such intense heat that the Vakin entropy soared into its highest degree of chaos. Ormidtz was forced to acknowledge that it would be impossible to still this turmoil, and abandoned his plan to create orderliness in entropy which would allow him to extract sufficient energy to tear away his essential being from the grips of Vakin.

He resorted to his second plan of action and willed his *atman* to traverse the murky depths for a tachyon which, with a velocity faster than the speed of light, could penetrate the darkness of Vakin. His noumenon waded through the shifting and viscous quicksand of Vakin that continually dragged it to a near standstill. But it didn't give up. Every time it was forced to stop, his *atman* restarted the search again, and again, and again. Its movements coming to a near stop due to extreme weakness, his *atman* finally located the tachyon and succeeded in merging with the particle.

The resulting burst of energy generated a radiation wave function that tore through the shroud of despondency that was holding him prisoner in Vakin. The frequency of vibrations of his essential being peaked and the faint glow which still enveloped it, flared up into a blinding explosion that propelled Ormidtz into an advanced evolutionary projectile, expelling him from the Vakin quagmire into an unknown void.

In this unfamiliar emptiness, life-creating subparticles began to adhere to his essential being like those that had first created matter by attaching themselves to the Higg's boson after the Big Bang. The strands of atoms coalesced and entwined through spacetime, twisting themselves to form Ormidtz's new life braid.

CHAPTER XVI

THE DECEPTION

Zenad Reality
The Polar Lab

Rescue helicopters hovered in the frigid air, waiting to transport the seriously injured to the nearest hospitals. Below, emergency medical technicians administered first aid to scientists and staff as they emerged dazed and confused from the Polar Lab Shelter. Against the blinding white snowscape, the bright yellow, fully-encapsulating hazmat suits of the first responders were clearly visible from the air. Wide polyvinyl chloride faceshields, flexible because of the added phthalates, permitted a broad range of vision but came at a price: the face of the wearer appeared distorted beyond recognition to anyone peering into the transparent window of the faceshield.

These emergency medical technicians and scene of accident investigators had arrived to find that the explosion at the Polar Lab wasn't as devastating as they had been led to believe. The underground Collider was only partially destroyed and, while several sections of the Polar Lab were badly damaged, the reinforced Shelter had wholly escaped any impact from the blast. Among the debris lay the scattered remains of an elevator, a wide gap in its shaft exposing Level 3, clearly the epicenter of the explosion.

Once the epitome of orderliness and efficiency, the lab at Level 3 was now a scene of chaotic disaster. Large computer screens hung drunkenly from the ceiling, some still emitting random readings as codes continued to stream down the cathode ray tubes. Almost all the workstations had been demolished and the floor was littered with shards of glass on which lay remnants of hard disk drives, graphic cards, audio cards, and motherboards. Thick layers of dust coated the area, while here and there loose wires discharged bright, electrical sparks giving a festive look to the dismal scene.

Since the Lab and the Shelter had been adequately heated, the survivors were all lightly dressed in clothing ranging from suits, jeans, jackets and lab coats, and now needed to be kept warm to protect against the biting cold and to counteract reactions to shock. As they filed out of the building, EMTs rushed forward to drape them in paper-thin solar blankets made from shiny sheets of aluminized polyethylene which from the air looked like supernovae glinting in outer space. Due to timely evacuation, most of the staff had fortunately escaped serious injury, and whatever first aid was being administered was mainly for minor scratches and bruises received in the stampede to reach the Shelter on time. Together with the blankets and first aid, the EMTs also handed out hot, sweet drinks to help the survivors overcome the shock and the cold.

Either too busy or still recovering from the trauma they had just experienced, none of the responders, investigators or survivors noticed a figure shimmy down a Douglas fir and slide shadow-like into the emergency response van which held all the EMT gear. He, or perhaps she, unhooked a hazmat suit, stepped into it and zipped himself up. He then grabbed a packet of solar blankets, casually jumped out of the van and briskly walked up to the milling crowd, a clone of the other responders.

The intruder's eyes scanned the crowd searching for survivors who were of special interest to him. The Director was nowhere to be seen, but at a distance he noticed Raj and Paul busy helping the responders minister to the injured. Neither of the young men appeared to be hurt in any way, and the man nodded to himself, reassured.

He continued to scan the crowd and was pleased to see Erlang Shen pacing up and down just a few feet from where he was standing. As he approached Erlang, the stranger heard the scientist mutter, "No, no. It can't be true. It just can't."

Coming closer, the intruder asked, "What can't be true?"

Erlang raised his eyes to an optically distorted face staring through the faceshield.

"What? What did you say?" he asked distractedly.

"Sir, you're in a state of shock and you're talking to yourself," said the man solicitously. "Please sit down and drink this hot chocolate. Or if you prefer tea. Would you like another blanket? Are you sufficiently warm?"

In a daze, Erlang obeyed the man and sat down on a nearby folding chair. "Yes, yes, tea please," he said.

"Here you are sir," said the man, handing Erlang a mug.

As Erlang wrapped both his hands around the hot cup, the man repeated, "What did you see? What can't be true?"

When Erlang didn't answer, the man continued. "I know you're suffering from shock, but I'm afraid I have to ask you a few questions. I have to immediately submit a report on what caused the explosion, and it would be very helpful if you could tell me exactly what happened at the Lab while the facts are still fresh in your mind."

"I don't really know what happened," replied Erlang vaguely. "I remember that the Veil Lifter, that's the project we're working on, was launched on schedule in spite of the controversy surrounding its level of safety."

"What was the controversy?" asked the man.

"Some scientists believed that the Veil Lifter was flawed so that, if launched, it would trigger a disastrous catastrophe. Others didn't agree."

"What made the scientists think there might be a catastrophe?" the man asked.

"It's all very odd." Erlang said in a reminiscing tone, the hot tea apparently reviving his memory. "As I recall, the Director informed us that a series of unexpected technical breakdowns had delayed the launch of the Veil Lifter. Added to that was the fact that I and my two colleagues who had developed the mathematical model for the Veil Lifter, had simultaneously suffered bizarre accidents that hospitalized us for several days."

When Erlang lapsed into silence, the man prodded, "Then what happened?"

Arousing himself, Erlang continued, "We had barely recovered from our ordeal, when the Inter Galactic Security Force dispatched us to the Polar Lab, informing us that there was an error in the model which must be found and corrected before the project was launched."

"Why did you think it was odd?"

"Because it's unusual for a non-scientific branch of the federal Administration, such as the Inter Galactic Security Force, to identify an error in the model without providing any supporting evidence. They just warned us that if the Veil Lifter were launched without making the necessary adjustments, the universe would be placed in great jeopardy," said Erlang.

"You didn't believe the Security Force?"

"It made little difference whether I believed them or not, for before we could locate any problem, the Director initiated the launch sequence," said Erlang.

"Why didn't he wait?"

"He said the optimal time slot for the launch was about to lapse, so he couldn't give us any time to modify the model," said Erlang.

"What happened then?"

"It's all rather confusing after that, for as soon as the Veil Lifter was launched, Paul and Raj, two young astrobiochemists who work on the project, declared a state of emergency and herded us into the Shelter," said Erlang.

"Was the Director with you?"

"I really can't quite remember. The announcement to evacuate, followed by the blare of the emergency sirens, created panic among the staff who made a mad rush towards the Shelter. In the confusion, it was hard to see who was or wasn't in that crowd. Besides, I had other things on my mind."

"So you joined the others in the Shelter?" asked the man.

"No, I stayed behind in the Lab."

"Why didn't you go to the Shelter? Weren't you afraid of the catastrophe?"

Suddenly suspicious of the stream of searching questions, Erlang asked, "Who are you? Why are you asking me such personal questions?"

"I'm part of the security investigation team, and as I just explained, I need to submit a report as soon as I've gathered enough information from eye witnesses," the man replied.

"Oh," replied Erlang readily accepting the investigator's explanation, his earlier misgivings evaporating as suddenly as they had arisen. Then striking off on a tangent he asked, "If you're from the Security Force, you must be knowing Commander Ormidtz. He was detailed to the Lab to provide extra security during the launch, but I haven't seen him anywhere since the explosion."

"The Inter Galactic Security Force is a huge organization with many departments, so it's not possible for us to personally know everyone working there," came the reply. "But the name rings a bell and I may have heard of him in some context."

"Where is he? Do you know if he has survived?" Erlang asked looking around as if suddenly aware of his surroundings.

"I'll search him out as soon as I can," assured the man in the hazmat suit. "I'm sure he's fine since most of the scientists and staff of the Polar Lab have survived. But tell me, why didn't you go to the Shelter like everyone else?"

Erlang turned away his face and replied curtly, "It was for personal reasons."

Realizing that pursuing this line of query was going to be unproductive, the intruder changed his interrogation tactics and said, "Well, I'm glad you've survived for the world always needs brilliant minds like yours."

"I'm not sure if my so-called brilliant mind will be of any use in the monastery," replied Erlang.

"Monastery, what monastery?" asked the man in a startled voice.

"As soon as I can leave this place, I shall return to Henan, to a life I had led a long, long time ago. I'll revert to being a Shaolin monk so that in my next reincarnation, I'm reborn in this mystical place of my dreams that haunts me even in my waking hours," replied Erlang. His eyes glazed over as he stared at the distant horizon, mentally far removed from the Polar Lab.

"What will your life be as a monk?" asked the man.

Erlang shrugged. "Praying, eating, sleeping, meditating."

"You're a scientist and a learned man," said the man. "So I'm sure you are familiar with the ancient texts which warn you that forsaking worldly activities and remaining in idle seclusion won't ensure transcendence to a higher consciousness and to the form of ideal existence that you seek. The direct path to higher human evolution is by fulfilling one's duties to mankind and the universe."

"I know whom you cite for I've studied many forms of meditation that lead to higher levels of consciousness," said Erlang. Then added, "Are you also into meditation? For a security man, you seem to have garnered a lot of unusual and esoteric knowledge," said Erlang, peering closely at the intruder.

Unwilling to yield to Erlang's scrutiny, the man stepped back and turned to leave. He called out to Erlang over his shoulder, "Thank you for the information, it will help me write my report. You're an exceptional physicist, so think carefully before you choose the life of a monk. Perhaps your karma is to make discoveries that will benefit both mankind and planet earth, and fulfilling that karma could lead you to that mystical place you are seeking."

δ

The man strode off, quickly blending into the crowd, one hazmat suit amongst the many. His search for witnesses continued and he peered into little knots of people who were standing around undecided what they should do next. He looked intently at their faces, then shaking his head, walked on. He meandered between the parked vans and vehicles, seemingly looking for someone in particular. He wandered past one of the emergency trucks, frowned and retraced his steps. Someone was sitting on the tailgate of the truck. A solar blanket hung from slender shoulders while another, clutched tightly under the chin, obscured the face.

He bent over and asked tentatively, "Ma'am?"

Ruari O'Connor cast him a glance before turning away. She pulled the blankets closer around her.

"Are you hurt? Do you need any first aid?" asked the man.

Ruari shook her head impatiently. "I'm not hurt and don't need any medics examining me. I'm just chilled to the bone and wish I had my fur coat with me, but I guess it's buried under all that rubble."

The intruder aware that people reacted differently to traumatic experiences, offered her a mug of hot tea, saying placatingly, "Here, this might help."

As she reached for the steaming mug, the blanket slid off her head, fully exposing her face. She said, "Thank you for the tea. Everyone else has been offering me cocoa and coffee, neither of which I much care for."

Now fully confirmed that he had found another one of his quarries, the stranger said, "So I was right in thinking you're a tea-drinking kind of person."

"Is that how you classify people – tea drinkers and non-tea drinkers?" asked Ruari.

The man deflected her question with a laugh, instead explained his need for data to write his report. When Ruari questioningly raised an elegant brow, he said, "Do you remember anything about what happened in the Polar Lab just before the explosion?"

She dropped her gaze but not before the man had caught a cagey look creep into Ruari's eyes. Then appearing to take control of her emotions, she lifted her eyes and stared into his faceshield. "I don't like talking to someone whose face is so distorted by his helmet."

"Oh, that can be easily fixed," said the man, as without hesitation he reached up to undo the fastening on the faceshield.

"But aren't you afraid of radioactive contamination?" she asked, surprised at his quick and unexpected acquiescence.

"Well, everyone from the Center is walking around without hazmat suits. I guess I'll inflate the number of those exposed by just one."

She heard a smile in his voice which inexplicably set her heart aflutter.

Before she had time to wonder at her odd reaction to this stranger, Ruari found herself staring at a finely chiseled, coffee-ground brown face. Red ochre tinted dreadlock braids were tied back in a ponytail and exotic, gold-flecked hazel eyes glittered peculiarly.

"Now that you can see me, can you tell me what happened

in the Lab?" the man said.

She took a sip of her tea. "I once knew someone with eyes like yours," she said, digressing from his question.

"Really? Who was he?" he asked, then added, "Or she?"

"No one you would know," she said dismissing his curiosity with a wave of her hand.

After a pause, the man again asked, "So, do you recall what happened in the Lab?"

"I'm not completely sure," she began, finally accepting that she couldn't escape the investigative inquiry.

"Whatever you can remember," urged the man. "Any small detail, anything that caught your attention. I need all the data I can get for my report."

She hesitated. Then taking a deep breath said, "I remember that we were trying to locate an error in our mathematical model for harnessing energy from dark matter."

She stopped, seemingly lost in thought.

"Then?" he prompted.

She gave herself a little shake, sighed and continued. "There were three people in my team and in spite of our efforts, we couldn't find anything wrong in our calculations. So there was nothing to amend."

"Your team thoroughly reviewed the model, didn't they?" asked the man.

She cast him a glance. "Of course we did," she said. "Anyway what would you understand about mathematical models? Are you a scientist?"

"Not exactly," he said, "But I handle security in institutions such as the Polar Lab and so need to have more than basic knowledge about accelerators, colliders and particle physics."

She looked at him reminiscently then gave a doubtful shrug and continued, "Actually, we didn't get much time to review the model because the Director unilaterally decided to launch the Veil Lifter without waiting to learn if the model actually needed any modification."

"Did anyone try to stop him?" he probed.

"Not really," she began, then seemed to remember something. "No, someone did try. He was a commander from the Inter Galactic Security Force. Ormidtz, yes, that was his name, Ormidtz."

"What did he do?" the man asked, amused to see a slow blush creep up her cheeks.

"He tried to stop the Director, but failed."

"Did you or anyone else try to help this Ormidtz?"

"Yes, I did," Ruari replied without any hesitation. "But it was too late. You see, just before the launch, Ormidtz had been severely injured in an elevator accident, so even though he tried to prevent the Director from initiating the launch, he was too weak to put a stop to it. I guess Ormidtz collapsed from the effort for I saw Paul and Raj, two young astrobiochemists, holding his hands, trying to revive him I suppose. I'm not sure what happened after that but his injuries might have proved fatal." There was no sign of sorrow or grief for Ormidtz in Ruari's voice.

The man cleared his throat and asked, "Didn't it worry you that the project was being launched without the necessary adjustments?"

"I wasn't particularly bothered because I'm confident that I didn't make any mistakes in my calculations. I was also quite sure that the Inter Galactic Security Force was exaggerating when it predicted that a flawed Veil Lifter would create a catastrophe of epic proportions."

The man appeared to be lost in thought for a moment then continued his questioning. "A couple of other witnesses told me that the Lab was evacuated as soon as the project was initiated. Did you join the others in the Shelter?"

"Oh no, I couldn't," she said. "Not right away, anyway. I wanted to make sure that my other two colleagues were safe. I waited for them so that we could walk to the Shelter together."

"That was noble and kind of you," the man commented, fascinated by the deep emerald of her eyes, faintly marred by a sly glint.

She returned his look and shrugged, "It was nothing."

"So the Veil Lifter is now classified as an unsuccessful project." he stated. Then following up with a question, asked. "Do you have any theories about why the Collider exploded, if it wasn't due to the defective model?"

Ruari again shrugged, a gesture that the man was getting to know well. "I don't care enough to postulate any theories because the Veil Lifter is no longer of any importance," she said. "However, I'm convinced that it was a mechanical, and not a mathematical failure that caused the explosion."

"Wouldn't you like to confirm your suspicions?" the man asked.

"Look," said Ruari in an exasperated voice. "The eruption has destroyed all relevant data, so it'll be at least a couple of decades before another attempt can or will be made to harness energy from dark matter. Who knows where my own team and the Polar Lab team will be by then, and whether funding can again be raised on such a massive scale."

"So you're quite sure that the explosion wasn't due to a mistake in the model?" he reiterated.

"Oh, I'm quite sure it was a mechanical failure," Ruari repeated with an arrogant toss of her head.

"Since the Veil Lifter turned out to be a resounding failure, will you abandon any further research in cosmology?" he asked.

"Oh no," Ruari exclaimed emphatically. "Not at all. I've many projects lined up and will start working on them as soon as I'm able to return to my job."

"And what job is that?" he asked.

"I teach mathematics and cosmology and also conduct research in areas no one has dared to explore," said Ruari.

"In which case you must have heard of the physicist David Bohm," said the intruder.

"Yes, I have. What of him?" she replied, puzzled at the sudden change in the nature of the questions.

"David Bohm postulated that the reality we experience in our everyday lives is really a kind of illusion like a holographic image. He believed that beneath the reality of our everyday lives, there is a deeper order of existence, a vast and more primary level of reality that's beyond time and space," said the man in the hazmat suit.

"Yes, but he hasn't been able to provide any tangible proof of his theory," replied Ruari. "Anyway why do you bring this up now?"

"Ah, I can see that the mystical significance of Bohm's postulate escapes you. In fact, your focus on yourself and your work brings to mind teachings from an ancient text which says that an inflated ego, forgetting the needs of the soul, chases after insatiable wants and desires," the man said, softening the stern message with a wry chuckle.

"So you think I'm egocentric and egotistical?" she said, her voice rising in irritation.

"I'm just paraphrasing some words of wisdom."

"In this world," she retorted, "To get a modicum of success in one's career, it's absolutely necessary to be egoistic. Among scientists, look at the lives of Einstein and Newton for example. They were engrossed in their work and spared little time for family and friends. Then take the famous warriors, emperors and kings in history such as Napoleon, Genghis Khan, and Emperor Qianlong of ancient China. Each sought fame, wealth, and power, and had to be egocentric to be successful in achieving their goals."

"True," said the intruder, "But while the leaders achieved their goals, the common man made the sacrifices and many lives were lost. One can also ask if achieving their goals was good for their souls for we don't know how these famous people fared after they died."

"Well," said Ruari, "Since I don't believe souls exist, to me such concerns are irrelevant."

The man stood still for a moment lost in thought. Then giving Ruari a half salute, he said, "I have to go now and try to collect more data. Good luck with your future projects."

He zipped up his faceshield and turned away, so she didn't see the sad and anguished expression sweep across his strange eyes.

Ruari stared at his back thoughtfully as a sense of *deja vu* washed over her. Although she didn't agree with what he had to say, she was deeply intrigued by the man. She felt that not only did she know him well, but that she had known him for a long,

long time. And then there was that strange magnetic attraction. Who was this man?

δ

Pained by Ruari's indifference to the state of a human's soul after death, but aware that he had little influence over her, the man continued the search for his last quarry.

It didn't take him long to spot Ameqran Izem. Wrapped in a gold solar blanket, Izem was sitting on a fallen log shivering and mindlessly rocking back and forth. The man stood watching Izem from a distance, swamped by memories that the scene evoked. After a while he approached the acoustics expert and draped a second solar blanket around his shoulder.

He said, "Sir, you are cold. This extra blanket will help."

Izem made no reply and continued to rock back and forth.

The stranger bided his time until Izem had stopped shivering, then said, "I know this is difficult for you as you are under shock, but I need to know what happened in the Lab."

"Why do you need to know anything?" asked Izem.

"Sir, I'm from the security force. I'm carrying out an investigation as I must immediately file a report. I'm questioning survivors in order to piece together as accurately as possible, the sequence of events that led to the explosion," came the reply.

"Oh, you're from security," said Izem. "Do you know Ormidtz? He's also a member of the security team and was in the Lab with us but I haven't seen him in a while. Has he survived the disaster?"

The intruder smiled fleetingly behind his faceshield and

replied, "I'm sure he's fine, but since you seem very concerned about him, I'll certainly find out and let you know."

"Why are you playing hide-and-seek?"

The intruder jerked back, taken by surprise at the harsh and sneering tone of the question.

"Who speaks? What is that?" he asked.

"I know who you are. Why are you pretending to be someone else?"

Disconcerted to discover that the words were coming from Izem's mouth, the man said weakly, "Why do you accuse me of pretense? How do you know me?"

"You are Ormidtz, of course," came the reply.

"Why do you call me by that name?" said the man.

"Do you deny you are Ormidtz?" retorted Izem. "Do you deny that we've met before?"

"I don't understand why you keep calling me by that name," said the man. "I don't recall meeting you before this moment."

"You are a poor liar, Ormidtz," shouted Izem. "But you cannot fool me. I'm Zepar and I can recognize *atman*s even when they're encased in different human bodies."

The intruder sighed behind his faceshield, conceding it was futile to try deluding a djinn. Then distressed to find Izem still under the influence of a hi-neg being, he asked, "Zepar, why are you still occupying Izem's body?"

"You've asked me this same question before and the answer is still the same. It's because I enjoy experiencing life as a human. So don't try to persuade me to release him because I'm here to stay," said Zepar.

"You understand the consequences of your indulgence and obstinacy, don't you?" said Ormidtz. "You know that as long as you continue to possess him, Izem will be struggling to live the life of two very different personalities. His medical diagnosis will be schizophrenia or multiple personality disorder and he will appear to others as experiencing hallucinations and delusions."

"You can give Izem's condition whatever labels you want," said Zepar, "But I'm not going anywhere."

"You know Izem will suffer intensely both physically and mentally," Ormidtz persisted. "And his ability to think in an organized manner will be impaired. If you release him from your possession Izem can continue to use his brilliant scientific mind for the good of humankind."

"Don't squander your sympathy on Izem," said Zepar with a mocking laugh. "Because as long as you refuse to face the truth, you too will suffer as intensely, if not more, my friend."

"You, who can't be trusted to tell the truth," said Ormidtz, "How can *you* know what's the truth?" asked Ormidtz.

"I may appear devious at times," said Zepar feigning contrition, "But I can always distinguish truth from lies. When I lie, I do it knowingly. But you, you lie to yourself because you don't want to face the truth."

"Since you seem all knowing, Zepar, do please enlighten me," said Ormidtz with sarcasm. "What truth am I not facing?"

"You're fully aware that your mental and spiritual powers are superior to most humans, yet you refuse to embrace the knowledge because you're afraid of the responsibilities these powers bring with them, and the inner conflicts that they raise within you. You prefer to be like a horse wearing blinkers, seeing only what's in front of you, remaining intentionally blind to what's around you. You're blissfully unaware that such weakness and cowardice invigorate your enemies for they thrive on such negative traits," said Zepar.

"I see," said Ormidtz, assimilating the deluge of irrefutable criticism. "But you once told me that hi-neg beings like Umani and yourself want to rule the universe. So why are you urging me to use my special powers against your own interests?"

"I know it's hard for a human to understand," said Zepar, "But unlike Umani, I'm not all evil. I was created with some elements of honor and integrity and when the need arises, as it does now, they come to the forefront even if I try to resist, for as you well know, I'm not endowed with free will like you humans."

"Zepar, explain clearly what you mean," said Ormidtz, not sure he really wanted to know.

"Well, since you ask me directly, I can tell you that you're the chosen Gatekeeper of the Ocyyst Barrier to preserve harmony in the universe and the Realities. The task is formidable and you will be tested and challenged by your enemies in every lifetime, in every Reality. I truly pity you, so I thought I should give you fair warning."

And with a flick of his blanket, Izem quickly disappeared behind a clump of fir trees.

δ

Zepar's revelation added to the despondency which already lay heavy on Ormidtz. After he had escaped from Vakin, Ormidtz had chosen to return to the Zenad Reality to try and gauge the physical and spiritual impact of the explosion on the three scientists placed in his care. What he learned from his brief investigation already cast a pall over him.

The personalities of Erlang and Izem had been so transformed that they would be of little use to humanity for the rest of their lifetimes in Zenad. As for Ruari, Umani had managed to mutilate her sense of right and wrong so drastically, that all that was good in Ruari was deeply buried and she was now dominated by her baser instincts.

There could only be one explanation to the radical transmutation in the three scientists. In the nanosecond lag between the instant of explosion and the discharge of the strangelets magnetic field, the universe had experienced an infinitesimal flash of destabilization. During that moment of disharmony, a few negative subparticles had filtered through the Ocyyst Barrier, creating a momentary imbalance in the positive nature of the universe. Using this to her advantage, Umani had syphoned off the surplus negativity and fed them into the minds of the three scientists.

As a result, Erlang's desire to return to Machim Reality overshadowed everything to such an extent that he lost the will to live. Since killing himself was against his beliefs, Erlang had opted for the life of a Shaolin monk in the hope that his next rebirth would be in Machim, an expectation which Ormidtz knew had a very low probability of being fulfilled. Erlang's hungering soul wouldn't find the peace and harmony that it was craving, while in the meantime, his genius was lost to humanity in Zenad.

In Izem's case, the surplus negativity that Umani had injected into him had multiplied Zepar's contrariness to a degree where he would never agree to vacate Izem's body and mind. Izem would suffer from a split personality that would torment him for the rest of his lifetime in Zenad, depriving the world of his contribution to knowledge.

And Ruari? Was she Megan's reincarnation or was she a hybrid descendent of a long-ago union between a hi-neg being and a human? Did Umani indeed taint Megan's essential being in the Etruscan passages? Were the black streaks that had darkened the lunar moth's translucent wings at its moment of death not dust, but Umani's depravity seeping through the moth's innocence and polluting Megan's purity? Wherever lay the truth, Ruari's brilliant, selfish mind, sullied by Umani's corruption, would hold Megan's blameless soul captive until Ruari died and Megan's soul found redemption in another Reality.

And the others? How had Raj, Paul, the Director and other humans whom Ormidtz may never meet, how had they been affected by the surplus negativity? How would they change their own lives and those of others on earth in the Zenad Reality?

δ

Ormidtz had ensured cosmic harmony in the universe and the Realities, but at what price and for how long?

He had thus earned the right to guide his own destiny, but which destiny?

If Zepar was right, and he was the chosen Gatekeeper of the Ocyyst Barrier, was he physically and spiritually strong enough to protect Zenad and the universe against Umani and the generations of humans tainted by evil hi-neg beings? Would he be able to guide Erlang and Izem, and others affected by hi-negativity back to the narrow path, the right path that would lead to their redemption?

At a spiritual crossroads and filled with self-doubt, Ormidtz didn't know which path to choose. As always, Waara beckoned temptingly. Waara where peace and harmony reigned, where he could look forward to an existence devoid of conflict, devoid of pain. An existence of spiritual ecstasy, of supreme aloneness. Or he could accept the mantle of the Gatekeeper, the Protector, forfeiting Waara to remain in Zenad.

In Zenad he would then revert to a lower evolutionary state, seeking fulfilment in physical wants and carnal desires like most humans. Complex creatures, humans in Zenad are beings of virtue and villainy, of saintliness and satanism, capable of the greatest sacrifices for love and duty, but also capable of violent hatred that spawns massacres, genocides, war and discord.

Choosing to remain in Zenad had other drawbacks. He would have to recommence his journey to transcend to that level of pure consciousness that would uncover the Ultimate Truth and the Seventh Reality. On the other hand, in Zenad he could help Ruari cleanse her soul of Umani's evil influence and revert to being the pure *atman* that is Megan. With the transformed Ruari, he could return to the life of bliss that he had once shared with his Megan.

Which path should he follow? Should he choose the joys and pains of being a human with both a body and a soul, or should he choose spiritual fulfillment through perfect union with the Singularity? Dare he once again expose himself to the ecstasy of living a normal human life with the reincarnated Megan? Was he strong enough to withstand the pain of parting when the time came for her transition to another Reality where he couldn't follow?

Ormidtz had proven that he is worthy of the power. Now he must choose the trajectory to his new evolution.

CHAPTER XVII

THE AWAKENING

Zenad Reality
Jerusalem

Jerusalem.

I sit on a crop of rocks which has witnessed the emergence of first beliefs, the first principles of the Oneness, the first call for the brotherhood of man. Yet, these unspeaking stones have also beheld unthinkable acts of violence inflicted by humans on humans over hundreds of Zenad years.

The message for humans handed down over the years, as in the Tractate, is always the same and always expressed in words, for words are the most powerful medium in all the Realities. Words can instigate savagery when a simple signature legitimatizes the slaughter of thousands of innocents. Words can initiate a catastrophe when a sermon twists a young mind, launching him on the path to destruction. But words can also be the most potent medium for peace and healing such as the benediction that enlightens the lost; the love poem that salves a shattered heart; the lullaby that soothes a fretful child to sleep.

Lost in thought, I watch the setting sun glance off the Golden Dome of the Rock and throw a tangential ray towards the grey-domed Al Aqsa Mosque, once deemed to be at the farthest distance from Mecca. A flock of swallows wheel overhead to the strains of vespers and evening mass. Church bells toll even as the muezzin's melodious call to prayer remind the faithful of their duties. The scent of incense fills the air over the stone-paved courtyard.

A sense of deja vu overtakes me for I recognize the sounds and smells that had nudged me awake from my soporific slumber in the primordial Vakin Reality. Yes, it was the summons from this very spot that had kindled my desire to escape Vakin and seek the evolutionary path that was right for me.

The crimson sky, the lengthening shadows, the stark magnificence of the place, all raised my awareness to such heights that unbidden, my third eye flutters open and what had remained hidden from me for aeons, is suddenly clearly visible.

I understand that I've been looking at the Universe through a framework of false perceptions which led me to believe that I had transitioned five Realities to reach Waara. My ego, my intense desire to merge with the Singularity, had clouded my ability to recognize the Ultimate Truth. It dons on me then that I had never really left Zenad.

My third eye continues to unlock more mysteries. I smile a self-derogatory smile as it becomes clear to me that I'm not a being separate from Umani. Umani is a part of me as I'm a part of Umani. We are positive and negative subparticles orbiting around the nucleus of my essential being, my atman, reacting to currents of energy that define the human psyche.

I must cultivate beneficial emotions such as love and compassion that have higher frequency and more energy than destructive emotions such as hatred and fear. So any increase in my atman's positive property will guide me towards a higher level of consciousness, while any decrease will drag me down to a lower state of evolution.

I begin to realize that to find my inner self, I must overcome the weakness within myself for it only serves to strengthen Umani's negative forces. I must increase my own positivity to nurture my internal equilibrium and counterbalance Umani's high negativity. I must fight evil, not only that which is around me, but also the evil that lives within me.

Like all humans, I too, am defined by two main emotions – Fear and Love. The wave function of Fear with its shallow peaks and deep troughs, breeds hatred, anger, despair, self pity and resentment. The wave function of Love, on the other hand, is the antiphase of Fear and sweeps humans to pinnacles of honor, purity and goodness. I must therefore pursue a horizontal path that will superimpose the waves of Love over the waves of Fear to create a composite waveform that will thrust Fear towards a flat-line.

As my new awareness crystalizes, I feel a ray of Enlightenment pierce my essential being and I laugh out aloud in joy. The Zen koan is solved and the meaning of the parable of my life is bared before me. It has taken me eons, but I now have a rudimentary understanding of the central concept of the Tractate. It's the same as all the spiritual teachings that have been delivered to man over the centuries. Love in all its forms is the only thing that can overcome evil to ensure universal cosmic balance.

The message is simple in its complexity. The ultimate goal of my quest for nirvana isn't self fulfilment or ecstasy through merging with the Singularity, but to acquire wisdom and power to help and serve others during my journey. To be able to do that, I must annihilate my ego and embrace the elusive, all-encompassing, often unrequited love, for the wound from this ardor is the opening through which knowledge and wisdom enters the soul. I must destroy my own negative emotions spawned from fear and enhance my positive characteristics through actions that erase human ignorance and wipe away arrogance that threatens the ethical balance of the universe and the Realities.

A human soul is, after all, just a droplet of consciousness waiting to return to the ocean of the Seventh Reality where it is first conceived. To return to his womb, all that is required of a human is to transcend to the highest level of consciousness which unties the knot that holds back this power. This realization suffuses me with a sense of elation and I know instinctively it is Thebitz expressing his pleasure that I have finally taken my first step on the long journey towards the Ultimate Truth.

As I savor the moment, a flock of shrieking swallows scatter in panic. A pale form flits across the golden dome and a breeze carries the scent of jasmine towards me. Shadows lengthen with the sinking sun and a familiar fear washes over me.

But I stand firm. I know what must be done. I turn my face to the sky glistening with pinpricks of stars and announce in a voice that carries all the way to the heavens.

"I choose the mantle of the Gatekeeper. I am the Protector of the Ocyyst Barrier."

Epilogue

The Tractate
{Σ∞}

Know ye:

There is no other universe but one.
The Whole is the Singularity
And the Singularity is the Sum of all Infinity.

There is no beginning.
There is no end.

There are six coetaneous Realities in the universe,
Each spawned of the Seventh Reality is a manifestation of It.

Deeds performed by thee awaken thy Consciousness,
Lifting the veils that obscure Enlightenment.

Deeds with positive mana draw thy noumenon
towards the Singularity,
Unto an evolution of pure energy and knowledge.

Deeds with negative mana create disharmony and obstruct
transcendence to the Seventh Reality.

Which deeds to perform is always thine to choose.

δδδ

www.ingramcontent.com/pod-product-compliance
Lightning Source LLC
Chambersburg PA
CBHW022139170626
46807CB00005B/2002